DUNCAN JEFFERSON

I0592711

THE
YOUNG
COUNTESS

THE RENAISSANCE BROTHERS

✦ BOOK 3 ✦

Cover by Jenn Reece at
WWW.TIGERBRIGHTSTUDIOS.COM
Interior design and typesetting by Ampersand Book Interiors
WWW.AMPERSANDBOOKINTERIORS.COM

9 8 7 6 5 4 3 2 1

PAPERBACK - 978-0-6480694-7-8

Prologue

IN A SIMPLE OAK bed lay an old man, gripping the white bedsheets with blue-veined fingers as life ebbed from his withered frame. With his last remaining strength, he turned toward his confessor. The young priest leaned close to hear his final whispered words. Then the priest withdrew, acknowledging the dying man's words with a final benediction. Returning to the shadows of the canopied death bed, he waited with the others.

The old man's frail chest rose and fell a few more times, before releasing one final sigh into eternity. By all appearances, he'd set aside a great burden and allowed his tired soul to relax into death.

The black-robed priest leaned forward once more, listening for any further signs of life. He muttered the required final absolution. Turning to the assembled throng, he asked: "Who is Rosso?"

One

THE ARTIST

LATE ONE SUMMER'S MORNING, a young mother named Agnes sat on a bench outside her home. She watched the retreating figure of a traveler. Fingering the envelope in her lap, fresh from the city of Rome, she tried to guess what the contents might be. She knew the handwriting, which made her fearful of what she might read.

Next to her was her redheaded daughter, Maria. The girl was feeding milk to an orphaned lamb from a horn fitted with a leather teat. Both the lamb and Maria were completely oblivious to anything going on in the rest of the world.

Agnes broke the seal and read the letter. In a few seconds, her misgivings were dispelled, and she gave a small squeal of delight.

Tucking the letter into her apron, she reached across to take the suckling lamb from its adoptive little mother, saying, "Run and get Papa. I've got some wonderful news for him."

Maria's face reflected her great reluctance to release her pet. "But Mama, he's not finished yet," she reasoned.

"I think I'll be able to manage, Maria," Agnes said lovingly. "After all, I've learned from the best." She smiled at her daughter. "And you can have him back as soon as you return. Go on." She shooed Maria off, whilst nestling the woolly mite in her own lap and feeling the milk slosh in its stomach. The disgruntled pet snuffled and sought out the leather teat that she proffered, before rapidly resuming his feast.

Agnes watched young Maria with motherly pride as the young girl scampered across the yard, and disappeared into the large wooden barn that Rosso had built some years back.

In just a few minutes, Maria ran back to her shouting, "He's coming, Mama!" She stood with pleading eyes before her mama, waiting for *her* little lamb to be handed back into *her* care. Agnes patted the wooden bench next to her, and Maria sat down, holding out both arms for her woolly orphan. Once the lamb was settled back into her daughter's arms, Agnes looked at her growing child. She was amazed at how her life and Rosso's had changed since they had become parents.

Some minutes passed, and still there was no sign of her husband. "What was Papa doing?" Agnes asked.

Without taking her eyes off her charge, Maria replied, "Oh, you know, the usual—painting."

"Then I think I'd better go and get him myself," Agnes said, preparing to get up. Just then, Rosso appeared in the sunlight. He was cleaning a brush with a cloth, and his face and clothes were a collage of colorful sprays and smudges. As he walked toward them, he had a happy smile on his face.

"Finished," he said. "I think they'll like it, too. What was the news you wanted to share?" he asked.

Laura waited for him to reach her, and they embraced as if for the very first time. "I'm so proud of you. Those people don't realize how much work you put into those paintings of yours. You should think of asking for a bigger commission, you know . . ." She'd said this several times before, but the answer was always the same: "My reward is seeing my paintings in their rightful place. Hopefully they'll inspire the people who see them . . ."

Rosso held Agnes at arm's length and gazed into her face. "I am the most blessed man on this earth. I love you so much, young lady. I'd never have dared to do any of this," he said, sweeping his arms around as if to embrace the whole world. "You believed in me right from the start. Even when I was that broken wretch whom you floated down the river on a log and then restored to life. No man could wish for a better wife than you are to me." He wrapped her in his arms for a few moments and then smiled at the smudge of blue paint that had appeared on her cheek. "Blue suits you," he said, wiping it off with his cloth. "Tell me, what's this news of yours?"

"I just got a message that Marco and Laura are coming to see us!" she said.

"That's fantastic news!" replied Rosso with genuine delight. "Do we have any idea when we might expect them? Are the children coming with them? Shall I clear out the spare room for Gino and Maria? Turning toward the barn, he shouted, "Toni! Marco and Laura are coming to see us! I'll need a hand cleaning out the spare room." He felt a light touch on his arm and looked back at Agnes. He saw the sad look in her eyes and remembered a terrible truth. "Dear God, forgive me," he muttered as he crossed himself. "I'm sorry, my darling, but I completely forgot. Do you think they're visiting because they want to get away from Rome? It must be around the anniversary of the boys' deaths?"

"It will be twelve months next week," said Agnes. "I can't imagine how they must have felt when it happened. It's beyond my comprehension. One day the boys are fine, healthy young men in the bloom of their youth, helping Marco in the forge—then within a week, they're both dead." Their attention was diverted by the arrival of Toni, who was leading their little son Gino by the hand. To see the tall, lean Toni with his slight limp and the dark, chubby lad trotting along next to him always made them both smile.

"He was helping me feed the cows," said Toni, with the pride of the godfather that he was.

"Ton-eee, let me ride him!" the little lad said, with all the seriousness that his three-year-old stature would allow. The grown-ups grinned.

"Did someone say Marco was coming?" Toni continued. For a moment, all eyes fell on the boy, as each of them remembered Bini and Rizo.

"Come here, Gino," said Agnes, reaching out to take the little boy in her arms and hold him close to her heart.

"We're not sure when they will get here, but let's make sure they have a memorable time. I wonder if Sara will be with them. She would be about twenty by now, wouldn't she?" asked Rosso.

"What about your Clare?" Agnes asked. "Do you think she'll be coming, too?"

Rosso scratched the nape of his neck as if struggling with the idea, then said coyly, "Of course she will. She couldn't miss seeing me, could she?"

Rosso and Toni left Agnes with the children and went off to see what needed to be done in the spare room. Most country dwellings had such rooms. At first sight, it usually appeared that all that was needed was a light dusting. But if someone opened any of the cupboard doors or peered under the bed, that person would find a jumble of broken toys and discarded childhood treasures that had been stored away 'just in case.'

"It shouldn't take too long," said Rosso, in a less-than-convincing voice.

"That's what you said when you were going to build that shelter for the cows," replied Toni.

In his early life, Toni had been more of a shirker than a worker. Despite this and the physical limitations inflicted upon him before they'd first met, Toni was Rosso's right-hand man, and he now performed more of the farm duties than his blossoming-artist friend and boss.

Rosso hesitated. It was all becoming a little more complicated than he'd expected.

"Perhaps we'd better ask Agnes what she'd like us to do, before we get too carried away and move the wrong things to the wrong places," Rosso archly suggested. "After all, this is her realm. Ours is out there with the sheep and the cattle and the canvases." Closing the bedroom door behind them, they returned to seek counsel from his all-wise wife.

They needn't have worried. The following week, another note arrived from Laura to say they'd been delayed, but would be there on the feast of St. Francis, and would it be possible to have a cot ready, as Laura was expecting her baby soon after that. The news about the baby's arrival lifted everyone's spirits, making the preparations for their dear friends even more special.

It was autumn, that time of year when the sheep needed to be brought down to lower pastures, pens prepared for them, and enough food and fuel stored for everyone in the house. Despite this, an air of great expectation lightened their work, so much so that the time flew and before they knew it, everything had been prepared.

One bright autumn day, Marco and Laura came down the track in their blacksmith's cart and stopped in front of Agnes and Rosso's little home.

Rosso was shocked when he saw Marco. His friend's hair had gone completely white, yet the same familiar smile illuminated his old friend's features. Laura had hardly changed one iota, and it seemed incredible to Agnes that she was pregnant at all. From behind, she was still willowy-thin, and it was only when seen from the side that her bump became apparent. Her face was unlined, but those who loved her dearly could see a visible remnant of pain haunting her beautiful eyes. Marco was as attentive as ever, as he helped her toward the little throng. Gino and Maria stayed close to their mother's legs, whilst Rosso and Toni helped unload the few possessions Marco and Laura had brought with them.

Agnes showed Laura into the house, with Maria and Gino following closely behind. Toni took the horse and unburdened cart to the barn to feed the animal and check over the wagon. Marco and Rosso were left standing alone, watching as Toni disappeared behind the building.

"Come, friend," said Rosso, gently taking Marco by the arm, "let's take a walk through the fields whilst it's still light. It's been a glorious day here. How was your journey?" The two of them chatted away about workaday things until they reached the shepherd's hut on the far hillside. The late afternoon sun had warmed the western wall, so they slumped down against it and looked back toward the farmhouse, where smoke drifted lazily from the kitchen chimney.

A few lingering bees buzzed them, and crows cawed as they flew home to their perches high in the woods nearby.

"I can't find the words to express my sorrow for your huge loss, Marco," Rosso said softly. His hand reached out and squeezed his friends' calloused palm. He was fleetingly aware of how broad and how hard the blacksmith's hand was against his.

"I miss them," said Marco. Rosso turned and saw his dear friend struggling with the waves of emotion that gripped his throat and threatened to flood his eyes with tears.

The evening breeze stirred the red berries in the nearby hedgerow. "It'll be a harsh winter by the looks of it," Marco mused.

"I never knew blacksmiths knew our countryside secrets," said Rosso, trying to sound casual.

"Blacksmiths hear a great deal. Some good, some not so good." Silence returned as the sun began to rest on the distant horizon.

"Come on," said Rosso, clambering to his feet and offering his hand to his friend. "Otherwise the ladies will be missing us."

As if awakening from a reverie, Marco asked Rosso, "So how's the painting going? If my memory serves me correctly, the last time I saw you, you were crushing colors for your maestro. That was just after you and Agnes were married, wasn't it? What was his name?"

"Raffaello," said Rosso, smiling at the memory of it all. "I learned a lot there, although at the time it was one of the most frustrating periods of my life. Almost as bad as being a novice monk!" he chuckled, which made Marco smile. "All I seemed to do was to mix colors, prepare canvases, and watch the other painters do the painting. I didn't actually see that much of the maestro, because he was spending so much of his time at St. Peter's in the Vatican . . ." When I did see him and ask when I could show him my sketches, he'd just say, 'Not now, my little firebrand, first you must learn the basics, then you build on them.' If he hadn't died so young, I suspect that I'd still be there mixing colors—and still waiting." Rosso plucked a long blade of grass and chewed on the end of it.

"Looking back on it now, though, it was probably the best thing that could have happened to me. He could see that I could draw, and I think he just wanted me to develop my own ideas and techniques. But he knew that I needed to learn the basics thoroughly, so I could develop my own style of painting—and not just try to imitate someone else! But it was Agnes who turned me into an artist." Rosso smiled at the memory of it all. Waving his arms and tugging his red locks, he went on, "You see, at first I'd get frustrated when something didn't work out, and walk away from it for days or weeks at a time. She told me that if I wanted to become a proper artist, then I should spend at least two hours each day painting, even when I didn't want to." Rosso slipped his arm through his friend's and continued, "The trouble is that once I'd developed the habit, I found I couldn't stop. Then bit by bit, things began to fall into place. Brother Julian came to visit once and saw what I was doing. He insisted on taking a canvas back to Rome with him, because he said it made him sing better every time he looked at it. And the rest, as they say, is history."

"I'm really happy for you, Rosso. It seems like a thousand years since you first walked into the forge with little Clare. What great hopes we had then."

Marco went quiet. "What a terrible mystery life is, eh?" he said, as they walked the gentle incline back down toward the house. "You were beaten by a bad father, almost killed in battle, found the love of your life, and went from being an almost-monk to the father of two gorgeous children. Then, as if by magic, here you are, a renowned artist! And me? I thought it would all last forever. Me and my beautiful Laura—my rock, my delight—and our children." Marco faltered and tears welled up in his eyes. He wiped his face with his sleeve before going on, "My beautiful children are gone." He spoke so softly that Rosso had to lean in close to catch the words. "The boys were always so close. They shared the same room and the same bed, even when they'd been arguing." Marco smiled at the memory. "And if you know young men, you'd know that happened most days. They'd planned to go off hunting for wild rabbits down near the river. It was still warm; some would say it was a perfect autumn day. They'd decided to camp out for a few nights. When they hadn't returned after four days, I went out looking for them. I met the Bishop—you remember him, don't you? He was the one that helped track us down when we were kidnapped. You'd hardly recognize him now. He's fully grown and become quite respectable, which I suspect is the result of Pietro's influence. But he still maintains his 'contacts,' as he calls them, so when I told him about Rizo and Bini not coming home, he said he'd make some inquiries." They stopped and looked up at the stars, which were just beginning to appear in the night sky.

"We found their camp. They were together in their shelter. Bini was holding his brother, but they were both dead. It was the plague. It was the worst feeling that I ever hope to experience in this life, seeing them there like that—and yet it was so beautiful, too." Marco wiped away a tear and said to Rosso, "I like to think of them arriving in heaven together, arm in arm, and giving St. Peter a hard time, too."

Rosso put his arm around his friend's shoulder and pointed to the evening sky, saying, "You see that star there? When my sister Anna died all those years ago, she put that star in the sky to remind me that she was safe now. It's good to think that somewhere up there are two more stars that your boys have put up there especially for you and Laura."

"Thanks, Rosso," said Marco, "that means a lot to me."

"But you said that all your children had gone. Surely Sara is still with you. And Clare?"

"Sara took it hardest of all. Laura was unbelievable. She cried until I thought her heart would break—but just on the brink, she stopped, looked up at me, and said that we must keep moving forward, and then everything would become clearer. Each day she watched and cared for the rest of us, but Sara seemed to shrivel somewhere inside herself, as if her heart couldn't cope with so much grief.

"A few weeks after we buried our boys, our friend Maria arrived from Urbino. Laura had written to her, and the good woman had dropped everything and come straight away. She's an amazing person. She said that perhaps Sara might like to come and stay with her at her uncle's palace. Remember him? He was the Duke of Urbino. Maria said she'd take very great care of Sara, as if she were her own child. So a few days later, the two of them left. Maria writes that the change seems to have helped, and the notes we get from Sara are sounding much more optimistic. She's started to write and tell us more about what is going on in the court around her. For a time, I thought she might enter a convent, but if my beloved wife is correct in reading between the lines, then I think there may be a young man paying her some attention. We'll just have to wait and see."

"And Clare," Rosso, asked with some concern. "She's OK, isn't she?"

"That girl's a survivor," said Marco, with life returning to his voice. "A few months back, a courier arrived from Ferrara. Her godmother whom you will never have heard of . . . . . . ," he said, looking conspiratorially at his companion. Rosso opened his eyes wide in mock horror and replied, "I know nothing of the woman."

"Well, this woman whom you know nothing about invited Clare to spend some time with her. Laura and I thought it would be good for her to attend court, as it might help secure a more comfortable future for her. By all accounts, she's settled in well and is getting tutored by the old Jew that once taught Maria. The world is such a small place, isn't it?" he said, looking at Rosso with his wise eyes.

"It's a very confusing place, too," Rosso replied, with a twinkle in his eye. "Who would ever have thought that a little ragamuffin who'd been abused and abandoned would end up in some ducal court, and mentored by . . . some lady whom neither of us even know." Throwing his grass blade away, he asked, "But you must be very excited about the new baby, Marco?"

"Not only is the world small and confusing, but every now and again it produces the odd miracle," the white-headed blacksmith answered. "I have to admit that the news caught the two of us completely by surprise! And yes, it's given us new hope. After the boys died, so many memories and ghosts seemed to haunt the forge. I confess that I questioned my God deeply during that period, and not everything I thought about Him was very Christian either! But Laura never stopped believing in His goodness. Women seem to be more forgiving, don't you think?"

"Perhaps it's because they practice on their husbands so much," Rosso chuckled. "Come on. We'd better go and grace them with our presence, or we'll be in trouble." The two of them walked up to the farmhouse arm in arm.

A sudden breeze had blown up, causing the last remaining leaves to dance a small gavotte just as the men closed the door behind them and entered the warm kitchen.

"That smells delicious," said Rosso, as the aroma of the evening meal sent savory messages to his salivary glands. "The soup *is* delicious," said Toni, from the corner of the hearth where he was seated. He tore off a piece of bread, dipped it in his soup, and offered it to the ever-present Gino, who sucked on it happily. "More please," the little lad said, looking up at his besotted godfather.

"He spoils that boy," said Rosso happily. "But then we all do," he added, crouching down before the two of them and tousling the young lad's curly black hair.

Laura was helping Agnes with the pasta until Marco suggested that she take a break and sit after their long journey.

Laura looked at him lovingly and said, "Once we've fed you two hungry men, then we'll take our food." She winced and placed her hand on her side.

"Is he kicking you much?" asked Agnes, who moved to place her hand on her friend's swollen belly. Another kick caused the two women to look at each other and smile happily. "It must be a boy, with a kick like that," Agnes said. "We girls are much more polite, aren't we, Maria?" The little girl nodded in that superior way that only a firstborn girl can, and continued to eat her own soup in silence.

It was a warm and happy reunion around their wooden kitchen table, which had mutely eavesdropped on so many tales over the years. As the light outside disappeared, the lamps were turned up and Agnes put the little ones to bed with minimal fuss. Shortly after, Laura said that she would retire early, too, as she was beginning to feel the effects of the journey, and no doubt her little lodger would do his best to keep her awake most of the night.

"Call me if you need me," said Agnes as she closed the door after Laura. Then she returned to the table to join the men. "How far gone is she, Marco? She's not very big, is she?"

Marco rubbed his head, as if trying to dislodge some information deeply hidden in its depths. "I may not be the right one to ask," he said, "but from what I can gather, her time should be up in the next couple of weeks. She never got that big with any of the others, especially little Bini." His brow furrowed as he spoke his dead son's name. "But it's all a bit of a mystery to me. As long as my Laura is OK and the baby is healthy, that's all that matters."

"Enjoy your sleep whilst you can," added Toni from the corner. "I don't even sleep in the house, and my little bambino still manages to wake me when he cries at night." Rosso playfully tossed a small crust in Toni's direction.

"You can start complaining when you start having them," said Agnes, joining in the fun. "Hopefully everyone will get some rest and recover from the journey before the baby decides to make his presence felt in the world. Do you have any plans for tomorrow?" she asked Rosso.

"Well, I've got a couple of things I'd like Marco to look at, and I've also got some work to do on one of the canvases that Brother Julian asked me to do for Santa Maria's. Toni will be busy with Gino and the sheep, but apart from that, my love, I'm as free as a bird!"

Shortly after, they all retired to bed. Laura's baby was kind to them that night and stayed put.

Two

A BABY IS BORN

TEN DAYS LATER, it was eerily silent as the grey dawn dissolved the blackness from the sky. Marco heard Laura call his name and immediately threw back the blankets to pull on her foot and relieve the cramps that she had been suffering for the past several weeks of her pregnancy. She giggled and said, "It's not a cramp, Marco, I'm in labor."

Marco gave her a confused look. "How do you know?"

"Because my waters have broken, you silly man," she replied, as she caressed his cheek gently. For Marco, the last tatters of hope for sleeping in were blown away. They held each other tight for a few seconds, and then Laura went on, "I think you'd better get dressed and call Agnes for me. There's women's work to be done here. I don't expect much to happen for a little while because my contractions haven't . . ." She gasped suddenly and began to breathe deeply and slowly. About a minute later, she added, "My mistake, darling, you'd better tell her that my contractions have started already. Go on," she smiled at him, "If all goes well, our baby should be here by midday."

Marco dressed quickly and went to wake Agnes. He needn't have bothered. She was already dressed and in the kitchen, boiling some water and taking down clean sheets from a cupboard in the corner by the fire. "Call it a woman's intuition, or just that the walls aren't very thick here, but is she in labor?" she asked Marco.

"She is indeed, and I'm afraid I'm about as much use to her now as a bumbling blacksmith."

"Your job is to feed the men, feed the fire, and say your prayers," Agnes said with quiet authority as she backed into Laura's room bearing fresh sheets and a change of nightclothes.

Just then Rosso appeared. "It's started then?" he asked, knuckling the sleep from his eyes and giving Marco a big hug. "I'd better call Toni, because we'll need an extra pair of hands with the children. What's for breakfast, Cook?" He winked cheekily at Marco and hurriedly exited toward the barn before Marco could reply.

The sun was peeping over the horizon and casting a crimson glow in the eastern sky. Marco looked out the window and wondered what sort of bloody warning such a crisp, clear sky would conjure up in the mind of a superstitious shepherd. The newborn day veritably bustled into life. Then the sounds of Laura groaning with each contraction reached his ears and caused him to wince in empathy.

Fortunately, hearing Agnes comforting her calmly had a calming effect on him, too.

The door opened, and Agnes quietly asked Marco to call for Rosso. He didn't notice her dilated pupils or the paleness of her face; her controlled manner kept him in a place of peace. Marco opened the door and shouted, "Rosso! Agnes wants you."

Rosso came over to the house. "Me? What would she want me for?" he asked in genuine astonishment. "I'm as useful here as a bull in a china shop." He knocked on the bedroom door and went in.

Laura was on the bed watching all that went on, her eyes darting from Agnes to Rosso and back again. A sheen of perspiration covered her pale features. A new contraction sent shock waves through her whole body, causing her face to change instantly from white to puce red.

Agnes turned to calm her through the contraction.

"What's happening, my love? Why do you need me?" Rosso asked in alarm.

"Just wait a moment," was the brief reply, as the contraction slowly released its grip, and Laura settled back onto the white pillow behind her.

"Something's gone wrong, Rosso. The baby's arm has come down first," she said, looking him straight in the eye.

"Is that not good?" Rosso replied in genuine ignorance. Agnes went to lead him toward the door, but Laura spoke out, saying "You needn't whisper, Agnes. It's OK to talk in front of me."

Agnes gripped Rosso's hand. She glanced up at him and then over at Laura. She studied the floor for a brief moment as she arranged her words. "The baby won't come out if the arm is down. It'll die." She paused before going on, saying in a soft voice to Laura, "And you'll die, too."

Laura blinked and then said, "Can you ask Marco to come in?"

Agnes looked back at Rosso and indicated that they should leave the room and leave Laura and Marco to talk alone.

Marco was completely confused as to why he was to go into the birthing room. "Everything's OK, isn't it?" he said over his shoulder as the door closed behind him.

Agnes had begun pacing around the kitchen with one hand on her waist and the fingers of the other running through her hair. Then she stopped, turned, and instructed Rosso to call Toni, "Now!" Rosso heard with great clarity her unspoken words, and his heart went cold. He touched her lightly on the arm as he immediately left to find his friend.

Toni immediately answered his friend's summons, dragging the two children in his wake. Rosso bent down and held Maria's face gently in his hands, saying, "I want you to take little Gino with you and feed the chickens."

"But Papa, you said that only Toni could feed the chickens," the little girl replied primly.

"Today, darling, you can feed the chickens and take as long as you want about it," her Papa replied, pushing the two of them toward the barn. Then he turned to Toni and said, "There's a terrible disaster looming. The baby's not coming out properly, which could kill Laura and the baby. Agnes wants to talk to you immediately."

"Me?!" said Toni with astonishment, just before Rosso pushed him into the kitchen.

"There is only one way we can save them," Agnes began, "and you two are the only ones who can do it."

Rosso and Toni looked at each other, their mouths open wide in utter disbelief. "Us?!" they said in complete unison. "We don't have a clue about women having babies," Rosso finished.

"I'm sorry, my beloved, but we don't have time to discuss this. Every second is vital. Any delay will mean certain death to one or both of them." She drew a deep breath before continuing, "The only way we can save either of them is if the baby is cut out of Laura's womb." She didn't pause to let the full horror of her words sink into their consciousness. "Rosso, you were once a butcher and know the insides of most animals. You also know how to use a knife properly, and you know how to sharpen a blade so that it cuts cleanly. Not only that, but you studied anatomy under Raffaello in Rome when you were learning about painting. In other words, you're the only one who would know what things look like inside a woman's body."

Before Rosso could offer even one word of challenge, Agnes turned to Toni, "And you, Toni, have raised hundreds of sheep and cattle, and you've saved many a calf and lamb by cutting it out of its mother's body." She paused to let her words sink in. She took a step toward the simple shepherd, saying, "And Rosso will need a steady pair of hands to help him. I'll need to be free for when the baby comes out."

The silence in that homey kitchen was palpable. Only the sounds of children laughing and happily clucking hens could be heard. "Now I need to know what you'll need, and I need to know *now*."

She looked at the two men, whose granite-firm bodies were matched by the stony silence of their minds. "Come on, Rosso, I need help. Laura needs our help, and Marco, too. We have to do something," she pleaded.

"It's a pretty bloody business cutting calves out of cows, and I doubt that it would be very different in a woman," Toni proffered, his mind stumbling back into the present. "I heard of a man in the mountains—he looked after pigs, so the story goes—well, he cut his baby out of his wife's belly when it got stuck." He looked at Rosso, whose mind was slowly sifting through an overload of seemingly impossible information. When the fog of emotion cleared, his thoughts really began to race.

"I'll sharpen some knives. We'll need some linen thread to tie up blood vessels when they spurt and to close everything up once we get the baby out," he said, with a look of sudden clarity in his eyes. "Getting the baby out shouldn't be the problem, it's closing the wound and not letting Laura bleed to death that terrifies me."

Agnes placed a gentle arm on his and said, "You're her only chance, my love, and I trust you. Is there anything else you'll need?"

They rapidly discussed what they might need, and Agnes returned to the bedroom to talk with Laura and Marco, whilst the men prepared themselves.

Marco was sitting on the bed with his arm around Laura's shoulders as she struggled through another fearsome contraction. Wisps of her blond hair stuck to her face, and her dry lips were pulled tight in a fading grimace. She relaxed and lay back against Marco. "That wasn't too bad," she said, closing her tired eyes. Agnes looked at Marco's terrified face and nodded slightly as if attempting to transmit her inner calmness to the poor man.

"We have a terrible problem here," she said. Laura opened her eyes for a brief moment and smiled faintly.

"I know," she said, her dry lips sticking together after each word.

"There is only one solution," Agnes continued, "the baby must be taken from your belly, and it must be done now," she pronounced with calm authority.

"Now?!" asked Marco in disbelief.

Agnes spoke forcefully: "Yes, *now*, Marco. It can't wait. The baby won't wait. It must be done now!" Then preparing to deflect the challenges gathering in his head, she said, "Rosso understands what it's like inside a woman's belly from his anatomy studies in Rome, and he knows how to use a knife. Toni has delivered more babies than anyone for miles around, so I am confident the two of them will do a good job."

"But Toni's a shepherd. They were baby animals . . ." Marco struggled to speak, but Agnes interrupted him.

"We don't have any choice, Marco," she pleaded. Laura reached out to her terrified husband and held his hand, twisting her fingers between his. "Don't worry, my dear, Rosso will do his best. We must trust him." She was cut short by the start of another violent contraction.

"Marco," Agnes said, "you'll have to hold Laura whilst this is going on." Her eyes acknowledged the terror he was about to endure. He nodded once, held his beloved wife, and wept.

Agnes went out to Rosso and Toni. Both had been busy collecting what they needed: knives, linen thread, sewing needles, and bandages made of sheets torn into usable pieces. Water boiled over the fire.

"Be as quick as you can," Agnes said to them, reaching up for a jar of virgin olive oil. "Use this on her skin before and afterwards. I've used it on the children's cuts, and they never seem to go fetid afterwards." She turned and went back into the bedroom.

The men were piling their tools on a tray when Marco appeared. He took one look at their equipment, picked up the knives and needles, put them on a shovel, and put them in the fire.

"What are you doing, Marco?" Rosso shouted in astonishment, "We need those things!" and he went to grab his instruments from the fire. Marco grasped his wrist with a grip of iron.

"Wait," the blacksmith said. "Trust me," he added, looking at Rosso with a fierce look. "She's my wife," he added, with such heartrending passion that Rosso stayed his hands and dropped his head. Composing himself, Marco stared at the live coals, saying "I know you're trying to do your best, and so am I." An ember spat out of the fire and Rosso automatically ground out the still-burning spark with his boot. Marco went on, "I cauterize animals with hot irons. It stops pus forming. Maybe the heat kills the pus. I don't rightly know, but it can't do any harm either." He pointed to the bedroom, "I'll bring them in once you've got everything prepared. Go on, Laura needs you." The two men hugged, then Rosso and Toni gathered the rest of their things and went into the room.

Agnes was at Laura's side. Laura was pale and drenched with sweat, but she still managed to smile at the two men. "Good morning, gentlemen," she said. "I have been praying to Our Father that your hands are as true as your hearts. I am ready whenever you are." Rosso couldn't speak, so he merely nodded in reply.

Toni helped Rosso set up their equipment on a small table next to the bed. Rosso noticed a small crib in the corner of the room and said over his shoulder to Agnes, "I'm glad to see everything is ready." Then he called to Marco to bring the instruments in.

Toni cleaned Laura's whitened dome of a belly with the oil before wiping off the excess. At first the simple shepherd blushed at the sight of her naked body. "No time for modesty now, Toni. I need you to have all your wits about you," Rosso whispered to his assistant, before they both noticed the small clenched fist between her legs. The knife Rosso picked up still felt hot, but it didn't burn him. He placed his finger and thumb on the skin just below her navel and before he made the cut he looked up at Agnes, then Marco, and then Laura, and saw the trust they had in him. He suddenly felt completely alone.

Making a firm vertical slice downward from her belly button to her pubic bone, he saw the skin open silently and was surprised at how little blood came out. Laura let out a small scream, her legs went rigid, and then she fainted into Marco's arms. Rosso sliced again and felt the thicker matting of the deeper sinews. On his final sweep, the sides of the wound parted, and the purple mass of muscle that was her womb, and which was crushing the life out of both mother and child, was revealed.

So far, so good. He looked to Toni for guidance.

"Don't cut there," the little man said, pointing at the higher part of the womb. "It's too thick and will bleed like a stuck pig. Try and go as low as you can and then pull the wound open sideways. It should tear quite easily. Don't be scared by all the blood, most of it'll be water from around the baby." He talked to Rosso as if he were in a stable discussing the delivery of a calf. "Remember, once you open the womb, you'll need to move as quickly as possible. Ready, my friend?"

It was the loneliest feeling Rosso had experienced in all his life. He paused, and then thrust the knife into Laura's womb. Bloody water welled up and filled the cavity. Toni worked steadily to mop it all up with the linen cloths. Soon there was a small pile of bloodied cloths at their feet.

Rosso put his fingers into the hole he'd made and pulled hard. The womb was tough, but ripped apart in an even fashion, and immediately they saw the baby inside. Without thinking, Rosso scooped in his hand and tried to lever the infant out. Between the oil on his hands and the white coating on the baby's body, he couldn't get a decent grip on the still infant. He felt panic rising in his throat. He tried again, but with no luck. He could feel the tension at breaking point within the room. Then Agnes began to hum a soft melody, and his body relaxed. Squeezing his hand into the bloody void once more, he cupped the baby's head in his hand and lifted it toward the light. He was surprised at how suddenly things happened next. Within seconds, the baby's limp blue body lay flat on Laura's immobile body.

"Tie off the cord," said Toni calmly. "Do you want to cut the cord, Marco?" he asked. Marco shook his head. He held Laura's limp frame even closer.

"Give the baby to me," Agnes said immediately. "You've still got a lot of work to do, Rosso." Rosso looked back down at Laura's belly and saw nothing. The pang of fear that the baby was already dead, and maybe even Laura, too, caused him to freeze and look over at Agnes to see what she was doing.

"Concentrate on what you've got to do, Rosso. Trust me to do my best here."

Toni's steady voice refreshed his focus, "What you have to do now, Rosso, is find the edges of the wounds and stitch them up," he said with simple wisdom. "If you're quick, we should have this finished in ten minutes." The seeming ridiculousness of his words made Rosso laugh out loud.

Toni worked steadily cleaning out the blood, as Rosso prepared the linen stitches. Suddenly he felt Toni's hand grab his arm. "We've forgotten something," the little shepherd said. "The afterbirth. We can't leave that inside. Pull on the cord firmly, and it should just come away." To Rosso's amazement, it all happened just as Toni had predicted. The afterbirth with its gnarled and twisted veins slipped out through the bloody hole in Laura's belly and into Toni's cupped hands. "That's amazing," was all Rosso could think at the time.

The two men then worked silently and efficiently, stitching up first the womb, then the sinews, and then the skin. In the silence, as they looked at Laura's white tummy with its ugly wound, they heard a baby's cry from the corner. All three men looked at Agnes, who was holding the chameleon infant upside down by the ankles. He, and there was no doubting his sex, was rapidly changing from a dusky blue to a life-filled pink as his lungs filled with air.

"Give him to me." Laura's words were barely audible, but her return to consciousness dealt a final blow to the bleak despair they had felt only minutes previously.

"It's a boy," said Marco.

"I can see that, silly," replied his fragile wife.

"I can't believe we just did that," said Rosso to himself, still mesmerized by the wound on Laura's tummy. The spell was broken by Agnes, who poured more olive oil on it and then covered it with a clean linen cover as if closing the whole amazing episode.

Three

UNEXPECTED VISITORS

"I THINK YOU two should go and wash yourselves," Agnes said, her eyes glowing with pride. The two men turned and left as if in a dream. Only as they took turns washing themselves under the pump outside did they look at each other. The smile that threatened to crack Toni's face wide open was the spark for a bear hug from Rosso. They danced a jig, laughed and whooped, then embraced and wept with sheer relief.

"What's going on, Papa?" little Maria said, having appeared as if by magic. "Are we having a party?" she added, her mounting anticipation mixed with quizzical innocence. Toni and Rosso stared at each other once more— and once more they burst out laughing and danced around the farmyard.

When they were finally exhausted, Rosso called Maria and Gino to him. He hugged them both and said, "Guess what?" When he beheld their two blank and besmirched little faces, he continued, "Laura's had a little baby, and Toni and I helped her to have it."

"I hope it's a girl," announced Maria in a semiserious voice. "Baby boys aren't half so much fun," she added, before glancing down at her little brother and tickling him.

"I'm hungry, Papa," declared Gino, when the merriment had subsided. His father winked at him and replied, "Well, let's go in and eat. In fact, why don't we have a party?" Both children's faces lit up with delight. Rosso and Toni followed the children back inside, and the noise level escalated along with their entrance.

Agnes appeared at the bedroom door, "Shh! Laura's trying to feed the baby; we need a bit of quiet out here."

"Can I see the baby, Mama?" asked Maria.

"Not just yet, my darling. Laura needs to rest. Maybe later, after she's recovered from her . . . er . . . ordeal." Agnes's smile softened her words, which had temporarily dampened the celebration.

There was a loud knock at the door. They stopped in their tracks and looked at one another. *Who can that be?* Rosso's unspoken words were echoed in Agnes's and Toni's looks. He moved to the door and tried to see who it was from the small veiled window next to it. "Looks like a rider of some sort," he said quietly, as he went to lift the latch.

Outside stood a mud-spattered messenger, who asked, "Are you Rosso?" Rosso nodded.

"Message for you," said the man He reached into his tunic for a pouch, which he handed to Rosso. The messenger's final words were "No answer required," as he turned and remounted his black horse.

"Who sent you?" cried Rosso into the autumn air. But the messenger was quickly disappearing up the track to the far-distant highway.

Rosso pushed the door shut, whilst staring at the pouch. His thoughts were interrupted by Marco, who appeared at the bedroom door and signaled for them all to come in. Rosso put the pouch on the kitchen table and followed Toni into the room. Agnes put a protective arm around the children's shoulders and led them in first, with the men bringing up the rear.

There, sitting up in bed, with a slight color to her cheeks, was Laura. Her son was serenely stripping milk from her breast. His eyes were tightly shut and his hands curled into fists, as if daring anyone to approach too closely. The glorious ordinariness of the scene belied the fear and panic that had pervaded the place only a short time earlier.

"Marco and I cannot begin to thank you three for what you did today," Laura began, reaching out to hold her beloved husband's hand. "You not only saved my life and the baby's, but you've given Marco and me a new future, too. Only God truly knows how much that means to us. Thank you from the depths of our hearts."

The two men shuffled in embarrassment, as only men can when in the presence of a breast-feeding woman. The memory of what they had just done seemed a million miles from their minds.

Agnes intervened on their behalf: "I think that's enough for now. You need to rest and focus on your baby, Laura." With that, Agnes ushered all her children—large and small —out of the room.

The pouch sitting on the table posed a mystery to Rosso: who could it be from? He was working through a series of possibilities when Toni interrupted, "It would be much easier if you actually opened it, my friend." He picked it up and handed it to Rosso.

Inside was a rolled-up scroll, which Rosso pulled out. He dropped the pouch back on the table, where it landed with a dull thud. He then undid the scroll, revealing a smaller scroll inside, and placed both of them on the table. He didn't recognize the seal on the inner scroll, but broke it and began to read.

> *"My dear Rosso. By the time you read this, I will be cold and in my grave. Pray for me.*
>
> *You will no doubt remember the mission that you undertook from Rome to Paris all those years ago and the stories that we shared at that time. As you read these words, the forces that have always opposed me will be moving to occupy my estates in France. I have named my granddaughter Clare as my heir, and she is to inherit my family titles and all*

the lands that go with them. With this letter, you will also find one introducing Clare and you to the authorities in Saint-Germain-en-Laye. You will also receive my ducal ring to prove her identity. Take care of her, Rosso. Ever since I met her, I have loved her from a distance and tried to do what I could to help behind the scenes. Remember to pray for me, a sinner, who tried to do his best, but suffered from all the faults and weaknesses that challenge each of us in our own lives.

Your humble servant in Christ,
    Cardinal Villepreux
    Vatican City."

Rosso reached for the pouch and searched its corners. He found the large ring with the Villepreux family crest etched into a precious stone embedded in its surface. He smiled as he looked up at Agnes and said, "I don't think we'll ever forget this baby's birthday!"

Marco came out and slumped at the table. "They're both sleeping," he said, running his fingers through his hair. He looked at the small group gathered around him, then hung his head as he said, "There is no way in this world that I could ever express what you've all done for us today. It seems like only a few moments ago that my world was about to disappear down a deep black bottomless pit. Yet now . . . I'm sitting here with my wife and son asleep in the next room." He looked at each of them, his face an open book, and said, "It's a miracle. Thank you for being a part of that miracle."

"It was all a part of the service," Rosso said, trying to deflect his embarrassment.

"No, it wasn't," Marco replied. "Something happened in there that shouldn't have happened. But it did, and the only way it could ever be described is, it was a miracle."

Toni broke the silence that followed. "Rosso is an artist. He's an artist with the brush, with the paint, and with the knife." Agnes moved next to her husband. "He's a good man here . . . and here," she said, tapping him first on his head and then over his heart.

"Shouldn't we be celebrating?" Rosso interrupted, "But very quietly so we don't wake Laura and the baby? Have you thought of what you'll call him?" he asked Marco.

"Donatello," he said. "Our gift of new life."

"That's beautiful," Agnes said. "Donatello," she repeated, as if tasting the joy in the name.

"May God bless him with a long and good life," Rosso added. "I wonder what sort of world he'll grow up into?"

They were interrupted in their celebrations by another knock on the door.

"What the . . . ?" said Rosso in amazement. "Has someone put up a sign directing the whole world to this house? I don't think we've had as many visitors as this for the past seven months." He went to the door and opened it.

"Your name Rosso?" inquired the new messenger. His garb was covered with the same grime as his earlier colleague, and his horse was just as tired as its earlier equine counterpart.

"Yes. That's correct," replied Rosso once more.

"Message for you," said the bored man, handing over a sealed scroll. Having completed his mission, he turned on his heel and headed for his mount.

"Any answer needed?" Rosso shouted after him.

"No!" was the succinct reply, tossed over the departing man's shoulder. Rosso was left once more with a message in his hands and a mystery in his head.

"If it wasn't so cold, I'd leave the door open so that the next messenger doesn't have to knock," he said, with a lopsided grin on his face. He handed the scroll to Agnes, saying "I think it's your turn to open one. Maria, you can open the next one, and after that . . ." He bent down and swooped little Gino into his arms and began to tickle him.

Agnes broke open the seal and read the contents in silence. "Your friend Cardinal Villepreux seems to have been a very organized man," she said. "This is from the duchessa where Clare is staying. She says that she's received some correspondence from a mutual friend and suggests that you meet up with Clare in Bologna as soon as you possibly can." She looked up at Rosso and handed the scroll of parchment to him. He scanned it quickly.

"Looks like she doesn't want to say too much, but it speaks volumes. She probably doesn't want to say anything that might raise eyebrows in inquisitive places. I wonder what the hurry is?"

Marco chuckled. "You wonder what the hurry is? I still remember being buried alive and saved by Toni here. People in power hate to let go of it. If Clare is an heiress, then that means that someone else loses out, and you can be certain they're not going to be very happy about it!"

Toni chimed in, "I'm hungry. It's been a busy day so far, and my brain needs food to think."

"Thank goodness for one sensible head amongst us," Agnes agreed, bustling around the kitchen. "We should be having a meal of thanksgiving for Laura and Donatello. After that we can talk and plan. I've no doubt that's exactly what Clare would want us to do."

Marco linked Toni's arm as they approached the table. "Do you miss our friend Gino's place?" he asked gently and quietly.

Toni shrugged. "I have family on both sides of Florence now. Rosso needed me more, and Gino had that lost soul called Rabbit to help him. But I suppose you've heard that he doesn't like to be called Rabbit anymore?" He gave Marco a sideways glance and tapped the side of his nose. "Apparently there's a young lady in his life, so goodbye 'Rabbit' and 'ello 'Bernardo.' This love, eh, it changes us all!" The two men pulled their stools from under the table and sat down happily. "But for me, I have children both here and at Gino and Maria's. They are my life. I am a very lucky man, eh?"

"You certainly are, Toni," Marco replied with great grace, "as are the rest of us who count you as one of our friends."

The blacksmith gripped his companion's arm and quietly added, "And for me, my friend, you're a man who's just helped save the lives of two of the most precious people in my whole world. I will never, ever forget that."

"Now stop your chatting and start eating," said Agnes. "Rosso? Will you bless the food and let the men eat, please?" She placed a large bowl of steaming pasta in the middle of the table, which was soon followed by a large bowl of rich aromatic sauce and two loaves with crazed burnt-brown crusts.

"How long would it take to get to Bologna?" asked Agnes, after checking that Laura and the infant were still asleep.

"It really depends on the weather, my love," Rosso replied, ladling some sauce over his pasta. "If the weather holds, then three to four days if I'm lucky. But if it snows early in the mountains, then it could take a week or more." Marco and Toni nodded in agreement as they hungrily ate their meal.

"Where do you think the duchessa's staff will meet you, assuming someone escorts Clare to Bologna?" Marco inquired, cleaning a spot of sauce from his face.

"I'm not really sure," Rosso replied. "I've never been to Bologna before. What about you, Toni? Do you know anything about it.?" He winked as he said it, which caused his little friend to almost choke on his food.

"It's a nice city to visit if you like walls and towers. And yet, it was a place I always enjoyed stopping at. Remind me to let you know of a couple of clean places that are safe to stay at," he said, returning Rosso's gaze. He then pointed his bread at the bowls of pasta and sauce, indicating that his stomach still had space for more.

Rosso let out a sigh. "I think I'm too old for traveling the countryside in winter," he said. "But I can't let Clare down. What do you think, Agnes?" he asked his dear wife, who'd come to sit next to him.

She kissed him lightly on the cheek and stroked his recalcitrant red locks with loving care, tucking them behind his ear. "I think," she began, "that you have no choice, my love. I'm needed here. Marco obviously cannot leave Laura. Toni needs to care for his fluffy flock and his two-legged lambs. So go where you're needed. We'll be waiting here for you when you get back." She kissed him once more and let her head gently rest on his shoulder.

Rosso put his arm around her shoulder and held her close. Toni and Marco darted glances at the two lovers whilst eating their food, and exchanged mock exasperation at what they were seeing. "Young love," said Marco, and Toni smiled.

Four

BOLOGNA

THE SUN WAS reluctantly beginning to rise as Rosso mounted his horse, which Toni had readied for Rosso's rendezvous with Clare. Agnes handed up his satchel with food for the journey, and the children were handed up to share the trip as far as the gate.

"Godspeed," Marco said, "and that comes from Laura and Donatello, too. The little lad sent his apologies. According to his mother, he has a ravenous appetite and refuses to miss breakfast!" Happy smiles lit the group's faces in the lantern light.

"I'll miss you all. Keep well, and keep safe," Rosso said. "Take care of my precious lady," he said pointedly to Toni, who gave a slight nod and moved one step closer to Agnes. Rosso stored the memory of the parting scene deep in the sacred space of his heart: his beloved Agnes standing in the golden glow of the lantern, looking so strong and so wise. He looked at her and tapped his fist against his heart, mouthing the words 'I love you.' Then pulling on the reins, he turned his horse's head toward the road.

At the gate, he lowered the children down from the horse, then touched the horse's flanks with his heels, urging it to "Ride on!". "We love you, Papa!" were the last words he heard as he disappeared around the corner in the lightening grey gloom.

Rosso had decided to call into Florence on his way to Bologna. He'd made a promise some months back to visit a friend of Brother Julian's. The man sang in the choir at the Baptistry of San Giovanni and, according to Julian, had the best voice north of the Tiber. To Rosso, it seemed reasonable to stop and greet the man, as it wouldn't significantly delay his journey.

Rosso arrived in Florence shortly before sunset and made his way to the Baptistry. Going in, he discovered that Mass was in progress. A large crowd was in attendance, so he eased his way through the crowd until he found a space close by the altar. It took only a few moments for him to discover the reason why the space was free. It was occupied by a disheveled young man who exuded the sickly sweet smell of stale alcohol. A quick survey of his clothes suggested the very real possibility that he'd also vomited on them, which added to the nauseating miasma emanating from him.

Rosso shuffled a few paces toward the nearby pillar, an action that only mildly diluted the stench. But the tiredness he felt after the excitement of the previous twenty-four hours, and the droningly monotonous voice of the priest, soon had him on the verge of sleep. He was stirred out of incipient slumber by the combined voices of the four men who made up the small choir. He had never heard singing like that before. The harmonies they produced were transporting and beautiful, which probably accounted for the large number of people in attendance. The abundance of people certainly wasn't because of the oratorical skill of the priest!

The youth next to Rosso was also stirred out of his inebriated haze and to his feet by the voices. Rosso was even more amazed when the youth joined in the musical harmonization with a clear and steady voice. It was a voice that augmented those in the choir and belied the young man's unkempt appearance.

When the Mass was over, the people left, each taking with them some of the glories of the music they'd heard. Rosso approached one of the choristers to inquire whether Brother Julian's friend was around. The man indicated with his head that the person Rosso sought was standing right next to him, so Rosso introduced himself to the chorister.

"Ah, Rosso," said the genial man. "Brother Julian told me to expect you. "I'm Francesco," he said, greeting Rosso with a light kiss on both cheeks.

"That was stunning, Francesco," Rosso said, "I've not heard singing like that since I left Rome. I thought I'd heard the most beautiful voice in the world when Julian sang, but now I think he's got some competition."

Francesco bowed and smiled, accepting the praise from Rosso's lips. "Ah, Julian. God surely only created one voice like that. It's enough to make the angels weep and smile at the same time. Ours is merely chicanery. We all sing the same stanzas, but it's the harmonies that make it sound so good. If only we could achieve that within our own lives," he added, looking across at the heap of clothes that was the young man who had once again slumped back down on the floor. "That poor man could have a voice as great as Julian's, but sometimes youth needs to suffer a great deal before they can see the world clearly. It's such a shame and such a waste of great talent."

The two men stood and stared at the sleeping youth.

"Who is he?" asked Rosso.

"He came from Ferrara. We have close connections with the choirs over there, and he was given a scholarship to come here and study music. But the mixture of a bigger city, money, wine, and a beautiful woman have all reduced him to this. We let him come, although few can stand the smell of him. We pray that one day his life may change for the better."

Rosso continued to stare at the youth and said quietly "Under different circumstances that could have been me." He paused and prayed silently. "If it hadn't been for the kindness of total strangers . . . ," his voice trailed off. Looking at Francesco, he went on, "Do you think there's any way I could help him?"

Francesco threw his arms up in an act of frustration. "We've all tried and failed, but there's no harm in you trying, I suppose. How long will you be in Florence?"

"I leave in the morning," Rosso replied "I have to reach Bologna and would rather not be caught in the mountains if the weather turns sour."

"Mario, that's the lad's name, comes from somewhere near there; you should take him with you." Whilst Francesco spoke with a smile, his words lingered on in Rosso's mind.

He went over to where the youth was. The lad was sobbing very quietly, and a great pity rose in Rosso's heart. Almost unaware of the stench invading his senses, he squatted down next to the desolate Mario.

"Hi, I'm Rosso," he said softly. This was met with no response. Slowly the heaving shoulders stilled, and the silence grew loud.

"Time to go home now, people!" a voice called out of the gloom. He jangled his keys toward them indicating that the Baptistry was about to be locked for the night.

"Come with me," Rosso said to Mario, and he helped him to his feet. A piece of paper fell unnoticed from the young man's pocket. Rosso picked it up and stuffed it in his own pocket, intending to give it to him later. "Where do you live?" he continued, as they walked out of the building and into the square. Flares lit the buildings and caused massive shadows to dance across the black and white walls of Il Duomo di Firenze.

Mario shrugged his shoulders and muttered, "Who cares?" Then after a pause, he said, "Anywhere dry suits me."

"Well, tonight you're in luck, because you're going to sleep under a roof, my friend." Mario made to pull away. But in the voice he used when correcting his sometimes errant children, Rosso said, "Young man, you're coming with me. After a hot bath, a square meal and, I strongly suggest, a change of clothes, the world will look a different place."

"I doubt it," came the swift, sullen reply.

They found Rosso's intended lodging, where he secured a room for the two of them. A bath tub was brought in and filled before the warming glow of a well-laid fire. "Get your clothes off and then get in. Then I'll leave you to it," Rosso said. The young man obeyed, dropping his fouled clothing in a heap next to him. Without his clothes, he looked vulnerable and thin. Rosso recognized the marks on his flesh left by a recent beating. No doubt some of the brave young locals had tried to prove their manhood by beating a half-conscious derelict. He bristled at the thought of it, but felt deep empathy for the young man before his eyes.

"Is there anything special you'd like to eat?"

Silence was all he got in return. Turning away from the sight of the youth, sitting in the hot bath, with his ribs and spine pressing through the pale skin of his back, Rosso left Mario to his ablutions. As he left to give the youth privacy, he scooped up the youth's discarded clothes. Mario rounded on him, shouting "Where are you going with my clothes? They're mine. Put them back!"

Rosso stood his ground and replied steadily, "They stink. They need washing, and I doubt even you would go out naked on a frosty night like this. So just enjoy the bath, and I'll go and get some food. Alright?" Pulling the door shut behind him, Rosso smiled to himself as he descended the squeaky wooden stairs. He found one of the servants who worked in the taverna and asked that the clothes be washed and dried before dawn as they were leaving early. The servant looked at the clothes and said, "Good-quality stuff, but they don't half-stink. Are they yours?"

"They belong to a friend of mine," Rosso said, but the look in the servant's face suggested that he wasn't entirely convinced. "Just make sure they're ready before dawn," Rosso said, and he went to find the landlord.

As he was settling his account for the stay, Rosso reached into his pocket for his purse. A crumpled piece of paper fell out. It was the one he'd picked up in the Baptistry. After he finished paying, he went and sat by a lamp to read the paper. He smoothed it flat and read:

She came with soundless slippered footfalls
And blessed the flagstoned souls beneath
     her passing feet.
Glassy-eyed I watched, with breath still
     stained by last night's excess
and stood and sang amongst the cloistered
     choir
Mouthing hollow words in that hallowed
     place.
Suspended in the silence of its own end
The holy canticle haunted the vaults,
Filling the empty spaces that fled-fear will
     oft leave behind.
One glimpse

One candlelit face
One tiny light to spear the bleak black
*   landscape that enshrouded my soul.*
Her gentle knees graced the wooden floor,
Her timid eyes shivered as simple earnest
*   prayers were mouthed to eternity*
By soft lips that spoke their words in
*   sensuous mime.*
Oh that blessed morn
When my soul was burnished bright by
*   such beauty.*
Green shoots of great and glorious deeds
*   took root in my mind,*
And my body thrilled at thoughts of a life
*   well-lived.*
All is ash now.
All is desolation.
All is darkness.
Hope has fled.
For she is taken from me.

Rosso sat stunned at the beauty of the words. As he sat, memories flashed before his eyes: Little Anna, his beloved little sister who'd been his only solace in his sad youth. Of Gino and the Dom, who'd guided him oh-so-gently along a path to goodness and hope. Of his dear Agnes, the very essence of love and life. Brother Julian, Marco, Laura, and his precious Clare. Each name was a milestone marker in his journey toward manhood.

Mario, he thought to himself, deserved as much un-looked-for help as he himself had received.

He climbed the narrow wooden stairs to return to his room. The bath had been cleared away, and Mario sat in his cot with a blanket around his thin shoulders. For the first time, Rosso had a clear look at his face. The lad had a head of dark hair, still glistening from the dousing it had received. His face was square, his jawline fringed by a strug-gling beard not yet certain of its own manhood. His dark eyes were sunken, edged with dark rings reflecting the harshness of a life lived in the shadows. He had a promi-nent, slightly hooked nose that sat snugly on his face and managed to bring the whole visage to a certain balanced completion. It was not a handsome face, but it was a very interesting and endearing one.

A knock at the door heralded the arrival of some food. The fragrant smell of the herbs and freshly grated cheese sitting atop the hot meat sauce, reminded the two of them just how hungry they really were.

"Help yourself," said Rosso. Mario's hunger overcame his obtuseness, and without any further urging, he ate with great energy. "Enjoy, my friend," Rosso said to the top of Mario's head, "we have an early start in the morning, so we'll need all the energy we can get."

Mario halted and looked at Rosso. "What do you mean by 'we'? I'm not going anywhere with you." He tried to meet Rosso's steady gaze, but faltered and returned to his feasting.

"Mario, my ravenous friend, that wasn't a request, it was a statement. I'm afraid you have no choice in the matter, at least if you know what's good for you. All you need to know is that we're heading for Bologna. I need the company, and you need the exercise. So, everyone wins, eh?" He finished his statement with a smile, whilst wiping streaks of sauce from his face.

Mario looked up from his plate, faltered, licked his fingers, looked again at Rosso, and came to a conclusion. "Alright," he said, "I'll come. Anyway, there's nothing to keep me here now." His face fell as he spoke.

Rosso reached into his pocket and handed the crumpled paper over to him. "I think this must be yours. It fell out of your pocket." He watched the young man's face as he read those first few lines. "My apologies, Mario, but I did read it. It's really beautiful," he said softly. There was a long pause. Rosso went on, "I think there are a few verses missing, though. Please God, you'll be able to write them soon. But now it's time for sleep." He walked across to where the candles were. With just a small puff, he blew them out, leaving just the embers of the fire to light the room. "See you in the morning," he yawned. With full stomachs, warm beds, and the reassuring glow from the fire, they were soon both soundly asleep.

The servant was as good as his word and left the dry clothes at the door; they were clean and wrapped with sprigs of rosemary. "Fresh as the new day," said Rosso as he handed them to Mario, who'd woken like a bear with a sore head. A grunt was all he received in return. "Come on,"

Rosso cajoled him, "get dressed, and let's break our fast as soon as we can. I want to be away from here before day-break. We've a long day's walking ahead."

"I'm not walking anywhere," grunted Mario, pulling his head through his shirt. "I think this has shrunk," he said, looking miserable as he tugged it down over his waist.

"No, it hasn't," replied Rosso, "It's just that your brain isn't soaked in wine anymore. I'd hazard a guess that this is the first time in ages you haven't woken with a hangover and can feel things." He headed out the door and crept quietly down the stairs, so as to not disturb other guests in the taverna. A big fire was warming the dining room, and a servant appeared with some fresh bread and warm soup. "Thank you," Rosso said, "What's the weather like outside?"

"Frosty, master," was the reply. "I'm glad I'm staying inside for now, although I reckon it'll be a gorgeous day when the sun comes up." Leaving the soup tureen on the table, the servant said, "Help yourself to as much as you want," then he left. As he was going through the door, Mario chose the same moment to come in from the passage. Bumping the servant out of the way, he gave the man a sour look whilst making a beeline for the warmth of the fire.

"Sit down, and have some soup, perhaps it'll put you in better spirits. At least it'll keep you warm and give you some strength. He was just telling me that it looks like it's going to be a beautiful day," Rosso said, indicating the doorway with his recently licked spoon.

"Who said I was going anywhere?" Mario retorted, "And even if I do decide to go with you, who said anything about walking? I thought you had a horse?"

"In the event you should choose to honor me with your divine presence," Rosso sarcastically replied, "we shall be taking a donkey with us to carry our supplies. It's at least a three-day journey even in the best of times, but at this time of year, anything can happen. I'd rather have a donkey to walk in mud, frost, or snow, than a poor horse to carry the two of us as well as our supplies." After a few more mouthfuls of bread and soup, he added, "Anyway, it's much cheaper."

He looked sideways at Mario, who was trying desperately to remain sullen, but was having great difficulty suppressing a real urge to giggle. He met Rosso's eyes, which proved fatal for his sullen mood: he spluttered his soup all over Rosso, which only made him laugh more. Then they both had the giggles and were interrupted only by the return of the servant who inquired, "Is everything alright?"

"Fine, thank you," Rosso replied, "but I want the recipe for this soup"—causing the two of them to burst out laughing like imbeciles once more.

When they had dried their tears and settled down again, Mario said, "You win. I'll come with you. But only as far as Bologna."

"That's fine by me," Rosso said. "As far as I know, that's as far as I'm going, too." He reached down for his pack and handed Mario a thick woolen cloak, one of two that Agnes had packed for him 'just in case.' "You'll be needing this because it's cold out there."

"Thanks," was the curt but well-meant reply.

They went to the stables, where a groom had laden the donkey with Rosso's personal effects and their supplies. As they led the donkey out through the small yard, the lad in charge shouted "Godspeed, gents," whilst fingering the small coin Rosso had dropped into his hand.

They made good time through Florence. On the main highway, the muddy track had been turned into an icy morass that made for slow and dangerous walking. The donkey, however, walked the treacherous terrain with insouciant ease as Rosso led him.

Some hours after sunrise when their cloaks were no longer needed to keep warm, they paused for some refreshments.

When they resumed their journey, Rosso gave the donkey's reins to Mario. "Here, it's your turn," he said, walking on ahead. Mario looked after him, but said nothing. Turning to the ass, he tugged on the reins, demanding, "Well, come on then." He was immediately halted in his tracks by the donkey refusing to budge. "Come on, you ignorant brute," he yelled, going puce in the face as he pulled on the bridle, "MOVE!" The donkey blinked at him, but didn't move one iota. Meanwhile Rosso had stopped. He looked back with a big smile on his face. "Anything wrong?" he asked benignly.

"Nothing apart from the fact that this stupid beast refuses to budge one inch. How come he's so good for you?" Mario complained to his companion. Rosso ambled back down the track to them. Going up to the donkey, he gave the beast a friendly scratch between its ears, before carelessly throwing his arm around its neck. The ass gave him a friendly push as if saying 'Good to see you, Rosso.' Then it turned its long-eared head toward Mario and gave the strong impression that it was thinking, 'And who is this idiot you left me with?'

Rosso put his hand in his pocket and took out the apple that the donkey had been smelling and threw it to Mario. "See if this helps," he said, and set off back down the highway whistling to himself.

"So that's how you do it," Mario said, offering the fruit to the now very friendly ass.

"Sometimes temptation can be turned to our advantage," Rosso shouted back to him.

"You can always learn something, even from fools," replied Mario, now happily leading the donkey by the reins along the rutted road.

Their path took them east, up and across the mountains. It was a well-used highway even at this time of year, so the two companions were not alone for long during the short daylight hours. The route led them through several small villages, where they and their donkey stopped for some well-earned refreshments. By this stage, they had named their four-legged friend Caesar, because of its omnipotent power over their progress. When Caesar thought it time to stop, not even the lure of an apple could force him to budge until he was fully ready.

On their journey across the mountains, they were blessed by relatively kind weather. No sun appeared, but neither did any snow fall. Occasionally icy winds from the east drove squalls of rain at them. But it was the dense morning fogs that were the greatest challenge. "No use trying to go any-where until this lifts a little," said Mario, who had begun to blossom in Rosso's eyes.

"Unfortunately, I agree, my friend," Rosso said, stretching his legs out before the fire in the taverna they were staying at. "No point in asking Caesar if he wants to go, at least not until I've bought some more apples." He smiled across at Mario, who was staring deeply into the embers of the fire. "What do you see there?" he asked.

"I was writing a poem in my head," Mario said shyly in return. "What do you see?"

Rosso looked at the fire. A log threw off a spark that landed near his foot. He lifted his boot and absentmindedly snuffed it out. Crenulated embers surrounded the glowing logs. Some dropped off and turned to grey ash before his eyes. Flames danced in their yellows, reds, and pale blues. He saw faces dance and spirals of smoke ascend the sooty chimney. "I'm not sure, really," he answered as if in a trance. "It bewitches me. I see log and flame, but there's something else there, too." He chuckled and without taking his eyes off the fire said to Mario, "You'd have to be here to under-stand it, eh?"

Tearing his eyes away from the mesmerizing hearth, he looked across at his young companion. *That wispy beard becomes him*, he thought to himself: *he actually looks like a poet.* "What lines were you dreaming up in that brain of yours?" he asked.

Mario stared fixedly at the flames and spoke softly to them:

Empty black boughs finger the grey skies.
Rutted roads rimed with hard frost
glisten with unlooked-for dangers.
Breath-ed dragon's-breath bedecks beards
with jeweled beading.
The ass snorts its indifference.
Winter walks tease and test,
Seeking out the committed from the fearful.
What makes a man walk on such a morn?
A hope?
A dream?
Some looked-for safety?
Or is it you, my friend? Is it you?

Rosso and Mario sat staring at the fire in front of them.

"Fog's lifting," a voice said from the open doorway. "You asked to be called, so I'm calling you. Looks like it's going to be a fine day after all."

The two travelers roused themselves and readied themselves for the last day of their journey to Bologna. "That was good. Quite the young poet, eh?" was all Rosso could say. Mario blushed as he settled his cloak over his narrow shoulders.

As they drew near to Bologna later in the day, Mario asked Rosso where he was going to meet Clare. "I'm not really sure," was the response, "but I expect they'll be on the lookout for me. There can't be too many redheaded itinerants arriving from Florence at this time of year." He

smiled broadly and removed his beret to reveal his russet
tresses in all their glory.

"Point taken," Mario replied.

"But tell me, young sir, have you any plans from here?"

"To be honest, I haven't really thought about it much.
Just waking up in the morning and feeling better about
myself is really nice, so no more wine for me. After that, I
suppose I'll go back to Urbino and rejoin the choir there.
Maybe I'll find some wealthy patron who likes my voice or
my poems and will pay me vast amounts of gold to live in
palatial luxury as I create great masterpieces."

"At least you've found your sense of humor," Rosso said,
giving his new friend a nudge in the side. "You never speak
about that woman you wrote about," he added after a pause.
"Do you know what became of her?"

Mario looked at Rosso with pain and confusion. "Her
father's a wealthy businessman from France. He'd brought
his family on a pilgrimage to Rome." Mario's gaze was far
away as memories seemed to float before his eyes. "After
that, they'd just been traveling around Italy." Mario chuckled grimly, "And for some reason, her father didn't think I
was quite good enough for his beautiful daughter."

"Maybe he didn't like the smell of secondhand Italian
wine," Rosso rejoined.

Mario stopped in the middle of the highway and held
Rosso by the arm. "We loved each other," he said, with such
earnestness that Rosso was moved by his words. "We only
met two or three times, and I can't even remember what
we said. But it was what we didn't say that meant so much

more." He linked his arm through Rosso's, and they continued toward the city. "She is the most beautiful creature on this planet. I almost couldn't breathe when I was with her, because we were both so happy. But her father's a strict man. Don't get me wrong, he's not a bad man, and if I were in his shoes, I'd probably do exactly the same. But Rosso, she's seventeen, and we love each other. What am I to do?" he pleaded of his new companion.

"I'll need to think about that. We'll talk later. First, we have to go through there," he said, indicating the looming gates of Porta Maggiore.

They passed under the magnificent archway of the Porta and entered Bologna. Above them, the two towers spoke of power and wealth. Papal troops stepped forward and asked them their business. They checked Caesar's load and then allowed Rosso and Mario into the city itself. "Same troops, different uniforms," Rosso said to Mario, as they walked along the porticos of the bustling city. "My friends tell me that the Venetian ones were better, but on this occasion, I think I'll keep that observation to myself."

They hadn't gone far before Rosso felt a tap on his shoulder, and a well-dressed maid asked, "Are you Rosso?"

Rosso bowed before the young woman, and Mario followed suit. The thin veil across her face couldn't conceal that her eyes switched rapidly from Rosso to his younger companion. Rosso also noted with secret pleasure that the young man seemed to blush in return.

"At your service," continued Rosso. "How may I be of assistance?"

"Mistress Clare said that you'd likely come in this gate, and I've been expecting you for the past two days. I've been watching from over there." She pointed to the garret window of a large building overlooking the nearby square. "She's expecting you, Signore," she said, as once more her eyes strayed in the direction of his still-blushing friend. "There is a room reserved for you, but I'm not sure about . . ." Her voice trailed off, but her tone spoke volumes.

"Forgive my rudeness," Rosso interrupted, "but allow me to introduce my traveling companion, Mario." Mario bowed once more. Turning to the laden ass, he added impishly, "and this is the leader of our group, Caesar." The donkey merely twitched one ear and chewed on a carrot. "May I have the pleasure of knowing your name, Signorina?"

"Lucia," she replied with a shy smile.

Rosso replied, "If you could tell Signorina Clare that first I must find stabling for Caesar. And then I will need to have a wash and change of clothes. After that I will be delighted to see my beloved goddaughter again."

"I will pass on your message to the duchessa," replied Lucia, shyly averting her gaze from Rosso's.

"Forgive me," Rosso interjected, "I defer to your duchessa, of course." Inclining his head to acknowledge his lapse in protocol, he inquired "By the way, where shall I meet the duchessa?"

Lucia pointed back to the tall building with the garret window where she had been standing watch for them. "That's the Palazzo Urbino here in Bologna. My lady attends you there." Dropping a slight curtsey, she gave one last swift glance in Mario's direction before turning and leaving them.

"She's so beautiful," whispered his companion, as soon as she was out of earshot. His words were immediately met by a loud bray from Caesar.

"Well-spoken, my friend," said Rosso, ruffling the ear of his asinine friend. "Our love-struck companion seems to change lover loyalty as often as he changes his clothes, which by my reckoning is about once a week."

"That's not fair," said Mario in a hurt tone. He looked Rosso in the eye before he went on, "Honest . . . , but not fair." The two of them gripped each other's shoulders as only good friends can do and led the ass away.

They found lodgings for themselves and secured Caesar a safe stall with fresh hay to eat. Having seen to their ablutions, it was less than an hour later when they found themselves knocking on the door of the Palazzo Urbino. The door was opened, and they were ushered in and told to wait for the young duchessa in the small drawing room. It was a homey room which had obviously seen the hand of a female in its ordering. They had just enough time to be impressed by their cozy surroundings when the door was opened to reveal Rosso's goddaughter, Clare, looking more radiant than ever.

Rosso stood there with his arms open wide to greet her. "You look stunning, Clare! Life in Urbino obviously suits you," he commented, soaking up the vision of courtly beauty before him." I don't think Marco would let you in the forge wearing that dress," he said, admiring the silken gown the young lady was wearing.

"The years have been good to you, too, dearest of uncles," Clare said, kissing him on both cheeks. Her eyes strayed toward Mario, a look of enquiry hovering around her eyes.

"Forgive my bad manners. This is Mario, my traveling companion, best known for his beautiful voice, his soaring poetry, and his ability to fall in and out of love every week." Mario bowed and blushed until his face throbbed, whilst Rosso and Clare impishly enjoyed his discomfiture.

"Come and sit by the window and let's talk. Does Mario want to stay, or would he prefer to take a tour of the house?" Clare asked. "I'm sure I could find someone suitable to show him around." She rang the bell and asked the footman to call for her maid. Clare turned slightly and gave Rosso a small wink. When the maid appeared and was given her instructions, it was difficult to work out whether Mario or Lucia had the redder expression. "She didn't stop talking about him from the moment she arrived back an hour ago," Clare said to Rosso when the door had closed behind them.

"But first of all, I want to hear all your news before dinner." She sat sideways on her cushion and drew her feet up underneath her, just as she had done all those years before when they were traveling to France, looking for her parents.

Rosso told her everything that had been going on since he had returned with Agnes to her farm. As he told Clare about their children, a light appeared in his eye, and a tear appeared in Clare's. She reached out to hold his hand and said, "You must be very proud of them."

"We are both so blessed to have two such wonderful children," he said, in a voice that rolled up all the hopes and delights of a loving parent.

Rosso went on to talk about his painting and how Julian had been such a help to him. He talked of Toni's arrival, and of how the children had taken him to their hearts, and how he loved them as much as any parent could. Then he came to Marco and Laura and his voice faltered.

"Nothing's happened to Mama, has it?" Clare said, with a sudden expression of terror. She looked into Rosso's face and saw anguish there. "No," she said, putting her hand to her mouth, "not the baby!"

"Hush, my little one," Rosso replied. "They're fine, although it was a very close call." He ran his fingers through his red hair, took a deep breath and began, "I can't believe any of it really happened. But it did and I was there . . ." He went on to describe the events that had led to him and Toni cutting the baby from Laura's tummy, and how they had both survived. "It's a miracle really," he said. When he'd finished his story, he became aware that his face was beaded with perspiration. "I still can't believe it really happened," he muttered.

Clare threw her arms around Rosso's neck and burst into tears. "I'm so very proud of you, Uncle," she sobbed joyfully into his neck. "You always seem to appear at the right time and be able to do the right thing. I am so blessed that it was you who found me all those years ago, when I was abandoned in the piazza."

Rosso held her close. "If I remember correctly, it was you who found me," he replied. They both laughed, wiping the tears from each other's eyes. "But tell me, my little Duchessa, what's been happening to you since I last saw you, and what are your plans now that you've inherited your title? And a French title at that."

"Well, Mama's probably told you that I went to my godmother after Bini and Rizo's deaths. That was so awful, so horribly awful," she said, looking down and fiddling with the silken tie around her waist. "Those two scallywags were always so full of life and mischief, it still seems unbelievable that they're both dead. I half-expect them to appear from some doorway chasing each other or plotting some mischief for Sara and me." A half smile crossed her clouded face, then with a struggle she returned to her story. " Afterwards, I went to Godmother's, which was a great learning experience for a simple girl like me."

"Anyone who thinks that you're simple must have rocks in their heads," Rosso teasingly interjected.

"I shall ignore that, Uncle!" She gave him a loving nudge before continuing, "Let me just say that court life is very different to being the daughter of a wonderful artisan in Rome and living in a loving family. Godmother was very kind to me and taught me so much about, how shall I put it . . . survival in that sort of environment, which was a very good thing, considering what's happened in the meantime.

"She'd intimated to me that she'd also been in secret contact with the cardinal, so she had a fair inkling of what my future was likely to be like. It was a real blessing for me to learn the myriad of protocols you have to follow when you live at court. You just can't imagine how many different clothes these people wear," she said, looking at Rosso with those innocent eyes of hers. "And food . . . Godmother's husband eats enough for six men when he returns from one of his hunting trips!" Clare paused as if trying to frame her next words correctly. "He's a harsh man, and I've no doubt he can be extremely cruel, too, but if you're straight and honest with him, then he's straight and honest with you, even if you don't always like what he says."

"I can see that you have developed the mind of a philosopher and the tact of a seasoned diplomat," Rosso said, with a wry grin. "Thank God you've got such a wise head on those little shoulders of yours. Mother in Milan was spot-on when she told me that all those years ago."

Clare's eyes widened with delight at the mention of the dear religious lady. "Have you heard from her?" she asked. "I haven't heard from her for months. I hope nothing's happened to her."

"I'm sure she's fine," replied Rosso reassuringly, "and even if she's died, there won't be a happier woman in Paradise."

"You're right as usual, Uncle," Clare said, "but I'm so looking forward to seeing her again soon."

"So you intend to head straight on to Paris, then?" Rosso enquired.

"That's what Godmother has urged me to do. By the way, she's pregnant again. I think that's the tenth—not including me," she added with a proud smile. "She said that as long as the château has no head, there will be carrion to feed on its body. She's been giving me a short course on how to survive palace life. Apparently, I'll be expected to attend Her Majesty and present my credentials to the king." She leaned in close to Rosso and whispered conspiratorially, "It all sounds like very cloak-and-dagger stuff. Apparently, the hard thing is trying to find someone whom you can trust and who can't be bribed, blackmailed, or beaten into betraying you."

"You be careful, my lass," Rosso said to her with obvious concern writ large on his face. "Who is traveling with you?" he asked.

"Just my maid," she replied, "I did hope that perhaps . . ." Her voice trailed off, and she looked pleadingly at Rosso.

"My most beloved goddaughter, there is absolutely no way that I can leave Italy at the moment. Perhaps in the spring we might be able to make it." He paused and returned her steady gaze.

"Please, Uncle. Please come with me. You know how wise you are and how well we travel together. I need someone I can really trust."

"Clare, my love," he said softly, "I cannot come with you to Paris. However, I will accompany you to Milan, even though every second away from Agnes is a trial for me. But she will understand, though she'll miss me as much as I miss her."

"I'm sorry, Uncle, for putting you in such a difficult position. Of course, you must go back to Agnes and make sure that Marco, Laura, and their new baby are well. It was selfish of me. Do forgive me, please?" she said.

Rosso looking long and lovingly at her. "Of course, I forgive you. You're too precious to me. I'm sure something will turn up when we get to Milan, and no doubt Mother will have some inspired advice as usual."

They embraced, then Clare said, "You must be famished. Come, let's get something to eat. I wonder what's happened to your friend Mario and my maid Lucia." A small smile danced around her lips as she said, "We'd better find them before they get into too much trouble."

She rang a small bell and a manservant appeared. Clare asked that he bring them some food and also send a message to Mario and her maid to join them. The manservant bowed and backed out of the room.

"You do that very well for a reformed ragamuffin," Rosso quipped. The sound of laughter came through the door, which burst open to reveal Mario and Lucia looking very happy in each other's company.

"Reminds me of home," said Mario with a cheeky grin, "although I found the stables a bit cramped for my liking."

"That's a shame," riposted Rosso, "because that's where you might be sleeping tonight! He looked at the three young people with him, and for a moment in that expensive room, the future of the world gleamed brightly. They arranged themselves around a small table by the window overlooking the piazza, much to the acute embarrassment of the maid Lucia, who was far from used to such cultured dining experiences. Clare reassured her and asked her to sit between Rosso and Mario. Food appeared, lights were lit and in a short space of time they'd settled back to enjoy the meal and each other's company.

"I hear you have a good voice, as well as a good way with words, Master Mario. Perhaps later you might entertain us with one or the other of them," Clare said, sipping her goblet of wine.

"It would be an honor and a delight for me, my lady," he replied, "though I feel that I could never do justice to such exalted company." His eyes darted sideways to where Lucia was sitting. She blushed furiously, whilst Clare and Rosso smiled indulgently.

"Pray tell me, Mario," Clare continued, "what are your plans now that you've arrived in Bologna?"

"Plans, my lady?" he said, scratching his head with his free hand. "The world is my plan. Rosso here has only recently liberated me from the demon bonds of drunkenness, and I am an infant rejoicing in life again. I shall go where I am needed and where I can spread my own vision of happiness. My plan, my lady? My plan is to be a lion of wonder, a veritable troubadour of love. I am at your service." With that he stood, bowed deeply, and sat down again.

"I think he means that he's free to come with us to Milan, my dear," said Rosso, picking up a chicken wing and chewing on the burnt bits.

"You have distilled my words perfectly," replied Mario. He was about to reach for his wine when a small hand touched him on the arm and pointed to the carafe of water instead.

"You promised to swear off all alcohol whilst in my lady's company," said Lucia softly to him.

"Ah, yes," Mario replied, "Well remembered. I shall be a beacon of sobriety to you all whilst we travel together. You never know, it might even become a habit." He smiled broadly at them all, then they burst out laughing.

Rosso and Clare spent the rest of the day talking, whilst the young ones went off to explore the delights of Bologna. It soon became apparent that there really wasn't a moment to spare as Clare needed to get to Paris as quickly as possible. "But first, my intention is to meet with Mother in Milan," she said. "I have need of her counsel. Godmother has been wonderful in preparing me for material matters and all things political, but Mother has an insight into this world that I respect and admire—one that I most wish to emulate."

"She is a very holy lady," Rosso commented, "and yet her feet are firmly placed in reality. If you hadn't decided to stop and see her, then I can assure you that I would have insisted that you do so." He smiled. "There is something very special about that woman that makes me feel so safe in her company—and her a frail old lady who probably couldn't even knock snow off a rope!"

Dawn of the following day saw them leaving in a small carriage and following the road to Milan. Having observed how sad Rosso and Mario were at leaving Caesar behind, Clare secretly organized for the ass to be taken to Agnes' farm to await their return.

"What are you smiling at?" asked Rosso as they went out of the city gate.

"Nothing," she replied, looking out the window at the passing countryside.

Five

THE JOURNEY TO PARIS

THE COBBLED SURFACE of Santa Maria Delle Grazie's small courtyard rang with the sound of their coach wheels. The low grey sky seemed to mirror the facade of the church itself. By the adjacent convent, a white-haired gatekeeper rose stiffly to his feet. Rosso helped Clare down from the carriage with Lucia following, aided by a much-subdued Mario.

They walked to the convent gate. "No Spaniards following you this time?" the old gatekeeper said. Rosso was both stunned and delighted that the man remembered him after all these years. "Not many tall, skinny redheads come along in this direction," the gatekeeper said, sifting the keys through his arthritic fingers.

"And this is the little girl who was with me then," Rosso said, indicating Clare with his free arm. The gatekeeper's eyes opened wide with happiness and delight.

"Well, signs and wonders, eh? Signs and wonders! Mother will be happy to see you again. Growed into such a beauty, too." Turning his back, he unlocked the gate and allowed them to enter.

Just as he was passing through, the gatekeeper held Rosso by the arm. "Remember that little fella who brought your horse around that morning?"

"How could I ever forget him? He saved my life. Do you know what happened to him?"

The gatekeeper grinned, "I'll tell 'im you're 'ere. No doubt 'e'll be round to see yer." With that, he gave Rosso a gentle push in the direction of the small group who were disappearing off in the direction of the refectory.

When Rosso caught up with the others inside that grand room, they were all standing with open mouths looking up at the fresco on the gable wall.

"He finished it," whispered Clare reverentially, half-turning her head, but not taking her eyes off the glorious masterpiece.

"It's nice, isn't it?" said a lilting voice. Rosso and Clare immediately spun around to feast their eyes on the little nun. "Mother!" they cried in unison, lovingly engulfing her in their arms.

"I don't think I've had such a greeting since I was a little girl," the slight woman said to them, her serene and happy face radiating love. Rosso studied her closely and found it difficult to see much change since they'd last been there many years before. If anything, there was a slight translucence to her skin that allowed her inner light to shine more brightly. As usual, her eyes danced with life and wisdom.

"It's so good to see you, Mother," Clare began. "There's so much news I've got to tell you, and I need your guidance so very much."

Mother's laughter was like the tinkling of silvered bells. "My dear, don't be in such a rush. In all things, calm yourself first." She pointed up at the fresco. "Leonardo did finish it, and I think he did a beautiful job, don't you?" Still gazing at the fresco, she commented, "But like all of God's creations, it has a flaw. Would you believe that the dear man forgot to paint it on the right surface. But that was Leonardo, always willing to take risks—even with beauty itself. If you study it carefully, you can see that some of the colors are draining from the figures, which means that we'll need someone to help restore it. It's a bit like our faith," she said with twinkling eyes.." We're all beautiful creatures, and yet we all need to be renewed every now and again, so we don't lose our luster." She paused for effect. "Now if only we knew of a painter who would be equal to the task," and her eyes fairly glittered as she turned to look at Rosso.

"Mother," he said, with eyes wide open, "you're not for one second suggesting that I . . . ," and words literally failed him.

"Calm yourself, my dear Rosso," she said, reaching out to touch him lightly on the hand. "The good Lord gave you a wonderful gift, maybe it's time to share it with the wider world. But let's leave that with Him for the moment.

"Now who's this here with you?" she inquired, turning to Lucia.

"Forgive me, Mother," Clare said, "this is my companion Lucia, who will be traveling with me to Paris."

"Ah yes, Paris," Mother mused, "your godmother has been telling me all about that in her correspondence. I'm so glad we'll have some time together to discuss your plans there."

"Godmother has been writing to you?" asked an impressed Clare.

"We've known each other for quite some time, you know. When she was just a little girl living in Milan, she used to visit me if she was sad or confused, and we'd walk in the convent garden together. She was a sweet child, and she's had such a difficult life. I hope she's found some peace at last."

"She was happy when I left," Clare answered, "although this last pregnancy has left her feeling very tired." By this time, Mother's eyes had fallen on Mario, who was sitting on a bench, his legs drawn up under his chin and with his arms clasped around his knees. He was lost in deep contemplation of the fresco high above him on the wall. To his eyes the figures danced in the light of the many candles that had been carefully arranged around it. Rosso made to go over and bring him across. "Don't disturb him, Rosso. If I'm right, that young man needs this moment. Our Lord may be whispering to him. It would be a pity to interrupt such a conversation just to talk to an old woman like me." They silently shifted their attention between watching Mario and then looking at the painting high above them on the wall. They all treasured the memory of this moment long after they went their separate ways.

"I think Lucia should go and organize your room, whilst the rest of us find a comfortable spot to exchange news and plans. How does that sound?" Before they could answer, she'd commissioned a passing nun to attend to her softly whispered instructions.

"Yes, Mother," the young sister said, turning to lead Lucia away in silence.

"Why don't we go and sit in the cloister? It's such a lovely day, and Cook can bring refreshments out to us." She led them along the corridor and out into the sunlight, where they found a shaded seat. Close by, a small fountain gurgled gently and speckled starlings hopped about, busily pecking at crumbs left out for them.

Mother and Clare immediately began to talk quietly with each other, so Rosso wandered off to explore the arcades surrounding the cloister on all sides. He walked past a gardener who was enjoying a break from his digging. The man was sitting on a bench and gulping down a cooling drink of water. Rosso acknowledged him with a nod as he walked past, yet his eyes remained fixed on the glorious statue of St Joseph at the far end of the arcade.

"Need an 'orse, mister?" a manly voice said to him, a voice that was both unknown and yet very familiar. Rosso turned to see the gardener looking at him with a big foolish grin on his face. "The gatekeeper said youse were 'ere. Funny who you meet when yer out and about in Milan, eh?"

"It IS you!" cried Rosso, and he rushed back to embrace his savior of so many years ago. "Thank God you're still alive." And holding him at arm's length, Rosso examined him from head to toe. "You've grown," he said foolishly.

"Still as sharp as ever, I see," replied the little horse trader-turned-gardener.

"Forgive me, but it's just so wonderful to see you again, and I don't even know your name."

"Pietro," the man said, and Rosso almost wept with joy at the name.

"That just happens to be the name of one of the dearest men I know in all the world, and now it's yours, too."

"It always 'as been mi name! But it's good to know it's been well-used by uvver 'olders of such a notable name," and he smiled back broadly at Rosso.

"I have so many questions to ask you, but have you got time to speak? I don't want you to get into trouble with Mother."

Pietro looked across to where the tiny nun was sitting and talking animatedly with Clare. "That little ole lady over there," he said, not taking his eyes off the two ladies, "I'd lay down my life for that little woman." Rosso knew then that the little boy he had met so long ago had grown into a great man.

Six

THE FAMILIAR ROAD
TO PARIS

THEY REMAINED AT the convent for a number of days whilst Mother and Clare discussed plans for Clare's arrival—and the inevitable challenges that she would find—in Saint-Germain-en-Laye. This allowed Rosso and Pietro time to visit those areas of Milan that Rosso hadn't had time to see on his last visit. Pietro for his part seemed to know everyone, and to be held in high esteem by them.

"Is your papa still alive, Pietro?" asked Rosso as they left the Duomo.

"Nah," his young friend said, as he kicked a rotten apple from the fruit stall into the gutter. "'E didn't last much longer a'rta you left. 'E tried to flog a dead 'orse to the wrong man. Trouble was, this bloke was a worse villain than mi ole man.

Pricked him straight frew the 'eart with 'is knife. The old man got a dreadful surprise, then 'e upped and dropped dead." Although he tried to sound lighthearted, Rosso could sense the sadness in Pietro's voice. "'E's no great loss to anyone. But you know what? I still expect 'im to be there when I goes home in the evening. Talking of which, do you fancy coming to the old place? And this time, I promise there won't be no one there wanting to do you no good." Saying that, he put his arm around Rosso's shoulders, and they went happily on their way, exploring the back alley-ways of the city.

A strange mood had come over Mario as he roamed the corridors of the convent deep in thought. "Let him be," Mother had counseled. So, they left him alone in his own inner world, chasing unseen visions and haunted by unknown thoughts. One morning whilst breaking their fast in the refectory, they were delighted to hear the glorious sound of singing coming down the corridor. It was Mario in full voice, and it was wonderful.

"You've certainly gotten out of bed on the right side," said Lucia as Mario came around the trestle table. He took her hand in his and kissed it passionately. "I am liberated at last," he announced.

Glancing around at the others, Rosso enquired with a broad smile, "Pray tell us from what demons have you been liberated, Mario?"

"The dagger of Dionysius, the blackness of Bacchus, or as some call it, the grip of the grape. You see before you, a man liberated from the demons of drink. No more will intoxicating liquor pass these lips," he said, placing a hand over his mouth. With that statement, he surprised Mother, who had just walked into the room and was delighted by the unlooked-for attention.

"The Lord moves in mysterious ways," said Mario, marching over to her and kissing her hand.

"And they are wonderful to behold," replied the little woman. "I'm hungry," she continued, looking toward the table where the remnants of the early meal were rapidly disappearing. "But I'm glad you are all well fed." She picked up a small crust, enough to keep a small bird alive, and beckoned to Rosso to follow her. He rose and followed her to her small room. He sat in the simple chair she directed him to. Drawing her own modest chair up next to his, she said, "We need to talk about a few things before Clare leaves." It was a statement of fact and needed no reply from the listener.

"Clare has inherited an ancient title, a large fortune, and a veritable mountain of challenges to overcome. She will need help." She paused to ensure that her remarks had registered in Rosso's mind. "She is a very bright and capable young woman now, and her godmother has given her some wise guidance already. However," she added, pausing, "Clare is still young, and court life in Paris can be a viper's nest. I hear the current queen has a good heart, so at least that should diminish some of her problems. But she will be alone." She paused again "My dear Rosso, if Clare asks you to go to her, then you must go."

A three-letter word beginning with b was forming in his throat; however, when he looked into Mother's tranquil, unchanging face, he could not say it. "Yes, Mother" was all he could manage.

"One more thing," she went on, "I mentioned dear Leonardo's fresco, which adorns our humble refectory. I meant what I said about it needing some attention, and you mustn't hide your light under a bushel. Brother Julian tells me that you're a very talented artist, and I shall be summoning you soon to come and give it your best attention. Just call it the simple wishes of an old woman." The smile that she gave Rosso would have melted the heart of the most black-hearted sinner.

As he was walking back to the others, Rosso smiled and shook his head at how this little waif of a woman had just led him by the nose into his current predicament. *How am I going to explain this to Agnes?* he thought. But in his heart, he knew exactly what her response would be. "Women!" he muttered aloud.

"They say it's the first sign of old age when you start talking to yourself," said Mario, who had appeared out of nowhere. "Have you got a moment?" he asked.

'I appear to be in great demand this morning," Rosso replied cheerfully. "How may I help you, my pure-hearted young friend?"

"I was thinking," he said earnestly, "which for me is often a very dangerous thing. But what would you say to me going to Paris with Clare? She needs company, and I can be very useful when I put my mind to it."

"Personally," Rosso replied, "I think she'd be mad to accept. But knowing that particular young lady, I'm sure she'll say yes." He stood in front of Mario before continuing, "Mario, when I was a bit younger than you are now, I doubt anyone would have trusted me with the cat, let alone their precious godchild. It was the goodness of decent people that allowed me to begin to trust the world in return. None of us can read the future, but as long as you promise to become the incredible man that I believe you can be, then you have my blessing."

"Thanks, Rosso," Mario replied. "I'm not sure that I know what my best is, but I promise you that I will strive to reach it."

"And Mario," Rosso said, looking his young protégé straight in the eye, "if at any time, you have any fears for Clare, or you think that she needs me, then you must get a message to me, and I'll come straight away. Understand?"

"Of course," the youth smiled back, "but I don't suppose that will be necessary." They both laughed at his bravado.

Their trip was to take them to the coast and then via Marseilles to Lyon. They'd decided to follow the river route before undertaking the final leg of the trip to Paris by coach. Rosso was impressed by Clare's organizational skills and how seamlessly things seemed to fall into place.

"It was watching Papa in the forge that helped. He was so patient and so orderly in the way he went about turning metal into things of beauty. And Mama was always so patient and understanding, even when attending the most difficult of customers. They always left feeling as if they were the most important customers that Papa and Mama had ever had. Before you found me in the piazza that day, I used to be terrified of the world, and then Mama and Papa helped me see that most of the people I came across were just as terrified as I used to be. 'All you need is a little patience' is Papa's favorite saying, and it has always stood me in good stead."

"Those two are the best examples of 'loving kindness' that I've ever met," said Rosso, putting his arm around her. "And now with your godmother and Mother here finishing the job, they've all crafted a most beautiful and talented young lady. I really am honored to be your godfather." He kissed her lightly on the forehead before they turned to welcome the others who were to accompany them on the journey.

"I wonder if I'll meet that little man we met in Genoa. What was his name?" Clare whispered conspiratorially.

"You mean Odysseo?" said Rosso. "It wouldn't surprise me if he turned up at the Vatican, whispering in the Holy Father's ear. But if your paths do cross, send him my best wishes and say that I'd be delighted to paint a portrait of him if he'd let me." With that he winked at Clare and stood back to allow Mother to take her to one side for a final few words of wisdom.

After what seemed like an all-too-brief period of bustling and packing, hugs and farewells, their coach had disappeared, leaving just Mother and Rosso standing by the entrance to the convent.

"Probably best for them that you stay 'ere," a voice said behind them. It was the gatekeeper, with his iron keys clattering on an iron hoop suspended from his belt. "It must be the red 'air" he added. "Attracts trouble, if yer gets mi drift." He put the iron key in the lock and turned it, shutting them both in.

Clare's journey to Genoa with her companions went without incident. Their major challenge was the boredom and trying to keep warm in the late autumn days. "I never realized that sitting down all the time could make you so tired," Mario whispered to Lucia. She smiled back at him as the carriage rocked to and fro.

"We won't be stopping in Genoa," said Clare. "Unfortunately, my inheritance won't wait for me, and I must get to Paris as soon as I can before some other relative appears and ensconces themselves in the château."

"Shall I go to the docks and secure our berths when we arrive?" asked Mario.

"No," said Clare with a strange look on her face, "I'll take care of that. If he's still around, then there's someone I think will be able to help us." Turning her face to the window, she smoothed a strand of errant hair back into its rightful position, and she had a bright glint in her eye.

When the coach finally reached the dockside, they all disembarked, and the luggage was handed down.

"Wait here," Clare said, before heading off to where tall wooden buildings peered down severely over the bustle of the dockyard.

"All very mysterious," said Mario, looking at Lucia. "Is she always like that?"

"I think we should be more interested in looking after the luggage than trying to work out what my lady is thinking," replied Lucia, who was growing uncomfortable at being surrounded by so many lecherous sailors.

Mario laughed as he drew her close, "If they think you're with me, they'll lose interest," he said.

"I think I'd be safer with one of them, thank you very much," the little woman responded. She pushed him away, much to the delight of the passing seamen.

"If you can't 'andle 'er, p'raps you'd better move away, and let a real man look a'rter 'er," said one man, supplementing his words with vulgar sign language. Mario tipped his hat toward the man, muttering, "Thank you, kind sir, but I think I can manage," before picking up the luggage and moving toward a nearby taverna. Lucia drew herself up to her full height, gave the impudent sailor a haughty look, turned on her heel, and followed Mario.

Clare swept through the throng like an unseen breeze, her heart pounding in her chest. It was a distant hope that she'd find the old ship that she and Rosso had sailed on all those years ago, but this was the moment she'd dreamed of nearly every day of her life since those early times. On two occasions, she thought she'd found it, but was disappointed when none there had heard of 'Puss' or of Kristopher, the cabin boy from the *Santa Maria*.

She caught sight of a fighting ship moored a little way out in the harbor. "What's that big ship over there?" she asked a man sitting atop an iron capstan. His craggy features were chiseled and burnished by many years at sea and his face wore a thoughtful, yet tranquil expression.

"That there is Admiral Doria's ship. Mighty fine, too, if I'm any judge of 'em." said the man, pointing with a gnarled and twisted finger in the general direction of the ship. He turned and studied Clare from tip to toe. "But what brings a fine young lady like you out along the docks, amongst all this 'ere riffraff?" he asked.

"I'm hoping to find an old acquaintance. I met him on a ship many years back when I was just little, and he was very kind to me. I was hoping I might find him again." To her acute consternation, Clare felt a blush spread across her face.

"Name of . . . ?" the man enquired in return, noting her embarrassment.

"His real name was Kristopher of the *Santa Maria*, but everyone called him Puss," she said, with a wry smile. "It suited him, too."

"Hah." the old man smiled back. "Little sprat with spike hair and shifty eyes?"

"No, he wasn't shifty at all," she said, turning on the man with a sense of injustice flaring inside her. She found herself looking at his toothless, grinning face as his shoulders silently shook with gentle fun.

"Easy, mate," he said. "You're mighty quick to defend 'im. Fond of 'im were you?"

"Sir," she said, her blush returning with a vengeance, "I was only twelve years old at the time." His laugh was both kind and understanding.

"Don't be afeared," the old man said. "I knows 'im as well as I knows this 'ere 'and o' mine." Pointing back at the warship, he continued, "An' 'e's the Admiral's right-'and man on that very ship out there. 'E ain't no cabin boy now, young lady. 'E's the captain of that mighty vessel. Captain of a famous ship that chases Turks and pirates all 'round the Mediterranean."

Clare followed his finger and stared at the massive boat, webbed with rigging and ringing with shouts.

"Can I get a message to him, sir?" she asked in a most reconciled voice.

"No need to send a message out there," the man replied, "'E's on shore." Twisting stiffly, he pointed to a building nearby where there was much coming and going by sailors, chandlers, and various merchants. "Don't you be a-going through the front door with all them other villans," he said. "You go 'round the side there. There's a door along there that leads to some stairs. Go up them stairs and give a knock on the door in front of you. Then feast your eyes on a great man." His hazelnut eyes looked straight at her as he said softly, "I remembers you from that time. Young Puss never stopped a talking about you for such a long time a'rter you left the ol' ship. 'E ain't ever walked out with any other young lady since, to my knowledge," he added with a knowing look.

"Thank you, sir," she said. She bent toward him and kissed him on the forehead. Now it was the sailor's turn to blush.

"Well if that ain't the best thing that's happened to me in many a long year. You're a blessing, young lady, that's what you are, a blessing."

Clare headed off in the direction of the building, side-stepping the human flotsam and jetsam that bobbed along the quay. Clare didn't hear the old sailor call out after her, "And whatever happened to that redheaded monk who was traveling with you?" His words were buried by the noise of the docks and the squeal of the seagulls that circled overhead.

She followed the sailor's directions and soon found the side door. Climbing the stairs, she paused, uncertain, with her small fist raised in front of the door. A small gasp of surprise escaped her lips as the door swung open to reveal an equally surprised face in the opening.

Kristopher was now a tall, well-featured man with a sun-tanned, lightly weathered face, yet Clare would have known his lively eyes anywhere.

"Hello, Kristopher," she said, with genuine delight. "I promised I'd find you the next time I came to Genoa."

Kristopher's mouth may have opened and even moved, but no sound came out.

"That's unlike the boy I remember," Clare said cheekily, "If I remember correctly, he was never at a loss for words."

Kristopher's mouth now clamped shut as his face heated with the emotion he felt. "I never dared dream—," he began, "I never dared dream that you'd ever return," he said. "Am I dreaming now?"

"No, you silly man," Clare laughingly replied, her face beginning to color. "It's the middle of the day, and anyway, it's far too cold in this hallway to fall asleep."

Coming to his senses, Kristopher stood aside and beckoned her into his office. "Come in. Come in." He bustled about and dragged a seat near the small fire in the corner, then begged her to be seated and to warm herself.

"Thank you, kind sir," she said, bowing coquettishly before sitting down. Kristopher went hunting for another chair, which he set down next to hers. "So, you do remember me?" Clare asked with a twinkle in her eye.

"How could I ever forget you, Signorina? I have thought of you so often since those times when we stood in the crow's nest of that dear old boat." He paused to take in what he saw before his eyes. "You are beautiful," he said, before hastily covering his forwardness and adding, "and life seems to have been good to you . . ."

"And to you, too," Clare answered, looking around the small room. "I hear you're the captain of a very famous ship and a friend of the great Admiral Doria. Is it true that you chase Turks and pirates all over the Mediterranean?" Kristopher blushed again. "I've been lucky," he said. "Most of the time life is very dull on board a ship. But tell me, why are you here? Are you going to Paris again?"

The two of them began to share their stories when a bell rang nearby. Kristopher looked at the door and then at Clare, "Excuse me for a moment, but I need to attend to a few matters. I will return immediately." He went to the door and called for his assistant. The summoned messenger ran up the stairs two at a time before receiving his orders in a low whisper from his captain. The assistant shot inquisitive looks over his master's shoulder at the young lady sitting in his master's office. When Kristopher was done giving instructions, he closed the door and resumed his seat by the fire.

"One of the few benefits of being a captain is that you can change your orders. Before you arrived, it appeared I had business to do this morning, but suddenly"—he snapped his fingers theatrically—"we have the rest of the day to ourselves."

Clare's hands shot to her face. "Oh dear," she said, "I forgot Mario and Lucia."

"Who are they?" asked Kristopher, mildly confused.

"They've been my companions on the road from Milano. They're coming to Paris with me." She hesitated before continuing, "You see, I've come into a small inheritance, and I need to go to Paris to present my credentials to the authorities." She looked down at her hands which were clasped together in her lap and fell silent.

"Well, come on then." Kristopher took her hand and helped her out of her chair. "Let's go and find them, and we can talk on the way." Suddenly they felt like the two young ragamuffins who'd run all over the ship those many years ago.

By the time they found the two patient companions, Kristopher and Clare had learned a little more about each other. They found that their bond from the past was little changed; if anything, it had become stronger and brighter.

Mario looked suspiciously at Kristopher, but when the captain held out his arms to embrace Clare's companion, Mario felt only the strong arms of friendship. And when he looked into Kristopher's eyes, he saw the look of a man he could trust. Said Mario, "You remind me a bit of Rosso. Apart from the color of your hair, that is . . . and the fact that you're much stronger, and you're about 15 years younger than him. But apart from that, you could be identical twins," he said. The others laughed at his unintended humor. Mario himself kept a straight face, because what he saw before him reminded him greatly of his recent benefactor and friend. He stored those thoughts in his head, thinking that perhaps one day he would weave them into a song or poem.

"Without wishing to state the obvious, Clare," Kristopher interrupted them, "but you will need to find a ship to take passage to France. May I modestly suggest that I may be able to help you there. My greatest regret, however, is that I won't be able to go with you, because currently Admiral Doria is not on the best of terms with our French neighbors. But times have a habit of changing," he added in a mysterious tone. "In the meantime, an old friend of mine runs a regular passage between here and Marseilles. With a gentle bit of arm twisting, I think I will be able to persuade him to offer you a comfortable trip to your destination. But first, let's take some refreshments." He led them outside and then pointed in the direction of a side street, encouraging Mario and Lucia to walk on ahead of them.

"You speak so very eloquently these days, Captain Kristopher," Clare said, raising a kerchief to her face to cover her smile and subdue the unpleasant smell they had just walked past.

"And you, my lady," Kristopher replied, doffing his hat to her in a mock bow, "seem to be dressed far more fashionably these days." They both grinned. Clare linked her arm through her old companion's, saying, "Can we stay with Clare and Kristopher, or should I still call you 'Puss'?"

"Kristopher will be fine, Clare," he replied smiling down at her. The moment seemed to be encased in crystal. "It really is so much better than I thought."

"What is?" she asked.

"Seeing you again," he said.

They were jostled to their senses by a passing porter with a large load on his back. Seeing that Mario was looking lost, Kristopher shouted, "Take the next left, and you'll see the taverna on the right." Looking back at Clare, he added, "Almost there now," and they finished their walk arm in arm in happy silence.

Over a meal, they all talked about the small and vital things in life. Lucia talked of her family and of how her father and two older brothers had died in the battle of Vailà when the French had defeated the Venetians. "They were mercenaries," she said quietly, her simple face undisturbed by any signs of pain or suffering. "Mama told them not to go, but Papa never listened to her anyway, and he took the two boys with him."

The others fell silent. "Won't you feel a little strange going to live in France, then?" asked Kristopher.

"No," she replied simply and brightly. "Mama taught us to serve others wherever we are. It wasn't the French who killed my family; there were just as many Italian mercenaries in their army as there were in the Venetian one. Who knows who was right or who was wrong? Not me with my simple head," she said in her open, simple way. "If my lady wanted me to go and work for her in Persia, then I'd follow her there, too. That's because she's always so honest and good to me—and as Mama said, 'Do unto others as they do unto you.'"

"You're a good child," Kristopher said, reaching out to hold and squeeze her hand. "I wish there were more like you in this crazy world of ours."

"I shall write a poem about you one day," Mario declared. "The only problem is that I think it would be difficult for one such as me to get into the mind of such an innocent as you." The others laughed again at his comment, but yet again, Mario did not join in the laughter.

Toward the end of the meal as Mario and Lucia were giggling over some private joke, Kristopher leaned close to Clare and softly said, There's something that I'd like to show you." She looked up into his eyes and again her heart melted and raced at the same time.

"Kristopher and I need to discuss the travel arrangements so we're going to his office for a little while. If you two could stay here with the baggage, please." She dropped a small purse into Mario's hand. "That should cover our expenses."

The young man nodded. "We'll wait here, my lady."

Kristopher took Clare by the hand and led her back to the storehouse. "Can you ride?"

"Of course," she replied happily, "but I'm not sure . . ." She indicated her travel clothes.

Kristopher flashed her a big grin, "Perhaps being a captain has more than one advantage," he said. "Wait here for a moment," he continued, before bounding up the stairs to his office. True to his word, he returned in less than a minute with a bundle of clothes. "Some of our best young couriers are about your size . . ."

Before he could continue, Clare put her finger on his lips to silence him. "You don't have to explain anything to me, Kristopher." Her simple, intimate gesture spoke to his heart and he inclined his head ever so slightly to indicate his understanding.

"The stables are around the back. You can change in one of the stalls. No one will disturb you, I promise." Taking her by the hand once more, he led her to where the courier's horses were kept on standby twenty-four hours a day. Whilst Clare prepared herself, she could hear Kristopher gently cajole the horses as he shortened the stirrups for her and adjusted the girths for them both.

When she appeared, his face couldn't suppress an impish grin. "Why do I always see that wild child in the crow's nest looking at me?" he said.

"It's strange that you should say that, Puss," she replied, pulling her hair tight behind her head and tying it in a knot. Lifting her left foot slightly, she said, "Perhaps you might help me up, kind sir," whilst grasping the saddle with her free hand.

Kristopher smiled. "Of course, my lady." Having helped her onto her mount, he handed her the reigns before mounting the steed tethered next to hers. "Well, are you ready for another adventure?" he called back over his shoulder as his horse moved into the cobbled courtyard.

They walked their mounts out through the docks and into the shadowy lanes. It wasn't long before the huddled houses gave way to the intoxicating freshness of the countryside. "Where are we going?" Clare shouted to Kristopher. He looked at her and then pointed to a small hill which was rapidly increasing in stature.

"San Benigno," he said. It was then that she saw the lighthouse for the first time. The building—for building it surely must be, even though it was pencil thin and rose over two hundred feet in the air—seemed like a needle thrust into the hill by some enormous giant. At its pinnacle, the housing for its flashing lens glowed with the light from a wood fire. But she had no time to admire it from such a distance. Kristopher urged their horses on until the shadow from the lighthouse seemed to tell time like a giant sundial.

Kristopher reigned in his horse, and the two of them walked their mounts to the summit of the hill, where he tethered them to a post near the lighthouse.

Pointing to a well-worn patch of grass, he said, "I've been coming up here since we first met." He paused, and even the gulls soaring lazily overhead seemed to acknowledge the beauty of the moment and remained silent.

Clare felt something inside her chest expand and race. Her face could not suppress a smile. She felt happier than she had ever done in her life.

"I have imagined this moment for so long" Kristopher continued, "and now it's arrived . . ." His voice tailed off and he fell silent. The breeze stirred the grass with a feathered touch for a brief moment before holding its breath once more.

"I prayed for this moment, too," Clare said, "but I thought God was deaf to my words." Again the silence of the world embraced them both. "But now I know he heard my every word. My prayers must have seemed rash to Him. I wanted to rush things, but He knew best."

Kristopher led her to the flattened grass and spread his jacket on it. He helped Clare to sit down and then sat down next to her. The two of them looked out over the sea and let their eyes scan its ever-changing form. Although the spicular patterns formed by the whitened surf swept their eyes from this point to that, they saw nothing. It was a moment of pure contemplation. They sat in silence as lovers do, communing in a private universe where words become unnecessary and being is all.

A bold gull landed close to them, bringing them back into the present with its pure white chest, beady black eyes, and sole orange-webbed foot. It stood on one leg and cocked its head to one side as if asking, 'Well, what are you going to do now?' The two smiled in unison before turning to each other.

"Clare . . . ," Kristopher began, but she dropped her gaze as a small furrow appeared on her brow. They looked back over the wide sea.

"I think we should get back" Kristopher said, "the others will be expecting us." He offered her his hand. With her smile restored, she grasped it and he pulled her to her feet. Now they were barely inches apart from one another, close enough to feel each other's breath. "I will wait for you," he whispered.

"As I will for you, Puss," she replied, and their lips lightly touched for a brief eternity. "Race you to the horses," Clare said, pulling back slightly and hurtling off down the hill. "I bet you can't catch me," she called back over her shoulder. Kristopher couldn't resist a smile and took off after her.

As they entered the cobbled area of the port, they stopped their mounts. In the silence of their own language, they reached out and held each other's hands, speaking only with their eyes. In the isolation of that silence, they pledged their troth to each other. When they released their grip, the noise of the world flooded back into their lives.

"I'll go and secure you all a passage," he said, "and will meet you back at the taverna. Leave the horse with the groom. He has instructions to see to your needs."

"Thank you, kind sir." Her eyes flashed with happiness. She held her hand out, and they touched fingertips to fingertips. Then Kristopher was gone.

Once she'd changed back into her travel clothes, she headed back to the taverna, flushed with the joy of life. She'd expected that her friends would read what had happened in her face, but they'd been too busy having fun themselves to notice any change.

"You're back," said Mario, before returning to his conversation with a fellow Italian—which naturally involved the use of hands and face to embellish various points. Lucia, meanwhile, was being courted attentively by a young officer who appeared to be French. Clare was left to her own devices until Kristopher reappeared a short while later.

'"It should be an easy crossing . . . ," he said. "But with the sea, I always say, 'Be prepared for the worst, then you won't be surprised by anything.'"

"Wise advice, Captain," interjected Mario, having observed his new friend's return, "wise advice indeed."

"One more thing." Kristopher signaled to them to stay seated and leaned in toward them, talking in a lowered voice. "Ports are always full of spies and troublemakers, so beware. My admiral is not the most favored person in French eyes, but that may change. Likewise, the French have created a lot of enemies recently, mainly because they've won so many battles, which makes the rest of the world very nervous." Looking at Clare, he added, "and you're a young Italian woman with very little protection who's going to live in France and claim a French title!" He placed his hand on her arm to stifle her defense. "All I'm saying is, be careful. You are very precious. Be nice to everyone, but trust no one —unless they happen to be a ship's captain and part-time pirate."

"Thank you, Captain, for your timely reminder," Clare replied, and a small smile lifted the corner of her lip. "Although I would suspect that fighting Turks on the open sea would present one or two more dangers than taking a carriage to Paris."

Kristopher looked around the crowded taverna and retorted seriously, "I'm not so sure, Clare. You be very careful."

He escorted the small group to their ship, and a porter was employed to transport their luggage to the embarkation plank. The captain of the ship appeared at the rails and gave a knowing nod to Kristopher. "You'll be safe in his hands," Kristopher said to his friends, "but when you get to France you'll be on your own. If things change here, then maybe . . ." He left the sentence unfinished but a seed of hope was planted in Clare's heart.

November weather was known for being unpredictable. Sometimes, the skies were blue, the air icy, and the seas mirror-smooth. At other times, an arctic storm would sweep down from the Russian steppes, turning the rigging into frozen webs of glacial stalactites. The travelers were shown to their small cabins, which were spare of furniture, but had plenty of blankets should the weather turn.

Clare returned immediately to the deck and stood at the railing, where she saw Kristopher still standing bare-headed, waiting to wave farewell. She smiled at him and pointed to the lookout nest at the top of the mast. He smiled back at her and tapped his chest over his heart before nodding, knowing exactly what she was thinking. "Ask him!" were the last words she heard from Kristopher before orders were shouted to prepare the ship for departure.

As Clare clung to the rails, she was unaware of Mario's presence as he came to stand beside her. "He's a good man," her companion said, as the sails filled with eager wind and snapped into position.

"He is the most precious of men," she replied, without taking her eyes off the shrinking figure standing on the dock. He gave her one final wave and shouted something into the breeze. His words mixed with the wind and were lost. "As long as he stays safe," she muttered.

Turning to Mario, she said with a glint in her eye, "There's something I'd like to ask the captain," and she headed off across the deck to gain the captain's attention.

Two days later, as the watery sun reached its zenith, Clare, Mario and the lookout stood on the platform at the top of the highest mast. Their faces were caressed by the warmth of the sun.

"It's so beautiful up here," said Clare.

"I feel sick," was all Mario could say, as his white-knuckled hands gripped the tarred pole as hard as he could. "This is suicidal," he went on. "Have you got a death wish?"

"Open your eyes and look!" Clare shouted. "You can see forever!" She opened her arms wide as if to embrace the whole sky.

"Beautiful, isn't it, Signorina?" the lookout said. "Best place on earth on a day like today. But even when a gale's a-blowing fit to rip the sails apart, there's nothin' like being up here lurching from side to side, seeing the foaming giants a-trying to smash this little lady down into the deep dark depths."

"Stop it," yelled Mario, "you're killing me." His two companions only laughed more at his discomfort. Yet slowly and surely, he too opened his eyes as he grew accustomed to the rhythm of the sea and the singing sounds of the ship's timbers. He, too, began to feel the emotion of what he saw and what he felt. He, too, became aware of the life in the air and in the water, and how fragile were all those who dared to sail across its surface.

When they finally descended and the lookout went to give his report, Mario stopped Clare and said, "Thank you. I never realized how dizzying heights and unstable ships could be so, well, exhilarating. For a moment, I felt so free and yet so vulnerable up there. It's difficult to describe . . ."

"But I hope you will try one day, Mario. You are an Alchemist. You use words, not spells, to create magic."

Seven

FRANCE

NOTHING HAD ALTERED, Clare thought to herself as Marseilles came into view. The docks were just as loud, just as busy, and just as smelly as she remembered. She'd hoped that she might glimpse an elephant with her little friend Odysseo leading it along the quay. But it was not to be. She also looked to see if anyone might be watching for her. All around her there were throngs with many faces sporting shifty expressions. None of them seemed the least bit interested in her or her two companions. So it was that on this occasion, she believed her arrival had occurred unnoticed.

Having found suitable accommodations for the night, they asked the innkeeper to arrange for river transport to Lyon. "Don't accept any cabins below decks," she said, "The last time I tried that, it killed my father." Mario looked at her askance.

"But I thought your father was alive. Didn't you say that he'd just become a father again?" he said.

"My real father was a Frenchman. He was heir to a dukedom, and he died from a fever he caught from one of the wretched barges that run up to Lyon from here." A fire seemed to sparkle in her eyes. She looked at Mario and added, "We'll sleep on the deck under the stars if we have to!!"

The journey to Lyon was tedious. Low skies infused the landscape with a monotonous greyness. A sort of early winter dullness and dampness seeped into their clothes, their bread, and their thoughts. A misty rain fell on them for most of the journey, and the black-fingered tree branches and reed wands were heavy with moisture, all waving back and forth in the probing winter breeze. Lyon came as a welcome relief to them, breaking the mind-slowing monotony of their journey.

Only Mario seemed to cope with the appearance of it all. On the last day of their boat trip, during a lull in the wind, Clare found him on the deck sitting cross-legged and staring at nothing. In his lap was a piece of paper. She came up behind him, but felt guilty about reading over his shoulder.

"What are you writing?" she asked lightly.

"Only some thoughts that for some reason took up residence in my head. My brain seems to do funny things in gloomy times," he said, looking up and over his shoulder at her. He was smiling as he said that.

"May I see them?" she asked.

He handed her the piece of paper. As she read it, a small gasp of wind lifted the corner of the page. It blew a strand of hair into her face which she unconsciously replaced as she continued to read:

Lapping waters lick the low-lined keel.
Misty miasmas make shrouds of sails
Whilst battalions of water-footed rushes
shiver and stir in the numbing cold.
Grey light, grey sky, grey world;
Color bled from every living thing;
Eyes leeched of light's transcendent weft
As we slide silently past,
Ghostly actors on this winter's morn.
A diamond drip of water drops from
     dipping branch
Sending dizzy circles to marry and mingle
     with others.
Small grey-coated birds with regal pose and
     great hearts
Dispel the gloom with sweet songs
From puffed-out chests brightly bibbed with
     rosy plumes.
There is a peace here on this wooden deck.
There is beauty to be found in this greyed-
     out world.

Just one small glimpse is all it takes,
One unexpected act of nature's grace
To illuminate the mind and warm the
    heart
of we who silently pass by."

Clare was moved by the words more than she dared describe. "Thank you, Mario. That's beautiful. Thank you." She handed the precious paper back to its smiling owner.

The river journey was slow and the wind fickle. Often the crew had to take to their oars to help the boat on its journey. Help was hired, too, from men with horses who patrolled the river banks for just such days. A line was thrown to them and they towed the reluctant ship against the flow, onwards toward Lyon.

When finally they saw the city through the parting fog, a small boat pulled out toward them. "Hold fast. You can't stop here!" a voice hailed them from a short way off. "We have the plague."

The captain of the vessel acknowledged the instruction with a spit into the water and informed his crew to sail on. As they passed through the city, they heard the plaintive sound of muffled church bells calling out their sad news. They saw thin threads of smoke from several sites on either bank indicating where homes had been destroyed in the hope of halting the contagion. Every now and then a body floated past, a grim reminder of their own fate if they had failed to heed the warning.

They passed glumly on and out past Lyon. "What do we do now, Captain?" asked Clare. "We were supposed to pick up a carriage to take us on to Paris."

The captain shrugged and spat once more into the river. "Reckon you'll have to try at the next stop, my lady," he said slowly, "though I doubt you'll be able to secure as comfortable a carriage as you would in Lyon. Depends, really," he said. His final expectoration indicated to Clare that the conversation was over.

About an hour past Lyon, they pulled into the wharf of a small settlement. "Any plague here?" the captain shouted to the lone figure sitting on a capstan.

"Not this year," came the reply. "There aren't too many left after it paid us a visit last year," he added.

"Could you ask if there's anyone who has a carriage for hire?" Clare asked him. A conversation was struck up between the captain and the capstan-dweller, the upshot of which was that he, too, spat in the river and walked off. Returning a short time later, he was accompanied by the sound of cart wheels, which stopped behind the large shed that acted as the jetty's storeroom. The capstan-dweller was in the company of a swarthy-looking fellow who was introduced as their new carrier. He stood silently watching as the three travelers descended via a narrow plank.

Their swarthy friend gave no hint of help, but turned and went around the shed to where a wooden tumbril stood. Sitting up in the front of this conveyance was a woman and her young child.

"Is this it?" Lucia asked Mario quietly.

"At least we won't have to worry about being cramped inside with other unpleasant companions," he replied weakly. "As long as it doesn't rain, we should be fine," he said, picking up a piece of their luggage.

The man stepped forward and in a surprisingly gentle voice stated, "I must apologize, milady, . . . but this is all that we have here in our poor village and if you wish, then I, Jacques, am at your service. My friend here tells me that you wish to go to Paris. If that is the case, then perhaps I can give you passage to Orléans." He paused and looked at his young wife before adding quietly, "We are going to live with her family. It is healthier there." Then he reached over to Mario and took the trunk from him, placing it in the tumbril. He then turned and held out his hand to help first Clare and then Lucia up onto the wagon.

"I am sorry it is not prettier," he said, and then joined the woman at the front of the transport. Once the travelers were settled, he gave the command, and the old horse began its stately journey along the well-used road.

The weather was mild when they began, and the threatened rain held off for some days, allowing them to climb the hills that confronted them in the early part of the journey. Often they climbed down and walked besides the tumbril, which proved a relief for the horse and for their bones! Even though the fields and countryside were bleak and bare, they still held a spare beauty which eased their tired minds and lifted their hopes. When squalls of rain hit them, Jacques gave them canvas coats from beneath his bench to help keep them dry. This simple act of kindness further ce-mented their budding friendship.

Lucia had struck up a happy banter with the young boy, who was also called Jacques, and who took great delight in her Italian words. When Lucia began to sing some lullabies intended to help him sleep, he would be reduced to fits of giggles, which were infectious. "Why is he laughing?" she asked Clare.

"I don't know," she answered, "but it's beautiful, isn't it?"

The mother's name was Claude, "The same as the queen in Paris," she added, blushing deeply at the sound of her own words. She was a quiet woman and seemed most devout, often reaching for the crucifix that hung around her neck. As they rocked along the road, Clare continued her educa-tion of Lucia and now Mario, about France, her customs, and her language.

"You speak very good French, milady"— Jacque said without turning round, "for an Italian, that is!" And he turned to see if his soft jest had hit its mark.

"It just so happens, Monsieur, that my father was French," said Clare. "It was a pure inconvenience that my mother happened to be Italian." She paused for effect before adding, "Well actually, she was Spanish, but my real parents were Italian."

Jacques looked totally confused at the conflicting infor-mation and replied, "As you wish, milady," before turning to tell his horse to walk on. The horse, being already in an ambulatory mode, looked around in mild surprise, then turned back and continued on its steady way.

They stopped at small market towns along the way where shelter and refreshments were available and much appreciated, especially by the horse. When the rain was heavy, they were forced to stay for longer than they wished. Jacques wisely chose to avoid flooded roads and bogged-down carts, preferring to sit by a warm fire in dry clothes. The travelers shared their stories with the little family and in those rain-soaked days, Clare and Mario told stories of Rome, of Milan, and of Florence to pass away the hours. But though tales of grandeur and splendor might impress for a moment, it was the daily struggle for survival, for employment, and for food just to stay alive that they all shared—and which brought them closer together. Life in bustling Rome, it seemed, was not much different from life in rural France.

Jacques and Claude had had four children. Little Jacques, however, was the only one of them to survive. The plague ravaged the population when it arrived from God-knows-where, killing young and old by the tens of thousands. The other silent killers that claimed infants' lives seemed to lurk in every household or hovel. One such silent killer was 'sour throat,' which swelled the neck and strangled the suffering child. Then there was 'convulsive coughing,' which wracked and weakened the wee ones to the point of death. An even more insidious evil came in the form of 'puerperal fever.' This much-feared, invisible adversary claimed not only the infant, but the mother, too.

Each and every town, city, and village through the land—and every family that dwelled in them—had been visited by such silent slayers. For Jacque and Claude, the loss of their three little precious ones at such a young age had naturally made them very protective of young Jacques. But secure within the embracing love of his parents, their small son grinned and prattled away in his mother's arms, blissfully unaware of the surrounding threats to his tiny life.

Just outside Blancafort on a bend in the road, and where the slope was gentle and helpful to the stout horse's heart, an unseen rock caused a wheel to rise and fall with a sudden jolt. It proved to be one insult too many for the cart's ancient timbers, and the axle snapped, causing the cart to discharge its load with great energy into the adjacent ditch.

"Is everyone OK?" shouted Jacques. Clare pushed a small trunk off herself and sat up. Mario seemed to be alright. He was holding his head and disentangling himself from a briar bush. When he was free, he turned his attention to Lucia, who appeared to have been knocked unconscious. A sudden scream from Claude sent icy shivers through everyone. "Jacques" was the word she screamed, but it contained all the horror that only a mother could truly understand.

Clare got to her feet and saw Jacque, the driver, scan the area looking for his son. That moment was a black abyss of pure dread. Then a voice piped up "Oui, Maman," and with those two words, fear fled the scene as joy and relief surged in, letting them all breathe easily once more. There was much hugging between mother and child, whilst Jacques stood beaming alongside them. Having assured himself of their safety, he went to examine the broken axle.

Mario, meanwhile, had cradled Lucia in his arms and was looking over at Clare with concern written on his face.

She went over to him just as a trickle of blood coursed down Lucia's face, painting a red line along the side of her nose and around her lips. Her left forearm was at an awkward angle, but at least she still seemed to be breathing. Picking up some clean linen thrown from the luggage, Clare staunched the blood on her young companion's head. Then she searched around the site, looking for a small branch or a broken piece of wood with which to splint the shattered arm.

Just then Jacques appeared next to them and quickly summed up the situation. "I think," he said, "we should fix that arm while the poor child is unaware," he said. "Once we 'ave it straight, it will mend much quicker and be of better service to 'er later." Mario blanched as white as Lucia's face when Jacques told him to hold her elbow whilst he pulled the arm straight. "Be ready, milady, with the splint and the bandages. The child may not be too 'appy with what we do, eh?" He looked grim as the three of them prepared to do what they could.

Claude held Lucia's head as they rolled her over onto her back. Jacques held the broken limb; Mario prepared to anchor the elbow. Clare gathered what she needed next to the unconscious maid and then nodded to Jacques to indicate that she was prepared. He took Lucia's hand in his and, looking straight into Mario's eyes, pulled with all his might whilst rubbing his fingers along the bones to check if they had moved back into a good position.

Her scream caused crows to flee from nearby trees and made them all flinch. Then blackness engulfed her mind once more, and all was quiet again. Jacques gave a grunt of satisfaction that he was satisfied, then indicated to Clare that she could splint the arm. Within ten minutes, Lucia lay on her back, her head cradled in Claude's lap and little Jacque caressing her forehead. The bleeding from a relatively small wound had been quenched. "So much blood from such a little cut," said Clare to Claude in wonder, "I hope there's no other damage done."

They were distracted from their line of thinking by Jacques, who'd checked the axle and reported that he could fix it. "If we are lucky, it should hold up as far as Orléans," he said. The less good news was that, apart from Lucia, the others would have to walk to lighten the load and give the cart the best chance of getting there. Orléans was a tantalizing two days away.

"I could travel in the cart with Lucia and hold her head, Papa," said little Jacques in a grave, sincere voice. His father smiled.

"That sounds like a good idea to me. What would you say, Mam'selle Clare?" Clare nodded in agreement, and so the little man was handed up into the tumbril, where he tenderly lay Lucia's head in his little lap. Claude fairly radiated maternal pride.

As they progressed on toward Orléans, the rain arrived and drenched them to the skin. Little Jacques made a canvas tent out of discarded covers and kept the worst of it from Lucia, who drifted in and out of consciousness throughout it all. They stopped for the night at a small relay station and rewarded themselves with two small rooms, where they changed into dry clothes and took some refreshments. Lucia was carried to Clare's room and put straight to bed, her face as white as the sheets that cocooned her. Clare, Claude, and even little Jacques took turns remaining in attendance in case she should awake and find herself alone.

In the early hours of the morning she awoke and let out a low moan. "Where am I?" she whispered.

"You're safe, Lucia," was Clare's immediate reply, holding a candle to dispel the darkness and to show Lucia her face. Clare looked lovingly at her, but was unsettled by the lost, unknowing look she saw in her companion's face.

"Who are you?" Lucia asked, "What's going on?"

She struggled to sit up, but let out a small cry when she tried to use her damaged arm. "What's happened? Who are you and what am I doing here?" she shouted, beginning to become quite agitated. Claude and little Jacques were awakened by the noise and came to the side of the bed, wiping the sleep from their eyes. Lucia's eyes darted from one to the other with deep suspicion. "What's going on?" she demanded.

Little Jacques, with all the calm innocence of the child he was, took her hand in his and reassured her, "C'est bon, Lucia. The cart got broked and your arm got broked and your head got broked, too." He turned his head toward his mama before adding in his serious little voice, "But my papa and Mario fixed you all up," he said, looking at her with big dark eyes, "so everything's going to be good."

Lucia looked at him with an uncomprehending stare, but then seemed to relax. A small smile crossed her face before she closed her eyes and returned to the safety of a deep sleep. Only then did it cross Clare's mind that little Jacque had been speaking in French, a language that Lucia hardly knew! Clare placed her hands on the little man's shoulders and whispered a sincere "Thank you" in his ear and gently pointed him toward his mother. Then Clare resumed her place in the chair by Lucia's bedside.

"The bang to her head has unsettled her mind, I think," said Claude. "She will need to rest if she is to recover fully. I am not sure if a long journey to Paris will be the best thing for her."

The two women looked at each other. "Perhaps things will seem more clear in the morning," Clare replied. "You go back to sleep, and I'll stay with her for now." Claude leaned forward and gave Lucia a kiss on the forehead.

"Till the morning, ma petite. Bon nuit."

Clare woke from a troubled sleep with her head on Lucia's bed. When she sat up, she found that her patient was wide awake and staring at her. "Who are you?" Lucia asked in a quiet but calm fashion.

"I'm Clare," she replied. "You are my companion. We're on our way to Paris from Milan. There was an accident, and you hit your head. It seems that you can't remember anything at the moment, but be patient and it will return. You are among friends." She turned and pointed to mother and son. "That's Claude and the little boy is your new best friend, little Jacques. His father's name is Jacque, too, and he was driving us to Orléans when the accident happened. Everyone else was OK, but you broke your arm and hit your head. Once we get to Orléans, we'll have to decide on what to do next, but in the meantime all you have to do is rest and heal. Hopefully your memory will return soon."

"Where am I?" Lucia asked in an uncertain tone.

"We're on our way from Italy to Paris." Clare repeated patiently. "At the moment we're near Orléans, about two-thirds of the way to Paris." Clare waited to see what the response would be.

"Oh," was all the girl said. "I see." Then she fell silent and looked across at little Jacques, who'd woken up and was stretching as only little boys can, almost dislocating every joint in his body in the ecstasy of the enterprise. He smiled spontaneously at Lucia, and she smiled back. Then she fell asleep once more.

Claude came and sat next to Clare. "What do you think? It doesn't look good, eh?" she said.

Clare sucked in a deep breath, saying quietly, "We'll wait and see how she is when we get to Orléans. In the meantime, all we can do is wait and pray." Pulling her shawl around her shoulders, she went to the corner to splash her face with cold water from a hand basin and brace herself for the long day's travel in front of them.

Three more dreary days of travel found them entering Orléans. "Is this the place that the Maid of Orléans came to save?" Mario asked Jacques in his halting French. He was walking alongside the tumbril, with Clare and Claude following along behind him.

"You 'ave heard of her in Italy!" exclaimed Jacques in a happy yet surprised tone.

"Of course," said Mario, "she must have been an extraordinary young woman."

"It is an extraordinary world that we live in, is it not?" mused Jacques, "And strange things happen all the time, eh?" He turned and nodded toward where his little son was sitting with Lucia, the two of them smiling happily at nothing in particular. "They do not understand each other's language. She has no memory, and yet . . . they can be 'appy together. Strange and simple," he said, then flicked his rein to speed his horse along whilst the weather was good.

They arrived in the older part of Orléans at a dowdy-looking merchant's shop. "We are 'ere," said Jacque, climbing down from his elevated perch and straightening out his aching limbs. Mario turned and waited for the ladies to catch up, whilst little Jacques scampered down and immediately disappeared through the open door. Small shrieks came from inside, soon to be followed by the appearance of a tired but happy-looking woman with two young scamps clinging to her skirts.

"Jacques," she cried, "It is so good to see you. How long can you stay with us?" More questions were delayed as she flung her arms around his neck, and the two hugged and kissed each other on both cheeks. Claude ran the last few paces and joined in the melee of happiness in the small street. Clare and Mario watched, soaking up the joy of the family reunion. Introductions were made, followed by "Come in, come in," as Claude's sister Joan ushered them all into the house. Mario helped Lucia down from the cart, whilst Claude whispered swift details of their trip into Joan's inclined ear. A fleeting look of pain crossed her face, and Clare knew instinctively that this was a good woman she could trust.

The inside of the shop belied its molding exterior. Inside all was neat and bright, with rows of haberdashery wares and an alarming array of needles and bobbins lined up in military fashion. "Where is Edwige?" asked Claude.

"Gone," came the concise answer. "She fell in love with a soldier. He was good-looking and promised her a new life in Normandy. Who can blame her? Life is still very tough here. It took a hundred years of fighting before we had any peace, and it's taken almost as long to find any prosperity. Still, life goes on, and with God's good grace, we are happy. My Pierre is away on business in Tours. I don't expect him back for another week, but I have plenty to do to keep me occupied here. Go through to the kitchen and make yourself at ease. I will be there in a moment." She herded her small flock through the low door and into the welcoming kitchen.

The room had a low, blackened ceiling from the fire grate that dominated everything else. A door was open to the backyard, letting in the sound of young voices exuberantly enjoying a game of hide-and-go-seek. The sole window in the room, with its freshly painted shutters framing the world outside, seemed to smile benignly on them all.

Mario went to the door and gazed upon a little piece of Paradise. There was an apple tree and a pear tree, each with a tiny platform swinging from one of its boughs to attract the small song birds that sought refuge and food there. Freshly turned brown earth with a pile of withered vines suggested that tomatoes and beans had once grown there. A naked grapevine clung to the far wall, making the most of its sunny spot as the last rusty leaves dropped into the musty mass below. The children were running around the trees and hiding behind clothes-wringers, emitting gleeful gasps as they avoided detection, and high-pitched screams when they were found.

"Oh, to be a child again," Mario muttered to himself.

"Who said you weren't?" Clare whispered in his ear.

Joan had followed them into the kitchen and went straight to Lucia, whom she embraced, then urged to sit by the fire. Joan fetched a fresh cup of milk and, offering it to Lucia, gently urged her to drink it.

"Sit down, everyone, and tell me your news." Obeying her request, the ladies and Jacques sat around the small oak meal table and exchanged their tales. Mario propped up the doorpost and watched the children play.

"I have to leave for Paris tomorrow," Clare said at the end of their conversation, "but I fear that Lucia will not be fit to travel further." Their eyes turned to where Lucia sat vacantly staring into the embers of the kitchen fire.

"And she will not leave this house of peace and love until she is fit to travel," interjected Joan. "I'm run off my feet now that Edwige has gone, and I need someone to help mind the shop when I'm busy out back. I'm sure that she'll be able to do that soon once she's got over her shock."

"But she can't remember anything, and she doesn't even speak French," replied Clare with legitimate concern.

"Then she'll be a blank canvas," said Joan with a smile. "The children will teach her and help look after her. She's only just out of childhood herself, if I'm any judge of young women."

"Are you sure?" asked Clare. "You've already got young children and a shop to run. Having a stranger who can't even remember who she is could prove a real burden."

"None of us know what to expect in life," Joan said. It was a simple piece of homespun philosophy which echoed the experience of most mothers—and some fathers, too! "No," she proclaimed, "you must go to Paris to sort out your family business. From what you tell me, you'll have little time to care for Lucia where you're going. Trust me, she'll be fine here with me and little Jacques." They all turned to look at Lucia. "Poor soul," Joan continued, "It's a mystery how that little lad and her seem to understand each other. But they do!" Another silence greeted her pronouncement. "So it's all settled," she said, with an air of finality. "Lucia stays until she is fit and able to travel—assuming that she does wish to leave then! In the meantime, Clare, you and Mario continue to Paris - that is, if you wish to take him with you." Her last words were said in a louder voice to attract Mario's attention, a ploy which proved successful!

"Did someone speak to me?" he asked, turning around as if out of a dream.

"I was just asking whether milady here would be better off going to Paris on her own without having to take you with her."

"What . . . ?" he blustered, trying to look wounded at the same time.

"We were only teasing," Clare replied, as those at the table giggled at his discomfort. "Weren't we?"

Eight

PARIS

THE FOLLOWING DAY, seats were secured on a carriage to Paris. Mario and Clare made their farewells to their new Orléans family, inviting them to visit at St. Germain once they had settled their affairs there.

"Perhaps . . ." was all Joan said. "But I think I would feel more happy in our humble shop than in a grand château," she suggested.

Clare paused and looked at this wise woman who was barely two years older than she was. "Then we must visit you," she said, embracing her friend warmly.

The travelers waved from their carriage windows until the streets of Orléans swallowed them up. They sat opposite each other, but soon sank into their own thoughts and reveries. In the carriage with them was a stern-looking man with bushy black sideburns that flanked his face with military precision. Opposite him was a small, well-dressed youth with a bundle on his knee. Neither spoke a word. It appeared that the military man's mode of communication was achieved by glowering, causing the boy to respond by cowering. It appeared that there was some relationship between the two, but to the casual observer, it was not one of a convivial nature.

In the long hours ahead, few words were spoken, but secret smiles began to flit between Clare and the youth. At one of the stops where the coach changed horses, the man extricated himself from the carriage like a mannequin with stiffened limbs and ordered his young companion to stay. All preparations by the boy to begin disembarkation were immediately frozen. When the military man with his military whiskers had disappeared into the yard, Clare asked the boy if he, too, was heading to Paris.

"Yes, milady," he replied very politely. "I'm going to school there," he added. A sudden sadness descended upon him that made his voice falter.

"It's nice that your father is coming with you," Clare continued.

The boy fiddled with the strap of his bundle before adding, "He's not my real father. He's my stepfather . . ." The bullied boy sniffed and wiped his nose on his sleeve.

"We're going to Paris, too. Actually we're going to Saint-Germain-en-Laye. My name's Clare Villepreux. If you are ever out at St. Germain, do come and visit."

"That's very kind of you," he said, but before he could say more, the military head appeared, framed in the car-

riage window, and barked, "Do not talk to strangers, boy."
Pulling open the door, he sat himself back down in his billet.
Drawing his lips into a cruel red line, he barked his orders
to the boy: "You may attend to your needs now. There's
a place behind the stables that should suit you nicely. Be
quick about it."

"Yes, sir!" the youth replied, darting a swift look in
Clare's direction.

When the boy had left, the man coldly saluted Clare.
Mustering his words like weapons, he said, "I'm sorry if the
boy upset you, Mademoiselle." But before she could stop
his verbal assault, he fired more words at her. "I don't encourage him to talk to strangers, so if you don't mind, Mademoiselle, please do not encourage him to speak." Closing
his mouth like the doors on a military prison, he fell silent.

Clare indicated to Mario that she was going to descend
from the carriage. "I think some fresh air is called for."
Mario quickly descended and helped her down the steps.

Clare contained her rage until she reached the safety
of the stables where she shook her fists and stamped her
feet as the words "arrogant brute" exploded through her
clenched teeth.

"Is everythin' alright, milady?" asked a startled stable boy.

"Don't ever grow up to be like him," she said, pointing
an accusatory finger toward the carriage where the military man was sternly gazing out of the window. The boy
nodded doubtfully and swiftly returned to the more comfortable companionship of the horses.

Just then her young traveling companion appeared from the rear of the stables and blushed deeply. Clare immediately softened and approached him. "What is your name?" she asked, straightening his off-center cravat in a motherly fashion.

"Jean-Claude, Mademoiselle," he replied, struggling to hide his boyishness behind his bravado.

"Jean-Claude . . . ," Clare seemed to turn the name over in her mouth as if tasting the morsel of an idea before it fully illuminated her thoughts. "Well, Jean-Claude, I want to share a secret with you. Can you keep secrets, Jean-Claude?"

"Yes, milady" came the swift reply, as his eyes glittered and his spine straightened.

"Well, mon petit ami, my real name is the Duchess Clare De Villepreux, and I am going to St. Germain-en-Laye. If you *ever*—" and she spoke the word like an arrow aimed at the deepest part of his heart, "if you *ever* need me, then you will find me there. Do you understand, Jean-Claude?"

There was a pause as the young woman and the lad looked at each other. Jean-Claude, valiantly suppressing a tear that threatened to flood his right eye, nodded. Clare gently laid her hand on his shoulder and added, "Then we'll say no more about it."

"Thank you, milady," whispered Jean-Claude, "you're very kind," as they returned side-by-side in silence to the waiting carriage.

If looks could kill, then Clare would have died from the dread and dead eyes of the stern stepfather. But Clare so disdained the man, that his arrogance failed to reach its target. Rather, his cruelty remained within his own black heart to ferment and molder.

The journey to Paris continued in silence. Jean-Claude occasionally darted secret looks in Clare's direction, but she knew that to acknowledge them would only make the poor boy's situation worse.

All the while, Mario sat in studied silence wondering where all this was going to lead him. For the first time in weeks he began to think that perhaps he might like a glass of wine to help steady his jittery nerves. *What on earth am I doing, going to Paris with a virtual stranger who seems to attract trouble and disaster wherever she goes?*, he thought. He looked up to find Clare looking straight at him. Her inquiring face softened into a warm smile. She held his gaze for a moment, and peace descended on his mind like a warm embrace.

Paris was noisy, it was brash, it was dirty, and it was confusing. The streets were narrow, and gutters ran down the middle of the cobbled ways in a vain attempt to remove the detritus from the previous day. In winter it only looked foul. In summer it would *be* foul, and the only living things that would thrive would be the flies. Hunger seemed to mark many of the faces of the small children who stopped midplay to watch the carriage go past. Men lounged in doorways, and some openly spat on the ground as they went past.

"Not a very polite welcome," muttered Mario in his native tongue. Clare's glare warned him to keep his observations to himself, whether in Italian or in French!

The closer they came to the center of the city, the more soldiers appeared on the streets, and the more the thoroughfares began to take on an air of order and cleanliness. Soon their coach stopped at its final terminal. Clare and Mario unwound their stiffened joints and prepared to descend from the vehicle. As she moved past the young boy, Clare held his knee briefly, seemingly to steady herself for the descent. She spoke not a word to the child, but the subtle nod of her head in his direction spoke volumes.

They alighted into the noise and bustle of a busy coaching yard. Mario took charge of the baggage and immediately gave orders that it be taken to the docks for transport by water to St.-Germain-en-Laye. His curt commands revealed his displeasure at being denied at least one night in this great city of so many delights.

"Don't worry, Mario." Clare chatted over her shoulder to him as she walked on ahead toward the Seine. "You'll get your chance to visit here soon."

On the river journey to their final destination, they both soaked up the pale-blue sky that had been hidden for so many days. The banks of the river still looked green, despite winter having tightened her cold, cloying grip on the countryside for some weeks now. Cattle lifted their heads and stared, snorting great clouds of steam from their indignant black nostrils.

"I don't want you to talk to anyone." Clare interrupted Mario's thoughts. "You are to be my eyes and ears. You must tell me everything that you hear or see," she said, still looking at the passing scenery. "If anyone asks, just tell them that you're my clerk and know nothing. It will soon become apparent to everyone that you're far more than just a humble clerk!" She smiled archly at him before resuming a somber expression. "Not everyone is going to be pleased to see me. I am sure that amongst my new extended family, there will be someone whose nose has been put severely out of joint." She paused, turned toward Mario, and finished, "It is possible that we may be walking into real danger, so be very careful."

Mario looked at this woman, who was barely older than he was and yet seemed so wise and so controlled. "As you wish," he said, and he pledged himself to keep his own counsel as if his life depended on it.

"Thank you, Mario. If all goes according to plan, then I can promise you a very exciting time in France."

Clare looked across the fields to the distant horizon and wondered what Kristopher was doing at that instant. "Take care, my love," she whispered to the wind.

They arrived at St.-Germain-en-Laye and took a carriage to the Villepreux estates. At the huge iron gates, they were greeted by a shifty-looking man wearing ill-fitting and unbuttoned clothes. When the window was lowered, it also became obvious that he had recently imbibed too much intoxicating liquor.

"Name," was the only word he could summon out of his hazy brain.

"Clare, Duchess of Villepreux," Clare said mildly. "And yours?" The words came from a soft, female mouth, but even the gatekeeper recognized the steel encased in them.

"Oh!" he replied, becoming flustered. "You're expected up at the château." Then he tugged the iron gates across the gravel road, leaving a perfect arc in the white quartz stones.

The carriage drove along the curved driveway between tall trees and winter meadows devoid of any cattle. "It looks like things have been let go a little, Mario. I think we may need to do some tidying up here." Her teeth clenched, and the light of battle glinted in her eyes.

They rode up to the front of the château, which was mostly boarded up. The empty fountain appeared desolate, devoid of sound or delight. Weeds grew where once fishes swam. The door opened, and a swarthy, sweaty man in a dark suit appeared at the top of the steps. He waited for them to descend from the carriage and ascend the steps.

"Welcome, Signorina Clare," the man said, in his native Roman tongue, "my master said to expect you." He turned to enter the house before them.

"Stop!" Clare ordered. Her voice was ice itself, and the power in her words caused even this blubbery serpent to halt in his track. "Don't ever turn your back on me again, Signore," she spat at him, "otherwise, it may be something more lethal than a sharp word that strikes you between the shoulders." Fear flickered in his face for a brief moment. Then he inclined his head and mumbled, "Forgive me, Signorina, I was forgetting my manners."

"My title is the Duchess of Villepreux, Monsieur, as you well know, so please do not forget it again, or you will be on the next ship to Rome." With this, she walked straight past him and into the château, with Mario following close on her heels.

She headed straight for the small drawing room, sat down by a dead fire and rang the bell on the small table by her elbow. She indicated to Mario to come and stand behind her chair, and then they both waited. She rang the bell once more. Soon the door opened, and the tall, aloof butler whom she remembered from her youth appeared. To her mind, he seemed to have shrunk. To her eyes, his hair had definitely gone completely white. And to her intuition, he seemed to be a little broken.

"You rang, Mademoiselle?" he said, yet to her ears, his voice had lost little of its imperious edge.

"I did, Georges. Come here." and she indicated spot by the cold fireplace. For a moment, the old butler's eyes opened wide in disbelief. All his life, he had participated in conversations from the framed portal of the doorway. His legs tried to move, but his mind found it difficult to coordinate his forward movement, giving the impression that he might not be quite all there.

Eventually he stood where he was commanded and waited.

"Things are not how you would like them to be since my grandmother—your duchess—died, are they?" Her soft smile shone at him, and his head dropped slightly.

"No, Ma'am," he replied, "standards have fallen."

"Well, we must raise them again, mustn't we, Georges?" and still she smiled at him.

As he looked back at her and studied her eyes, he felt a strange sensation trickle through his veins. It was the sensation of youth. He found himself straightening his spine and lifting his head higher. "We must, Mademoiselle," he said, with a hint of delight returning to his voice. "What are your orders?"

Still smiling, Clare went on, "Well, George, I find myself in need of someone I can trust. Someone who knows this house and this family. Someone who loves both of them. I believe that you are that person. Am I right, Georges?"

Georges blushed, probably for the first time since his youth. "I believe I am," was all he could find to say.

"Then I would like you to go and draw me up a list of things that need urgent attention, and then I would like you to go through that list with my clerk Mario so that we can determine where to start."

"Certainly, Mademoiselle!" Georges almost smiled.

"And I'll need it by tomorrow morning."

"Certainly, Mademoiselle," he said, and the corners of his mouth arced upwards for the first time in many a long year. "Will you be consulting your cousin about this?" he added mildly.

"I don't believe that we need to discuss it with anyone else, do we?"

They regarded each other calmly in those few silent seconds, cementing their understanding. Then bowing slightly, Georges left the room.

After the door latch had clicked shut, Mario let his breath out in a long whistle. "What was that all about?" he asked.

"It begins," Clare said, tapping her fingers on her knee, "but we need to be very, very careful. I suspect that my cousin will have more on his mind than delight at meeting his long-lost relative." She was silent for a minute and then, as if coming to a conclusion continued, "And seeing as the weather is so nice, I think we should take a turn around the garden, don't you? Being cramped up in coaches and barges was not how I was brought up." She turned to Mario and smiled. "If you understand what I mean."

Mario smiled back at her and with a mock bow replied, "As you wish, Duchess."

The next twenty-four hours saw Clare becoming reacquainted with the château she had briefly entered all those years ago. The small drawing room reminded her vividly of her grandmother. It was a place of paradox: splendor, yet spartan; brightly lit with the shutters open, yet melancholic in its gloom when the light began to fail. It was formal to the point of fragility, as if lives would shatter if protocol were to be abandoned. Human hands might have formed this mighty house, but "Madame Château" in return molded her occupants into her own image: grand, forbidding, and cold.

Upstairs, Clare paused with her hand on the golden handle of the door where her father had died with his head cradled in Rosso's arms. She was unaware of Georges standing further along the long landing in the shadows. She stood for what seemed like minutes, trying to comprehend the maelstrom of emotions she felt, before she finally turned the handle and went in. Surprisingly, the door hinges gave out a sharp squeal, which startled her mind into the present moment. She immediately made a mental note to add another item onto the list she had for Georges.

The room was immaculate. It was so perfect, it reminded her of a museum piece. Clare was almost disappointed that the bedsheets weren't still rumpled and her father's clothes thrown over a chair. She went over to the shutters and threw them wide open. Motes of dust danced with drunken delight in the unexpected light, and black spiders retreated to dark corners, no doubt muttering at the insanity of all this light appearing unexpectedly.

Clare was smiling at the thought of spiders complaining like humans when the ghost-like Georges appeared silently behind her.

"His Lordship has arrived, Mademoiselle," he said. He was becoming most impressed, in his own deadpan way, with how this young person seemed to understand the unspoken parts of his conversations. Her manner reminded him very much of her uncle, the cardinal, and from Georges's point of view, that was a very good thing.

"Everything is prepared for him?" she asked.

"Everything, Mademoiselle," was his bland reply, as he stepped to one side and let her pass.

As she descended the stairs, she looked at representations of her forebears and saw nothing immediately recognizable in them. Then she thought of Laura and Marco, and immediately she knew who she was and where she had come from. Sweeping into the library, she found her cousin sitting behind the large desk with his muddied boots besmirching the tooled leather surface. He was not a big man, and neither was he an unpleasant-looking man. About his mouth, he had the look of his grandmother, yet his eyes were black with mischief, and his blotchy skin spoke of a life of indulgence and debauchery.

"You have me at a disadvantage, sir," Clare said, "I am unused to addressing the soiled under-surface of riding boots. Perhaps you would like to explain." Her acid words eroded the man's confidence, but his boots didn't move.

"Ah, sweet Cousin," the man said, "Speaking of shoes, what price are horseshoes in Rome these days?" Remaining seated, he boldly tried to stare her into submission.

"I doubt I could find any that would be small enough for a man with such muddy little feet, sir," she shot back. "Perhaps when you've dismounted the desk, we can meet in the drawing room and take some refreshments after your obviously very tiresome ride here. Or did you walk?" With that, she turned on her heel and left the library.

She settled herself in her grandmother's favorite position by the fire. Georges had summoned and placed refreshments as she had requested. Some minutes later, her cousin, obviously tired of his own company, entered the room and draped himself on the sofa opposite her. "I suspect that you will find things here much different than they are in Rome, Cousin," he said disdainfully, whilst picking the remnants of his last meal from his teeth.

"The house is larger, the customs different, yet I find both of them to be cold."

"I have no doubt your servants can provide more fuel for the fire, Cousin," the man replied, sounding rather bored by the whole proceedings.

"Fires are easy to light, but the warmth of a loving family is seemingly harder to ignite," she said, looking straight at him, searching for some mutual understanding in his eyes.

He laughed. It was a mocking laugh, and shrill. "Loving families are pretty thin on the ground when you are part of a royal court, Cousin."

"Please call me Clare," she interjected.

"The only families who survive this court are those who watch their back and trust no one, dear Cousin. There's no room for love here." He roused himself to a sitting position. "But enough of this feathery talk of love and families, I have work to attend to." And rising to his feet, he said, "I have to see to my hounds." He knocked some mud from his boots with his riding whip and headed for the door. Stopping with his hand on the handle, he looked back and, as if an afterthought said, "By the way, the king expects to see you tomorrow afternoon at court. Do bring your credentials with you. You can't trust anyone these days, can you?" With a sickly smile, he ever so gently inclined his head and left.

Clare waited for a few seconds before she collapsed as if all the air had been let out of her. She bit her lip to stop from crying as Georges entered the room.

"I assume my lord Philippe has left," he said. "He's not an easy man, is he?" For such as Georges, this last sentence was a veritable chapter of information. Clare looked at him. "Shall I clear the tray, your ladyship?" This was the first time he had used those words, and the first time she had felt happiness since she arrived.

"Thank you, Georges." was all she could manage. "Thank you."

"I must find Monsieur Mario and discuss the items that need urgent attention, my lady." He bowed his head and left the room.

Clare sat in her chair by the fire, lost in thought. She tried to remember all the things her godmother had taught her during her stay in Ferrara, and what Mother Superior had said to her in Milan. But it was far easier to recall the wise words and loving counsel she had been given all her life by Laura and Marco. And in that moment, she missed them so very much. Kristopher's image flashed into her mind, but she slammed the door on it immediately. If she were to allow her heart to rule her mind, then there was no knowing what chaos would result.

Clare let the tears fill her eyes. She needed that moment to release her pent-up emotions, which was far better to do now than in the presence of His Majesty, the king.

She spent the rest of the day in her grandmother's room, going through her clothes and her jewelry. She picked out a simple outfit which she thought would suit the occasion, embellishing it with a plain necklace and matching drop earrings. Later she stood in front of one of the large gilt mirrors and rehearsed words that she might address to the king himself. Whilst she practiced her words, she observed and adjusted her own posture to that which she thought would be more appropriate to the French court than to Roman sensibilities. Some hours later, she closed the door of her grandmother's room behind her and turned the key in the lock. Her face betrayed none of her emotion. She had come here to do something, and tomorrow that mission would begin.

The next day's weather did not bode well for a visit to the royal palace. The rain descended in vertical sheets from a leaden sky. Certainly it looked as if the deluge had no intention of ceasing for several hours. Clare took all the precautions she could to stay dry, but even though Georges risked a severe drenching as he struggled to protect his mistress from the deluge, the hems of her skirts were soaked in the few short steps from château to carriage. Fortunately, she had worn overshoes to protect her fine shoes, and her feet were dry.

Settling back inside the carriage, she found a snug, dry, and warm Mario waiting for her. "One of the privileges of the lower classes is that you can stay under cover between the kitchen and the stables," he smirked.

She was torn between shouting at him or bursting out with laughter. In the end, she settled for shaking her cloak all over him, and the two playfully wrestled before Clare settled back again and said, "I don't think I should do that to the king, should I?"

"Not if you want to keep your head attached to your shoulders," Mario replied, and a serious tone crept into his voice. "I'm not sure I'm ready for this, Signorina Clare," he said suddenly, dropping his chin to his chest. "It was only just a few weeks ago that Rosso found me drunk in the cathedral in Florence, and now, here I am headed for the royal palace in France." He looked imploringly at her. "Perhaps you have made a dreadful mistake in bringing me along."

Clare held his gaze steadily. "Only you can plumb the depths of who you really are, Mario," she said, "but I believe that you're brave enough to dare to find out how great you really can be. Don't be afraid of making mistakes." Clare let out a light laugh which seemed to lift the gloom inside that dark carriage. "The Lord knows how many times I've gotten things wrong. Marco used to say that your biggest mistakes teach you the most about yourself, and that the measure of the person is how they respond to those mistakes."

"Were you always so confident?" Mario asked, as the carriage lurched forward.

"No, Mario, I wasn't," she said, reaching out and touching his hand reassuringly. "When Rosso found me, I was a terrified little ragamuffin who was scared of her own shadow." She looked out through the window and watched runnels of rain stream down at an angle as the carriage moved down the driveway. "I was an orphan who was used very badly." She paused as her wounded child inside relived those dreadful hurts, "And I thought that the only way to survive was to build a wall between me and the world. But I was wrong. I was lucky enough to meet some beautiful people who taught me that there were other ways of looking at things." By now Clare was almost talking to herself. "Laura and Marco might be called mild people, but believe me they are the strongest people I've ever met. I do hope they're safe, and I pray their new baby gives them the joy they richly deserve after such awful agonies."

At the thought of the death of her two brothers, Clare could not stop the tears welling up in her eyes. "My brothers had so much life in them," she said, before a smile rose in her face as she wiped the tears from her cheeks. Turning back to Mario, she said, "You'd have liked them, Mario. In some ways, you remind me of them, except that they couldn't sing to save their lives, and you, I understand, have the voice of an angel."

It was Mario's turn to smile. "You have to be holy to be an angel, and I am far from being holy, my lady," he said quietly.

"I never would have described my brothers as holy, either, and yet now I can only imagine them in heaven, causing a great deal of mischief . . ."

Clare looked out the window again and became aware of the bare trees marking their passage as the rain drummed on the roof of their carriage. "When we get to the royal palace, I think we're both in for another soaking," she said as she absentmindedly rearranged her cloak to cover her skirts.

The journey to the king's palace took them through countryside dark with freshly tilled fields, and woods dense with ferns and thickets. The Forest of Cruye seemed to go on for miles and miles. Every now and then, they caught sight of deer standing like sentinels, sniffing the air for the first signs of danger.

They passed through the small hamlet of Versailles, where the marshy ground looked desolate in the late-morning rain. Then their route met with and continued on the well-rutted track that was the main highway to Paris.

Francis was a king with many palaces. Currently, he was staying in the gloomy fortress of the Louvre Palace on the banks of the Seine. But according to Mother in Milan, Francis had sounded out Leonardo himself about coming to France to help with a château he was building in the Loire valley at Chambord. Mother had also told her that Francis liked the work of several Italian artists and writers, so perhaps the thought of having an Italian duchess at court might not seem strange to him.

The carriage rocked into the city amidst the bustle and turmoil of humanity. Most people were too busy struggling to survive to take much notice of Clare as she passed by, watching them out her window. She couldn't tell whether they seemed happy or not, as most were covered by canvas shawls or headgear to keep off the relentless rain. Sheets of it ran down the roofs and poured into the streets, creating a maddening maze of streams that filled and followed each new wheel track.

A dab of mud splatted against the window, causing her to jerk away. "What was that?" she cried.

"Mud," replied Mario coolly. "I'm glad the window was shut; otherwise, the king would get a surprise!" he said, trying to make light of a frightening event.

"Not all is perfect in the city of Paris, it seems," said Clare.

"It's no different than any other city," said Mario grimly. Clare looked at him and thought to herself that he was a much more enlightened person than she had taken him for.

The coach driver navigated the labyrinthine streets with care, until they finally emerged into the vast concourse opening out before the Louvre Palace. They stopped at the canopied entrance, a royal footman descended the marble steps to usher them onto dry land. Curtains of rain fell around the colonnade like waterfalls. Clare looked at Mario, who shot her a brief smile.

The young duchess ascended the steps and at the entrance was relieved of her cloak. She adjusted her skirts and her hair, took a deep breath, and nodded at the footman to proceed. Once inside they encountered more stairs, long wide corridors, and in the background, the constant sound of workmen emanating from behind closed doors. Tradesmen and artisans walked past. Some acknowledged her, while others were too preoccupied to worry about the young beauty, who seemed so serene and yet had adrenaline coursing through her veins.

They halted before a tall, ornate set of doors. The footman knocked and entered whilst Clare waited. The footman re-emerged and held the door open wide for her to enter. It wasn't the throne room, merely the antechamber, but was imposing enough in and of itself. To one side was a very ornate gilt desk, behind which sat a severe-looking man dressed all in black. For a moment, she took him for a priest.

"Ah," he said, rising, "We meet at last, my lady. Stopping in front of her, he bowed his head and held her proffered hand lightly in his. "How would you like me to address you? Duchess, milady, or perhaps Clare?" he said.

"I don't know how formal people are in France, Monsieur, but where I come from, I would be addressed as Duchessa or Duchesse," Clare responded with practiced civility.

"As you wish, Duchesse," the man answered. In an instant, he had changed his mind about this young woman. This was no country bumpkin who had struck gold; this was a beautiful woman with a clever mind—a woman who could prove a vital ally or a formidable foe. "His Majesty has asked me . . . ," he paused as if reconsidering his words. "His Majesty has suggested that you might like to meet with Her Majesty first, if that meets with your satisfaction, as he has some unexpected business that will occupy him for the next hour or so."

"I would be honored to meet Her Majesty," replied Clare, who continued to tremble inside her frosty exterior. Moving around the desk, the man moved toward the door, but was stopped in his tracks by Clare.

"A moment, Monsieur," she said, "I don't believe you gave me the pleasure of your name."

Monsieur paused at the door and replied, "Forgive my omission, my lady. I am called Pauthier, Jean Pauthier, one of His Majesty's secretaries." He feigned humility as he said this, but he was yet again interrupted by Clare.

"If my information is correct, Monsieur, I believe you are His Majesty's most private secretary," and she moved silently past him through the now-open door.

It was obvious that Queen Claude was with child. Her belly was greatly swollen, giving the impression of a fruit fit to burst. Her face was flushed, her ankles a little thickened, and she wore no jewelry, all of which magnified her natural plainness. Every now and then, she paused and clutched a piece of nearby furniture whilst holding her sides as if in severe pain—which she was. "One would have thought my sovereign lord had enough heirs by now, but still he seems to want more," she said to her lady-in-waiting, with a weak attempt at humor. Noticing for the first time that Clare had entered the room, she asked "And who is this, pray tell me?"

Jean Pauthier walked over and whispered in her ear. At the sound of his words, Queen Claude straightened her stance, and a light shone in her eyes. "Ah, our Roman duchesse has joined us at last. Welcome, young lady. Come," she signaled, "come and sit by me. We have much to discuss, no doubt." Clare dropped a curtsey and went and sat in the designated seat. Queen Claude's aides helped her to the more ornate one next to Clare. "Stop fussing," she ordered her aides, "and leave us in peace. There are more ways of letting fresh air into a palace than by just opening the windows." She signaled her ladies to leave them.

Without looking at Clare, and smiling as she spoke, the queen said quietly, "My dear, I think you know that you've just walked into a viper's nest." Clare blinked.

"Your frankness is refreshing, Your Majesty," she replied. "But I believe that vipers hibernate in winter. I'm not so sure that the ones you refer to ever sleep." The queen stole a glance at her new companion and was reassured by what she saw.

"I see that you've been well instructed, Duchesse."

"By the very best," Clare replied, and it was her turn to face the queen. "But tales of your goodness travel far and wide, and all say that I may confide in you as a penitent would confide in their confessor." The two women looked at each other for a few moments. The courtiers, who were out of earshot still, stared and wondered what this conversation was about and how it might affect their position.

"I know you will have much to do in the next few weeks and your time at court will be limited, but I would like you to attend me every Tuesday and to join me for Mass in my chapel." Clare was about to answer when the queen continued, "The men in this world are always talking of war and alliances, which are both costly and dangerous. I am led to believe that your estates are worth a great deal of money, and that makes you of great interest to the king himself. If it were only of interest to my husband, I wouldn't be concerned for you, but there are some," she hesitated and searched around in her mind for the correct phrase, "some less-than-honorable persons who may try to take advantage of the situation."

"I am fully aware that some men may see me either as a weak woman or a prize to be plucked. But believe me, Your Majesty, I am strong where it counts most, in my head and in my heart."

A spasm of pain interrupted their conversation, and Clare involuntarily reached out to hold the queen's hand. The contraction that creased the royal face settled fairly quickly, and she smiled back at Clare. "This child is in a hurry, even though it's not due for another six weeks. Perhaps I can rely on some of that strength you talk of to see me through these last few weeks, Clare. Do you mind me calling you Clare? It's so formal with all these titles, and after all, you're only a few years younger than me. It would please me if you allowed me to use your Christian name," she whispered, with a most unregal wink.

A lady-in-waiting approached and hovered expectantly nearby. At a glance from the queen, she approached. "His Majesty is ready to receive the Duchess de Villepreux." The queen nodded and turned to Clare.

"Perhaps we can continue our conversation another time. But one thing before you go," and she pulled Clare close. "Be wary, Clare. There are men in His Majesty's court who would see you as more of a threat than a prize—and depending on who has his ear, that may include my husband, too!"

Clare couldn't hide the color that rose in her face when she heard the queen speak thus, but her face remained impassive. "Thank you, my queen. I, too, look forward to our next meeting." She stood and dropped a curtsey before turning to follow in the wake of one of Her Majesty's ladies-in-waiting. At the door, she was met by one of the king's courtiers, whom she followed down the long, cold corridor.

In front of two large, ornate gilt doors, they paused whilst the courtier knocked. Both doors opened wide, and Clare entered into the king's private chambers. There were several men in attendance helping His Majesty prepare for the day. She immediately recognized one of the faces. As Lord Philippe smiled at her, Clare was aware of his handsome good looks, but also an arrogance which, in her eyes, distorted his prettiness. He leaned in toward the king's ear and whispered something. His Majesty looked up, and a rapacious smile briefly crossed his face. "You are correct in your description of your cousin, my lord," he said, not taking his eyes off Clare, "she is indeed a pretty sight. Come here, my lady, and kiss my hand." Her legs felt like rubber as she crossed the room to him. His bed was still unmade, and the royal chamber pot was only now being removed from the bedchamber. It helped remind her that this was only a man, one who just happened to be the King of France.

Clare curtsied formally before the king and kissed his outstretched hand. "She smells nice, too, my lord Philippe," he said in a loud aside. The men present laughed knowingly.

"Where I come from, my liege, the ladies need to wear scent to mask the corrupt smells of the marketplace. It appears that here, we weak ladies need to wear it to mask other forms of corruption."

The king laughed uproariously. "My lady has steel for a spine, eh, Philippe? It will take a mighty man to tame this one." This time the accompanying laughter was less ecstatic.

Clare stood in icy isolation with fire in her eyes and in her heart. "Present your credentials, my lady," the king said, seeming to lose interest in the game. He instead turned his attention to deciding which surcoat to wear that day. Clare reached into her purse and pulled out the letter and the ring that the cardinal had sent her. Francis looked at both of them, then back at Clare. "It seems that His Eminence was of sound mind after all. Gentlemen," he said, garnering the attention of all his court, "please show your respects to Clare, La Duchesse de Villepreux." All the men inclined their heads and gave a sweeping bow in her direction.

"How did you find my wife the queen today, Duchesse?" he asked.

"She is in good spirits, my lord, although I think she hides the strain of late pregnancy well."

Francis glanced at her with a piercing look. "My court is enriched by your presence, my lady," he said. "Tomorrow we go to the Loire, to the Château de Blois. Her Majesty is overseeing the refurbishments, and we intend to hold a ball there in a few weeks to celebrate Advent. You will join us there." Then, having come to a decision about his surcoat, he turned to her almost as an afterthought, saying distractedly, "You may leave now." With his concentration spent, he turned to admire himself in the mirror held up before his face.

Philippe, who had been watching all this with the air of a spider observing its prey, sent her a parting, but cruel, grin. Clare acknowledged his look with the barest inclination of her head.

Returning to her château, Clare gave instructions that she needed to see both Georges and Mario immediately. "I leave for Blois in the morning," she told the two men. Georges's expression remained fixed, but Mario's eyes opened wide with incredulity and then fear. He was about to explode into an Italian response, but the look that Clare gave him slammed into his conscious mind. His tongue and his hands fell limp, as he waited for what was to come next. "I take it that you two have settled on what needs to be done here at Villepreux?" she asked the men. The two exchanged looks before Mario answered for both, "Yes, my lady."

"Good," she said, "then one of you will need to stay here to make sure those instructions are carried out, and the other will need to accompany me to Blois with the royal party. I will need several outfits whilst I am there, which means that I will need a maid to accompany me." She turned to Georges, "You will choose the most appropriate person to be my maid, and you and she will accompany me. You will need the rest of the day to prepare, so please prepare well. You may leave."

Clare could see that Mario was about to explode if not given the chance to speak; she smiled as he waited until the door had clicked shut before his arms, his voice, and his whole body erupted into action. "But my lady," he began, "how can you leave me with all these French people? I know nothing about running this house or this estate. These people will not obey an Italian poet who can barely speak their language."

More words were about to pour from his mouth, but Clare stopped him with the mildest of gestures. "I know you, Mario. I know that fear is your first instinct, but it's not fear that inspires you, it's passion." The word seemed to confuse and calm him at the same time.

"Of course I am a passionate man. I'm from Italy," he said, spreading his hands wide and allowing a smile to soften his features. "We men from Italy suckle passion with our mothers' milk," he said. He waited for Clare to continue.

"At some point, I have to trust my instincts, and my instincts tell me that this is your hour, Mario. Whilst I travel to be with a foreign king, surrounded by strangers, some of whom do not wish me to succeed and others who openly covet my title and wealth, you will be deciding which Mario I will meet when I get back." For a moment, her face looked vulnerable and very young. "Our success depends on me finding the passionate Mario when I return. The intelligent, thoughtful, passionate Mario who will be my right hand here in France."

"You humble me with your trust, my lady," he said quietly, "I pray that I will be worthy of that trust."

"Rosso told me that he saw a great deal in you that reminded him of himself when he was a young man," Clare said to him. She came closer and put her hand on his shoulder as if in a benediction. "If he is right—and I have never found him to err in his judgment—then you have the mark of greatness in you. Because of all the men I have ever met who walk this earth of ours, there is none better than Rosso of Florence."

The two of them stood for a moment to let the words settle into their minds. "We have little time to waste," she continued in a businesslike manner. "We need to go through your list and decide on priorities. I expect that it will be early in the new year before I return, so you will need to discuss with Georges who will be the most reliable of the servants here, and who will be your enemies. I have no doubt that my cousin will already have bought off some of the workers as spies. So tread lightly and carefully." Clare

paused for effect before finishing, "And stay sober and celi-
bate, too." In a lighter tone, she added, "When I return, you
may travel to Paris and experience life there if you wish."
She gave Mario an impish look, which he returned with a
look of mock horror.

Nine
CHÂTEAU DE BLOIS

WHILST GEORGES'S FACE was generally impassive during the course of his duties, this was more than compensated for by the clarity of his mental activities and his ability to activate the staff under his authority. He and Mario had come to a rapid understanding that made for an unlikely pair of collaborators: the Italian, full of suppressed passion, and the Frenchman, whose icy arrogance concealed a warm and loyal heart. Though both were surprised by Clare's decision about who should go and who should stay, they accepted her orders with equanimity and ease. Georges filled Mario's brain with details about the functioning of the château, warning him about those who might be in the pay or service of Philippe. In exchange, Mario gave Georges a brief biography of his duchesse and confessed his admiration for his fellow conspirator's lack of emotion on hearing about her genealogy.

"You're not surprised?" Mario asked Georges. "A bastard daughter, brought up by a blacksmith, becomes your duchesse?" he teased his unflappable friend.

"I have had the unfortunate displeasure," Georges replied haughtily, "to have met far worse than that under this roof. In fact, if I were ever to judge a person's character," he continued after a pause—when for a brief moment, Mario thought he detected a fleeting hint of emotion in the man's face—then I would say she is one of the finest persons ever to have graced this château in all the years I've been here." Concluding his speech, he gazed impassively at Mario, who was subdued by its obvious honesty and sincerity.

Georges spoke to the maidservants and selected one to attend Clare on her journey. He directed the maid to Clare's room and gave her instructions as to which clothes she needed to pack and which jewelry she should take. "She's an honest girl," Georges confided in Clare, "but she's what I would call flighty, my lady."

"She's pretty, too," said Clare after the girl had left the room. "I'm surprised she hasn't been snapped up already by some handsome lordling."

Georges appeared to ignore her comment before adding, "I do hear that there is a young man who has shown his affections. A military man of lowly rank currently on duty somewhere in the countryside. She should have no distractions whilst in your service, my lady." Bowing, he left the room and returned to his lair belowstairs to meet up with Mario.

The grey dawn broke, bringing with it a dismal, bone chilling drizzle making their coach journey to the Loire valley dreary and dull. The sky was dull, the countryside looked dull, and even the spire of the Cathedral at Chartres seemed to point to the heavens and say, "Look there: it's very dull isn't it?" Clare had hoped that they might take the Orléans route so that she could find out how Lucia was. But that route was unsafe, so she sent a message instead.

Late in the afternoon they stopped at Vendôme, where Clare's maidservant asked if she might visit an aunt who lived in the area. The last-minute request irritated Clare, and she answered shortly, "If you must, but don't be long as we have to prepare for an early start tomorrow." The young girl dropped a curtsey, and a flush appeared on her cheek. Clare thought the girl might be about to respond, then Clare turned away and headed toward the lodging house where they were to stay. Georges, who had remained his immutable self during the journey, gave the departing servant the mildest of nods as she walked past.

On her way into the lodging house, Clare passed a rosy-cheeked woman who was standing by the entrance holding a carpetbag. The woman dropped Clare a curtsey, and her round face hinted at innate happiness. Georges followed his mistress with the night bags as their host showed them to his best suite.

Being tired from her journey, Clare took her evening meal alone, but was becoming more irritated as her maid had so far failed to appear. Her hand was poised over the small silver bell when Georges miraculously appeared in the doorway. "It appears that love has had its way, my lady," he said.

Clare stared at him. "It's unlike you to speak in riddles, Georges," she replied.

Georges cleared his throat, "It appears, my lady," he continued as if Clare had not spoken at all, "that your maid does indeed have a beau in the military, and it appears that the military concerned is stationed at Orléans where there is currently some, er, disaffection with our sovereign, the king."

A light appeared in the dim recesses of Clare's mind. "Go on," she ordered, settling back into her chair and suppressing a smile.

"In short, my lady, she's gone!"

"And . . . ?" asked Clare, beginning to see her butler fumble in his storytelling. "You know I can't appear at court without a maid, Georges, so how are we going to resolve this sudden disruption to our household?"

For an instant, Georges hesitated. "It just so happens that a relation of mine, a spinster lady of impeccable references, is waiting outside for your ladyship's perusal." Georges blinked like an barn owl.

"What an amazing coincidence," Clare commented with a straight face. "Perhaps you'd better show the lady concerned in, Georges," she said. As he went to do so, Clare called him back. "I never took you for a matchmaker, Georges," she said, studying him.

The barn-owl blink returned. "The lady's name is Marionette, my lady." Georges left to bring the lady in, as Clare relaxed into her chair, fascinated to see whom Georges was to present to her. Clare immediately recognized the woman whom she'd seen with the carpet bag on her way in. Marionette gave her obeisance to Clare and advanced to stand in front of her.

There were several questions that Clare should have asked of her. However, there was something about the woman's eyes that reminded her of Mother in Milan, except that several 'Mothers' could have stood behind Marionette and remained invisible. She seemed to be transparently honest, yet simple and wise in the same moment. Clare liked her instinctively and found herself asking Marionette, "Will you look after me, Marionette?"

Those kindly features blossomed at the question. "It would make my heart very happy to serve you, my lady." Tears appeared on her beaming face, which she dried with a lily-white handkerchief that she kept in her sleeve.

Clare turned to Georges, whose invisible presence had so far been ignored. She thought to say something to him and then checked herself. Georges looked back at her and gave another barn-owl blink. "Thank you, Georges," she said. "Thank you."

Clare and her party arrived at Blois the following day and were directed to their accommodation in the château.

Workmen were busy everywhere, but thankfully, most of the building was going on in the far wing of the huge palace.

On arrival, Clare had received a message from Her Royal Highness Queen Claude to attend her as soon as conveniently possible after Clare had refreshed herself. Marionette took charge of unpacking, preparing Clare's toilette and generally fussing about her as if Clare were her own daughter. All this Marionette did with great happiness, and her round, smiling face never altered from its naturally optimistic attitude.

"You are very kind, Marionette," Clare said, as Marionette brushed her hair, just as Laura used to brush it when she was a child.

"Such hair as this, my lady, is a delight to care for," Marionette trilled back.

Clare turned on her stool and faced Marionette. "Would you mind calling me Clare when we're alone together? It would make me very happy if you would."

"Of course, my dear," she said. "'Clare' it is, in here. And out there," she nodded in the direction of the door, "it'll be 'my lady.'" The conspiratorial nudge that she gave Clare made them both laugh out loud.

Clare returned to face the mirror. "I'm not so sure everyone here will have my best intentions at heart, you know," and she glanced at Marionette. The good lady continued to sweep through Clare's tresses before saying, "Georges did mention that perhaps I should keep my eyes and ears open. Just in case."

Nothing more was said, but they both knew that the château was not a palace of dreams, but a cage of fear where trust was the most treasured jewel. Looking at Marionette in the mirror's reflection, Clare thought that perhaps this trip would not be as bad as she'd anticipated after all.

The Duchesse de Villepreux was led to the royal apartment and taken straight into the queen's presence. Her Majesty was standing behind a tall armchair and leaning on the back of it. Her free hand was gently rubbing her pregnant abdomen in the attempt to sooth a minor contraction. Clare waited until the pain had passed. "Welcome to Blois," Claude said to her, with obvious delight in her voice. "I love this place, and the king has kindly allowed me to help with planning the new extensions. We've even got people from Italy here to help with the latest fashions. There are some wonderful artists and architects who have brilliant imaginations and ideas. Have you heard of Leonardo?" she asked.

Clare dropped a curtsey. "I actually met him once a long time ago. I doubt that he'll remember me, though. I was very little then."

"Well, my husband has convinced him to come and live nearby, so you will see him soon. He's coming to the ball, and we'll see if he remembers you then." Claude held out her hand to Clare. "Come and sit with me. It's so good to see you here. How was your journey? I hear you had to hire a new maid in Vendôme. How distressing."

Clare concealed her amazement that the royal ears had heard such minor details of her own household. *If they knew such inconsequential information, how much more do they know of my affairs?*, she thought to herself. As if Claude had read her mind, she said quietly to Clare, "Be very careful here, my dear. Everyone will be watching you, and all information eventually ends up in the royal ears." They both looked out the vast window over the château's gardens which, even at this late time in the year, were manicured to perfection. "The ball is tomorrow evening. I hope you have a suitable mask with you," Claude said to her pretty companion.

"Oh. I never thought it would be a masked ball!" Clare replied. "Perhaps Your Majesty . . . "

"Please call me Claude when we are alone," the queen said, "it allows me pretense that I am me and not some dressed-up trophy to be paraded in front of other dressed-up actors." There was an edge, and yet a tinge of vulnerability, in her voice. "I do get so tired of playing at being queen." She placed Clare's hand on her bursting belly and said, "Can you feel him kick? I'm sure it's a boy. Girls are much better behaved, aren't they?" They giggled like sisters sharing a secret. "Don't worry about a mask. I'll have my maid bring a selection to your room this afternoon."

They chatted away for some time about the lives they'd lived growing up. Claude was fascinated by Clare's story and said wistfully, "It would appear that neither of us had many choices when we were growing up. But whereas you eventually found love and acceptance in your new family, my lot was to be a pawn in a much larger game. Even though I am Queen of France, it still seems immoral to me that a six-year-old girl can be betrothed to another child purely in the interests of securing the dynasty of kings. Sadly, I had no say in it at all. My only hope back then was that he would prove to be a good and loving man." The flow of her story was interrupted by her unborn child, who seemed to want to heighten his role in her destiny. When the pains had passed, she smiled, "But it wasn't all bad. Most of the people I've known have been good people caught up in difficult situations—people who were just trying to do the best they could for themselves and for others, too." She shot a sideways glance at Clare. "But a few of them frighten me. Your cousin . . . ," her voice drifted off, but at the mere mention of his name, Clare's senses leaped into full alert.

"My cousin, Your Highness," she mumbled, returning to strike formality.

"Yes, your cousin. He is, how shall I put it, of concern to me. As you might have noticed, he has the ear of my lord the king, but what he whispers in that ear, only the two of them know. But there is something about him that frightens me." Another contraction, more stunning than the previous few, caused the queen to stop talking and concentrate on the rock-like hardness of her belly. "Such talk appears to upset my child," she said, with a weak attempt at humor. "Perhaps I've said enough already, my dear Clare." She said nothing more on the subject.

When Clare returned to her room, everything had been put away neatly and her personal things laid out on the dressing table. Marionette came in from the adjoining sitting room carrying the gown Clare was to wear to the ball. She read the look on her mistress's face and then gave the dress a firm shake. "I hear Her Majesty is a good woman," she said, giving the frock another firm rustle.

"She is, Marionette. She is a good lady and one I think I can trust."

"She didn't happen to mention anything about your cousin, did she?"

Marionette's comment roused Clare from her preoccupation with what she'd heard from the queen. "My cousin?" she asked. "Why should she mention my cousin?"

"More like the king's shadow, I should think. The man never leaves his side, whispering all sorts of nonsense in the poor man's ear from morning to night. Gives me the creeps, especially when he gives you one of those leering smiles of his." All this was said to the dress, which if it had been alive would surely have suffered a head injury from the shaking it received.

"How, what . . . ?" Clare stammered in benign wonder, "how do you know about my cousin?" Clare relieved Marionette of the poor dress and laid it on her bed.

"Poor Georges has had a terrible time with that man since your grandmother died: Always plotting with some people and squeezing others until they're dry. Always oozing around the king with obsequious smiles and putting temptation in that poor man's way. It's a miracle his queen puts up with it all. The Lord knows how many women's beds that man has led the king to. In my humble opinion, your cousin should be locked up and the key thrown away," the good woman harrumphed.

Clare smiled and threw her arms around an amazed Marionette. "Oh, dear lady, how blessed was the day when Georges brought you to be by my side." They hugged as Marionette reached into her sleeve to retrieve her kerchief to dry her eyes. "From what you've said, I take it that you don't like my Lord Philippe too much," but before the good lady could reply, Clare held up her hand and said, "I think we can agree on what that gentleman is like. And like your good self, I think we should be prepared for the unexpected, nay, even the very worst from that particular man."

"Do you have any idea who is coming to this ball?" Claude asked Marionette, deftly changing the subject. "I imagine you hear much more belowstairs than we do up here in our gilded cages."

"Well, they do say that just about every noble from here to Paris is coming, and that's not including the bishops, either. I hear that we can expect the ambassadors from England; the Vatican, plus some other Italian ones that I forget, but none from the Emperor or from Aragon. There's talk of alliances and war against the Holy Roman Empire, which no doubt will drain the king's coffers and cause thousands to starve. Men!" she finished and looked around for something else to shake.

Clare went to her dressing table to remove the pins from her hair and shake out her glorious mane. Marionette appeared behind her with a brush and began to untangle the knots. Clare let her mind think about what Marionette had said, and began to explore some of the possible treachery that her cousin might be planning for her. If Clare was indeed a wealthy person in her own right, then the king might need that money to fight his wars. She would have to tread very carefully if she were to secure her fortune and keep it out of the hands of warmongering men!

A knock at the door heralded the arrival of a maid with three ornate masks for the ball. She placed them on the bed, curtseyed, and then left without a word.

"Ooh," gushed Marionette, "I like that one," she said pointing at a mask with a plumage of plum and violet feathers about its pretty sequined face. But what caught Clare's eye was the large, pale-blue gemstone set in the forehead of the mask.

"Me, too," she said, as she picked it up and held it in front of her face.

"Oh that's stunning, my dear," Marionette said, standing back and admiring her mistress from a distance. "I wonder where it came from.".

"If I were a guessing person, then I would say it came from Venice, judging by the workmanship and the boldness of it." Clare gave a swift pirouette with the mask in front of her face, and Marionette clapped her hands together in sheer joy. "You will look wonderful, my lady." Clare lowered the mask and tried to put a stern look on her face as she said, "It's Clare in private, Marionette." She then held the mask in front of her friend's face and urged her to join in the fun. The two of them were so busy giggling as they twisted and turned that they failed to hear the door open as the silent figure of Georges appeared.

They stopped to gather their breath. Georges waited as if they were just finishing their afternoon refreshments. "A message from His Majesty," he intoned. After a brief pause, he added, "He wishes to see you."

"When," replied Clare, instinctively reaching to settle her hair.

"Now, my lady," Georges replied without emotion. "I am to lead you to his chambers at once." He moved to the door whilst Marionette and Clare exchanged questioning glances. In a couple of minutes, Clare felt confident enough to leave the room and present herself to His Majesty.

She was shown directly into his rooms, where his attendants ceased their conversations and stared at her. Clare held her own and stared straight back at them. ""Your Majesty," she said, dropping a low curtsey.

"What kept you?" the king snapped back. Clare thought of attempting some sort of apology, but thought better of it and tried to channel Georges's impassive facial expression. "We've been discussing your future, Duchesse," he went on. Clare remained mute and expressionless. "You will need a husband to protect you." Clare bridled at the very thought of someone choosing a husband for her, but stifled her retort until she'd heard the king out. The king seemed unsettled by her silence and looked around askance at his companions. Then Clare spotted her cousin lurking in the background. *You*, she thought to herself. *I bet I know who's behind all this*, but she remained silent.

"You have until Easter to find a husband suitable to me and to your position, otherwise I will make the decision myself." As he said that, he couldn't stop himself glancing at Duke Philippe, her cousin.

"As you wish, Your Majesty," she replied in a controlled voice. "Was there anything else you required of me?" The king looked slightly perturbed by her attitude and brushed her away with, "No. That's all. You may leave now." Just as she reached the door, he called to her in a slightly mollified tone, "I hope you find your accommodation to your liking. Her Majesty seems most fond of you." Despite the trappings of supreme power, for a moment his voice was that of an uncertain young man, who at heart was kind and considerate.

"Everything is to my greatest satisfaction, Your Majesty," Clare replied, and dropping a modest curtsey, she left.

When she got back to her apartment, she slammed the door and seethed at the whole experience. "The arrogance of those men!" she fumed. "How dare they tell me who to marry?" and she hit her small fist against the closed door, grazing her knuckles.

"What in God's good name has been going on?" asked Marionette, appearing from the other room.

Clare flounced down on a chair, related everything that had happened in the king's chambers, and promptly burst into tears. Marionette came to her, holding her close until the sobs had ceased. "There, there, my dear," she soothed, "that will have done you the world of good. Now tell me once more what the king actually said." Once she had repeated her story, Clare's mind was clear and her tears a receding memory. She went over to the casement window and looked out. The sky was as dark as her current situation seemed to be. 'Where are you, Kristopher?' she called quietly into the night sky. 'I need you so much.'

"It seems to me, my dear," Marionette continued, "that these men are playing a pretty game with you." Clare turned her attention back to her companion. "But you know what powerful men are like: they're arrogant, they're full of bluster, but at the end of the day, they all have a weakness. All we need to do is to discover those weaknesses and exploit them to our advantage." Clare looked in admiration at her companion.

"I like your line of thinking, Marionette. But we also need to build our own alliances to counter their power. The queen likes me, but she's with child, and I'm too new in court to put much faith in her being on my side. But what the king needs is money to fight his wars. He also needs to make alliances to help him prosecute those wars. And they need bankers to squeeze so that they can pay for their damned wars. But the one thing they all want is a pretty face to tell them that they're real men." She paused and looked archly at Marionette. There was a suspended moment before they both started laughing again.

Ten

THE BALL

THE LARGE BALLROOM at the royal château was brilliantly illuminated with thousands of candles in dozens of spectacular chandeliers. The women dazzled in their splendid and sometimes outrageous outfits. All wore masks, but most could not conceal the owner's identity, due to her girth or height, and in some cases, her smell. The men were almost as glamorous as their female consorts, with sashes, powdered wigs, and jeweled pendants signifying important status for some and sheer power for the feared few.

Clare appeared at the door, and her name was called out. There was a quietening in the chatter as she entered. Many heads turned to see her for the first time. She paused, and for an instant the whole room seemed to hold its collective breath. Some could be seen nudging each other and nodding in her direction. Clare looked absolutely stunning! Even the king shifted on his throne to gain a better view of the duchess as she came forward and knelt low before him. Queen Claude then summoned her to come close, and Clare obeyed. She knelt at Claude's side whilst the queen whispered, "You look wonderful, my dear. I don't think you will be short of suitors." She shot a swift glance in the direction of her sire, who was feasting on Clare with his own eyes.

"You do me great honor, my queen," Clare murmured, "but I intend to choose a man who loves me and not my money." Claude looked at her in silence as the noise in the room escalated once more. "I will do what I can," she said, then winced in pain. "That's if my little man inside gives me a moment to think for myself." The two women smiled as Clare rose and left.

Philippe appeared at her side like an unctuous servant. "How may I help you, Cousin?" he asked. "A refreshment of something perhaps?"

"I wouldn't accept a glass of water from you, dear Cousin, even if I was dying of thirst in a desert." She spoke the words in a low voice and with such genteelness that those nearby would have thought that they were the best of friends.

"As you wish," he replied. He bowed his head, turned, and left.

Clare let out an audible sigh and as she spun around to move away, she bumped into a masked pirate. "Forgive me, sir," she exclaimed, "I didn't know there was anyone behind me."

"The apologies are all mine," the pirate replied, "and so is the pleasure." There was something about the playfulness in the man's eyes that made her heart leap in her bosom. But before she could speak, the music began for a pavane, so he offered his hand and led her over to the set. As they moved around the dance floor in the ordered moves of the dance, he whispered to her on one pass, "You are in great danger."

An icy fear replaced the momentary flutter, yet her graceful movements belied any emotion. At the next pass, he said, "But don't worry, that's why I'm here." An irrepressible hope drove out any fear. There was something about him that was so familiar that, as she stood waiting for their next pass amongst the spinning bodies, her face was smiling behind her mask. On the final pass, he said nothing, but she felt him press a small object into her gloved hand. Then he was gone.

Clare was searching the room for signs of her masked pirate when Philippe suddenly appeared, saying "Is everything alright, Cousin? You seemed a little lost."

Clare cast him a disdainful look. "I am a little tired after my travels, Cousin. Perhaps you could lead me to a chair." The obsequious man bowed, took her arm, and led her to a chair. "Get me a cold drink of water, too," she ordered, causing his neck to flush red at her obvious insult. As soon as he'd gone, Clare opened her fist to see what was there. It was a small golden charm in the shape of a cat. For a second, her mind went blank, then she shot to her feet and searched the room once more.

"It was you!" she said to herself as excitement and anxiety swirled through her head. Philippe returned, bearing a goblet of water. "Thank you, Cousin," Clare said, "but I think all the excitement of the past few days has been too much for me. Please excuse me." She then made her way through the crowds and left.

A man dressed in black with the mask of an ass approached Philippe. "I'm glad to see you came as yourself," Philippe sneered.

"I have news for you, my lord," the other said, ignoring the barbed comment. "We've, er, detained the man who was dancing with your relative. He appears to be from Genoa. What would you like us to do with him.?" A terrible smile crossed Philippe's face.

"Take him to the usual accommodation we accord our more unusual guests," he said. "I'll see him in the morning. Perhaps your men could ask him a few questions in the meantime. Politely, of course." His companion let his mask drop for a few moments as a look of mock surprise crossed his features.

"We always show your guests the utmost respect, my lord. I am sure that he will appreciate our attentions." Bowing his head slightly, he too left the ballroom. Philippe stared for several minutes at the door through which Clare and the man had left. "Sweet Cousin, the game begins. Winner takes all." He tipped the water into a nearby flower vase and joined in the dancing.

Eleven

BATTLE OF WITS

CLARE RETRIEVED HER cape and called for Georges
to attend her as she was about to leave. She wisely sent a
message to the queen to inform her of Clare's sudden in-
disposition and apologize for her swift departure. Georges
appeared and followed her down the steps to her carriage.
She indicated that he should join her inside for the ride
on that cold night. "As you wish, my lady," was all he said.

Clare's excitement was palpable. She was thinking of
how to tell Georges about Kristopher's unexpected appearance when Georges coughed discreetly. "Yes, Georges," she
said, grinning with happiness in the gloom of the interior.

"There was a slight disturbance before you left, my lady,
and I thought you should be informed of the matter." The
ensuing silence was disturbed only by the crunching of
gravel and the jingling of the horses' harnesses.

"Go on," she said, fearing what the good man might say.

"It appears that the gentleman with whom you were dancing has incurred the displeasure of your cousin, who saw fit to have him taken into custody." Silence returned.

"Go on, George," Clare said in a steady voice, but icy fingers were already beginning to squeeze her heart.

"That's all I know, my lady." The silence enveloped them both. "Except that when your cousin has done this in the past, those he has detained are often much the worse for wear for their experiences." Silence again. "I trust the gentleman was not a close associate of yours."

Clare could not move. She could hardly breathe. Her mind was filled with white-hot rage, yet an icy grip tightened on her heart.

"How dare he!" she seethed. George sat in shadowed silence, so she could not see the haunted look in his eyes.

"How do you know all these things?" Clare asked, her face rigid with anger. "Is this some sort of plot to frighten me? Well, if it is, then they've got another think coming!" She sat like a caged wild thing ready to spring on any unsuspecting creature, and Georges was her only victim. "Are you with them?" she shot at him, cruelty poisoning her words.

Georges blinked like an owl. The silence in the carriage was fraught with pent-up anger. Georges blinked again, then cleared his throat as if some lump had appeared without permission. "No, my lady," he said, with the greatest of control. "I make it my business to know all things that pertain to the good standing and safety of my lady. That's all." He sat straighter, and for the first time in years, he sniffed as if he had a head cold.

Clare looked at this stiff man who couldn't conceal the tears in his eyes, and her heart melted. Her own great grief could not be contained any longer, and she threw her arms around his neck and sobbed her heart out. Georges was totally unprepared for such an exhibition of emotion. For minutes, he sat rigidly in his seat as she wept on his uniform. Then, ever so slowly, he put his arms around her and consoled her. "You can be certain, my lady," he whispered in her ear, "that I will never betray you, as long as I have life in my body."

Clare's sobs slowed. She looked up slowly into the eyes of the old bachelor and smiled weakly. She sniffed and said, "I believe you, Georges, and I will never doubt you again." Georges blinked once more and produced a white handkerchief for her.

"You may need this, my lady," he said, and loosened his hold on her. "Is there anything else you need, Mademoiselle?" he inquired. Clare looked at him again and burst out laughing.

"Oh Georges," she said, "what would I ever do without you?" She reached up and gave him a light kiss on the cheek. "Thank you."

The last time Georges had been kissed by someone of the fairer sex was long lost in the mists of time. Yet that memory returned to him now, and he treasured it as the carriage rocked them back to their apartments.

In the morning, a message arrived from the royal château. Her Majesty was inquiring as to Clare's health, and was most concerned about her new companion becoming suddenly indisposed the previous evening. She asked if Clare might call upon her that day if the duchess was well enough, as the queen's baby seemed eager to enter the world. Clare replied politely by return message that she had recovered fully and would be delighted to wait upon Her Majesty later in the day.

"There's nothing I can do here until I get more news, Georges," she said, staring out the window after the messenger had been dismissed.

"I have taken the liberty of engaging certain reliable persons to discreetly make enquiries as to the current whereabouts of your friend," the good man intoned softly.

"Thank you, Georges. Thank you," she replied. "Please let me know when my carriage is ready." Georges nodded and left. Clare remained at the window. Speckles of rain told of a recent shower. A larger drop slipped crazily down the window pane, picking up collaborators and speed as it went. It landed in a puddle on the lower sill and became anonymous. Clare traced her finger along its path. She blew a puff of breath against the cold window and drew a love heart on the foggy surface. That, too, disappeared as the mist on the window dissolved.

"I'll find you," she whispered to the window. "Just stay alive."

Twelve

LIFE AND DEATH

QUEEN CLAUDE'S ROYAL bedchamber had the dimensions of a ballroom. In that now very public place, a black flock of officials had gathered to await the impending birth. Heavy damask curtains around the bed allowed a certain amount of modesty for the lying-in of the queen, and incense burners attempted to dispel the sickly sweet smell that lurked threateningly in the air. Interspersed amongst the ladies-in-waiting were officers of His Majesty's court and a smattering of holy men in their robes. Though the windows were uncurtained, many candles sputtered around the room as the lowering skies blocked any spare light from entering.

When Clare drew back the heavy curtains, she saw Claude's white face contorted in pain. Something tightened in her own chest when she saw her new friend thus. The queen slowly recovered from her contraction and looked around for someone—anyone—to help her. Her eyes fell on Clare, and she beckoned her friend closer. Another pain gripped the queen, who let out an animal-like scream as her eyes opened wide with pain and fear.

She gripped Clare's arm as pain ripped through her pelvis, her rock-like womb trembling beneath the white dome of her belly. "This is not right," she panted, whilst Clare wiped the sweat from her brow. "I've never had pains like this before." She stared at her friend with fear-filled eyes.

"Perhaps if I gently massage your tummy, it might help," Clare said.

"Anything would be better than the tortures these infidels are threatening to do to me," the queen said, fiercely stabbing her finger in the direction of the black-frocked men on the other side of the curtains.

Clare lifted the sheet. She almost vomited at what she saw. A giant pool of blood covered the mattress and the queen's upper thighs. Clare couldn't restrain a horrified gasp.

"I've been bleeding like this since my waters broke, and no one seems to know why." Even as the queen spoke, a large clot of blood flopped out and onto the bedsheets.

The curtains were drawn back. "She needs to be bled again," the royal physician announced, with just a hint of fear in his voice.

"Hasn't she lost enough blood already?" shot back Clare. The tone of her voice was enough to make the man stop in his tracks and retreat a few steps. Meanwhile, the queen held firmly onto Clare and commanded the man to leave them both. "I fear this will not end well, Clare," her queen said, sinking back into her sweat-soaked pillow. "The child has not moved these last several contractions." She looked at her friend with a pleading look on her face, which slowly melted to resignation. "It appears that my baby and I will meet our Lord together: an innocent angel and one who tried always to be innocent of intent."

Claude's face was now deathly pale. Her womb rose again with all its power, trying to force the dead, unborn child out into the bloodied bed, but she could barely respond, despite the suffering that contraction brought. When it had settled once more, Claude turned her plain face to Clare. "I'm so sorry," she said, "I won't be here to protect you, either. Do what you can for my children, Clare. Forgive my husband. He is weak, but he has a kind heart." Her eyes closed, and Clare thought she would speak no more. The queen's eyes opened one last time. "No one has any power over me any more except my God, and I surrender my soul unto Him" Then Claude, Queen of France and wife of Francis, died.

Clare remained transfixed, aware only that someone had left the room. Soon there was the loud sound of footsteps advancing down the corridor toward the bedchamber. The door was thrown open. The king stood there in his finery, but his features trembled with barely suppressed devastation. He advanced to the side of his queen's bed and picked up her cold white hand. He looked questioningly at Clare, who still held Her Majesty's other hand. She shook her head, and the king's face contorted in pain. He let his head fall on his dead wife's chest, as he began sobbing in anguish.

King Francis then suddenly rose to his feet and glared at the gathering. "Get out." he said, in a controlled voice. There was a shuffling of feet, but little movement. "Get out!" the king screamed. "Get out of here!" he yelled, and picking up a loose towel, he made a whip out of it and chased them all out of the room. Clare stood like a sentinel at her queen's side, still holding Her Majesty's hand. Francis slammed the doors of the chamber shut, came back to the bedside, and fell to his knees. "She was too good for me. She was too good for this world."

For some minutes the king cried like a small child, until he fully regained his senses. He looked up at Clare, his face tear-stained and so very childlike. "How am I going to be able to stand up to them?" he pleaded. She had no answer for the grieving man-child before her. He wiped tears from his eyes with a frilled sleeve. "She kept me from making so many mistakes. They're just like feral dogs!" he added angrily, pointing in the direction of the doors and regathering his tattered manhood once more. "How will I survive without my moral compass?" His eyes searched Clare's for an answer.

"Her voice will always be in your memory, my liege," she replied, "and your children will remind you of the great gift she was in your life. Her Majesty thought you were a great king, but an even better man."

Francis looked at Clare as if he'd seen her for the first time. "Thank you, Duchess. Thank you." He smiled at her, and then looking back at Claude's white, now beautiful face said, "I'd like to be left alone now." Clare dropped a curtsey and left, closing the doors very quietly behind her.

Dozens of pairs of eyes followed her down the corridor, but the pair that burned into her back like flaming torches were those owned by her cousin Philippe. Clare kept her eyes focused straight ahead on the only face she could trust. The impassive face of dear Georges had mysteriously appeared at the far end of the long corridor, accompanied by several liveried members of the royal household. There was no trace of emotion on his face, yet Clare felt as if the man was carrying her down the corridor step-by-step.

"I have arranged for some refreshments in your apartment, my lady," he said, as he pivoted to lead her to the safety of their rooms. When Georges had clicked the door closed behind him, Clare sat quietly on the edge of her chair and thought. She didn't notice Georges place a small table next to her with some dainties for her to eat. His subtle throat-clearing brought her back to the present. "You need some nourishment, Mademoiselle," the good man said. "I'm led to believe that it's been a very trying time for you. You must keep up your strength."

"I think we've just lost our greatest ally in court, Georges," she said, unconsciously picking up something and eating it. "The king was right. The queen was a really good and moral person. She'll be sorely missed in this court, and I'll miss her, too. I'm not sure if the king has the spine to survive all the temptations that'll be placed in his path by those who seek his patronage."

"I hear that two days ago, the king had an emissary from an Italian gentleman, my lady." Georges spoke as if repeating someone else's lines. "It may be that His Majesty might not look on it too kindly, if he knows that the gentleman in question has been sequestered away by a certain relative of yours." He dusted a speck of something from his sleeve and then continued to look straight ahead as if in a trance.

Clare's mind moved rapidly. "You mean Kristopher is an emissary? From whom, Georges?"

"I believe that I heard the name Genoa mentioned, my lady," the good man said.

As if a light had suddenly shone in her mind, Clare shouted and clapped her hands together. "Of course. He's Admiral Doria's captain. So that's why he's here," and her eyes sparkled with happiness. Then, as if all her good thoughts had fallen off a cliff, a mad panic gripped her mind. "But Philippe knows all this, and he has the king's ear. He'll turn all this to his advantage and make out that it's all my fault." Her frantic face stared at Georges, "What shall I do, Georges? I don't know what to do."

Not one tiny muscle twitched on his face, but the good man serenely replied, "I suggest you try a tisane, my lady. It will refresh you and clear your head. Marionette has a wonderful gift for such things. Then you should give yourself some time to consider and reflect on your situation. I am certain everything will work out alright. In your case, life has an uncanny knack of working out that way." He inclined his head and silently left the room.

Clare's mind was a whirlpool of thoughts. The smell of the tisane reached up through her consciousness, causing her to pause and taste it. "Mm, nice," she whispered to herself and took another sip.

Clare sat staring at the fire, her mind numb from attempting to solve so many problems at the same time. Her very energy seemed to have drained away. She became fascinated by her inactivity and inability to even think. The flames, large and small, danced gavottes in the orange glow of the coals. When a draft from under the door kissed the coals, they turned briefly black before the passion of the fire engulfed them once more.

Clare sat motionless, observing herself from the inside. *I need to do more than just sit here*, she thought, but she found it so easy to become accustomed to this numbing inertia. With a great force of will, she pushed herself to her feet, whilst still watching those hypnotic flames. Finally, she wrenched her eyes away from the fire and took a pace toward the door, whose edges were illuminated by outside lights. Her sloth fell away, and her mind began to purr once more. She paced up and down the length of the room, oblivious to the pattern of the carpet beneath her feet, or her mirrored likeness on the walls. Ideas and plans came and were dismissed from her thinking. Then she stopped. All was still. Only the soft collapse of the ashen firewood broke the silence.

Clare went to the door and called for Georges. "Bring my carriage around to the front, please, Georges. We're going to visit my cousin."

"As you wish, my lady," was his soft response. "Will there be anything else?"

"Just the carriage, please, Georges."

Georges inclined his head and went in search of the driver, hoping beyond hope that the man was still sober. He returned shortly afterwards, his face his usual mask. "I am sorry to report, my lady, that there are no carriages available. It appears that your carriage has been appropriated by a member of the king's retinue, and there are no others available."

Clare paused in putting on her gloves. "I'm so sorry, Georges," she said, looking at him after a brief pause.

"Mademoiselle?" he asked quizzically.

"Well, I don't like to ride by myself at night, so you'll have to come with me. You do ride, don't you, Georges?" she asked lightly.

The good man blinked. "Certainly, my lady. I'll see to it straight away," Nodding once more, he retreated, leaving Clare to smile at his broad-shouldered back.

Thirteen

A RIDE IN THE DARK

GEORGES HAD ALWAYS looked old, even when he was born. As a child, he lived a lonely existence, mainly because he found the company of others confusing. In those early years, there was talk that he would enter the Church, as he served Mass on a regular basis, and indeed he was a favorite of the local priest. However, it was not the religion that enthralled him, but the absolute order of it all. Georges loved ritual and found security in it.

In his youth, he had been thought by some to be almost handsome in a cold, diffident sort of way, and he did manly things with great ease. No one ever picked a fight with him, despite him being a figure of fun. He was too big and too strong for most of his tormentors. But the simple fact was that Georges never even noticed them, those petty irritants. If ever he found pleasure, it was in his isolation: watching the morning sunrise, tidying up the priest's small library in an orderly sort of fashion, and riding to the bishop's palace with occasional messages from his kind benefactor.

However, Georges could be extremely stubborn. Most of it was beaten out of him by his father. But then, most young men of his era suffered such "straightening out," as it was called. In fact, it straightened Georges out so much that he could withstand the withering sarcasm of the most puerile of students without batting an eyelid and still complete the job at hand. So when he found himself in the stable asking for two horses to be saddled 'immediately,' the usual stable-yard wit was lost on him.

Having secured two mounts, he led the horses to the side door of the château, where neither he nor Clare would be noticed leaving. Clare appeared shortly thereafter, covered in her cloak. Georges assisted her into the saddle before mounting his own horse, and they proceeded to walk slowly down the driveway with the pebbles crunching under the horses' hooves. Nothing was said. It was if they were holding their breaths, hoping that no one would hear them. Cold breath came from their nostrils, but their mouths remained tightly shut.

The gatekeeper gave them a knowing look as Georges's tall figure accompanied by Clare's slight figure concealed in her cloak gave vent to his lewd imagination. "'Ave a good ride!" he shouted, as the gate rang shut behind them. His words were lost in the drizzle of rain that had begun to drift down.

"Do you know where we are going, Georges?" Clare asked from under the hood of her cloak.

"Yes, my lady," he replied, and once again they both descended into their own thoughts.

After some miles, Georges cleared his throat, his normal outward sign that something was worrying him. "Do you have a plan for when we arrive, my lady?" he inquired, as if asking about what refreshments she would like to take in the parlor.

"I shall demand that my cousin release my friend immediately," she replied animatedly. Another pause. Another clearing of the throat.

"And what if he refuses, my lady?" Georges quietly asked.

"He wouldn't dare refuse me!" Clare retorted haughtily.

Another silence. Another clearing of the throat.

"Your cousin can be difficult on occasion, my lady," Georges intoned. "Perhaps if I made some enquiries belowstairs before you went in, that might help," he suggested quietly.

"You may enquire as much as you want, Georges," Clare snapped back, "but I'm going to order my cousin to release my friend immediately."

"As you wish, my lady," Georges replied with admirable equanimity. They completed the rest of the journey in silence as the drizzle turned to a steady fall of wintry rain.

By the time they arrived at the darkened château, it was late at night, and only one light was visible from the front of the building. Both riders were soaked where their outer garments had failed to protect them. "Take the horses around the back, Georges. The poor things need a warm blanket and something to eat. I'll deal with my cousin myself." Slipping off her horse with the help of Georges's strong arms, she adjusted her cape and marched up the steps to the front door. She searched for the bell pull and gave it a venomous tug. A muted response came from deep within the house.

Georges waited until the door had been opened before leading the horses around the deeply shadowed side of the building.

The great wooden front door opened to reveal a young man in an ill-fitting footman's coat. He carried a single lantern aloft in a callused hand. It was not the usual hand of those who work in magnificent mansions. He looked taken aback as Clare attempted to bustle past him, but he stood his ground. "What do you want?" was his coarse question.

Clare stared at him. She mastered her anger before saying, "Tell your master that the Duchess of Villepreux has come to visit and needs to see him immediately." This news unsettled the young man, and he was unsure as to what to do next, being new to his position. He was rescued by the unexpected appearance of Philippe.

"Well, well, well. What an unexpected delight, dear Cousin!" he said. His sarcastic greeting was accompanied by a miasma of stale brandy. "Go back to your kennel, dog," he barked at the footman, pushing him roughly in the direction of the stairs. The young man shot them both a look that spoke volumes about his hatred of them as he stumbled toward the blackened stairwell.

"Come, come," Philippe said, putting his arms around his young cousin's shoulders. "Let's get you to the fire to dry off. You must be soaked through." Clare shrugged him off.

"Where is he?" she said. "I know you have him somewhere."

"Cousin," he said, aping a look of shock on his face, "what can you mean?"

Clare halted on the cold tile floor. The only sound was the quiet tapping of raindrops as they hit the hall window above the great front door.

Clare shot him a furious look before heading to the open door of the library, where a menacing light beckoned from the candles within. Inside, two huge arm chairs were drawn up close to the fire. Even in these early hours of the morning, the fire was still banked high.

Clare went and stood warming her hands in front of the fire. Philippe came and stood beside her with his back to the fire. "I don't think you've met my friend, have you, Cousin?" he asked. Clare turned to him with a questioning look on her face. Philippe merely nodded to one of the huge armchairs she had just passed.

"Forgive me for not getting up, Mistress, but these chairs weren't made for normal people like me."

Clare knew the voice before she saw his face hidden in the dark recesses of the wingback chair. Her heart leaped before her face froze. Philippe was quick to mark the look on her face. "Ah," he drawled, reaching for his goblet and taking a long draft, "so you know each other already."

"Of course I know her, you bloody idiot. Odysseo knows everyone and everything," the dwarf seethed. An evil grin crossed his face, "What a strange thing coincidence is, eh, mistress?" He stood up on the chair and began to bounce up and down on it, singing, "Oh I like this, I do like this," and he clapped his hands loudly. "What delicious games are you playing with my friend here, Philippe? Such a beautiful prize. Such a wonderful catch for someone with the right rod, eh," he shouted making lewd gestures as he bounced and clapped in such a hideous fashion that Clare turned to the fire with a deep hole in her heart.

"The trouble with you, Odysseo, is that you're so damned ugly." Philippe laughed cruelly at the dwarf, who ignored his insult completely. "The other problem is that you trust no one, and no one likes you." Philippe drained another deep draft from his goblet. A small stream of red wine dribbled down his chin, which he wiped clean with his stained sleeve. "On the other hand, it makes you the perfect spy, and the price you charge for your services is so very reasonable." There was a silent hiatus as the two men glared at one another, then they both burst out laughing.

"That's why I like you, Philippe, you're so devious—and lie so easily—that not even you know when you tell the truth. I may be bent and twisted," he said, contorting his oversized face into a gruesome smile, "but you're bent and twisted through and through." The little man then bounced and roared and clapped till he fell in a heap on the chair gasping for breath. "Oh, I do like this," he finished off, reaching for his own goblet.

"My little cuz here seems to think I know the whereabouts of some acquaintance of hers. Don't really know what's she's talking about." Philippe gave a great yawn and stretching his arms wide said, "I feel dreadfully tired all of a sudden. Time for bed," he said, shaking himself. He made for the door. "Are you coming, Odysseo?" he said, in a languid voice. Turning to Clare, he belched a foul cloud of stale wine at her. "As for you, my little blacksmith's whelp, I don't care a damn whether you stay or go. Whichever you do, just know that I despise and disown you, and I'll personally see to it that you leave France with your bastard Italian tail firmly clenched between your pretty thighs." Leaving the door wide open, he departed, the click of his heels echoing over the hallway flagstones.

Clare, who had maintained an impassive face so far, was about to explode into Odysseo's face when he put his finger to his lips and urged her to remain silent. Motioning to her to come close, he whispered, "I don't trust that man one inch. He'll probably come back to listen at the door. Meet me tomorrow morning at the blacksmith's place. It's on the edge of the village you came through last. You'll know it when you see it." He winked. "Now leave." These last two words were spoken with great urgency. Being unsure what to do next, she was shaken into action by Odysseo suddenly bursting into a loud bray of laughter, whilst all the time shooing her toward the door.

On her way out, she met her cousin still at the foot of the stairs, "Came to see what all the noise was about," he smiled. "Sounds like our friend enjoyed your company."

"He's not my friend, Cousin," she replied. "No one in this devil's den is a friend of mine." Heading for the front door, she opened it and left, hoping she would never have to return.

At the foot of the stone steps, she paused and thought before heading around the side of the château to find Georges, who was with their horses. The loyal man was in deep and earnest conversation with the footman who had opened the front door for her. The footman lifted his head and gave her a confused look. He inclined his head in her direction, and after a few more words with Georges, he retreated into the dark shadows of the great house.

"Any news of your friend, my lady?" Georges asked quietly. Clare shook her head, but her features spoke volumes.

"None. But I met someone . . . someone who I met with Rosso many years ago, and who I think may still be a friend. He wants to meet me tomorrow morning at the blacksmith's place near the local village. I think I can trust him, and he's the only lead we have."

Georges absorbed this crumb of information before saying, "May I suggest that we find some shelter for the night? I suspected that you wouldn't want to rely on the hospitality of your cousin. That being the case, I made some inquiries and found some simple accommodation for us about a mile from here. I am led to believe that it's clean and will have a warm bed for you."

Clare looked at Georges. "Why are my friends so kind, and yet my family is so horrible to me?"

"Such is the lot of many, my lady. But we seem to survive it, don't we?" The good man's smile was infectious, and by the time their horses had made it halfway down the long driveway, they were already looking to the future with hope.

From his window in the château, Duke Philippe watched the pair of them blend with the shadows and disappear. "Au revoir, Duchesse. Good riddance and damn you to hell."

Fourteen

UNEXPECTED HELP

GEORGES HAD NOT wasted his time belowstairs. His time in service had taught him to read his colleagues well. He'd quickly discovered that the young footman was actually a local farmer who'd fallen behind in his tithes. Philippe had taken his farm and put him into service until he'd paid off his debts. It transpired that the farmer had a young family, and they had been forced to leave their small cottage and move in with his wife's aged parents. The parents had been sheep farmers and managed their frugal income well. Over the years, their small savings had grown enough to make them independent. They had bought the small farm for their daughter and her husband, and it was to the parents' house that Clare and Georges were now heading.

The rain had ceased, but the roads were treacherous. A frost threatened from the starry skies. "It's beautiful," said Clare, looking up to the heavens. "It's just so vast and pure. Not even my cousin's evilness can reach those stars, Georges." There was a long silence as they both absorbed the beauty above them.

"No, my lady," he agreed quietly. "Many great minds have looked to those same skies and been stunned by their magnificence."

"I didn't know you had the heart of a poet, Georges," Clare said, in a teasing fashion.

Georges cleared his throat before saying quietly, "Neither did I, my lady." They continued up the lane toward the old parents' house. Georges slipped off his horse and approached the front door. He was about to knock when it opened before him, revealing a vision in a white nightgown holding a candle above her head. Her smile reached across the space and into Clare's heart. For a moment, she thought she'd arrived at Laura and Marco's forge. She'd half-expected to find a bent old lady without any teeth. The only indication of age in this lady was a wisp of grey hair that had escaped her nightcap and which cascaded down over one cheek.

"Come in, please," the lady called, holding the door wide and welcoming them in. Once Georges had helped Clare from her mount, the lady fussed over her until Clare had her cloak off and was sitting and warming herself before the glowing embers of the kitchen fire "Such an awful night to be out traveling on the roads," she said, "let me get you something warm to eat, to drive out the cold."

"Please don't trouble yourself," Clare urged her hostess. But her words fell on deaf ears as the good woman found some soup, put it in a metal pot, and nestled it amongst the rejuvenated flames of the fire.

"There," the good woman said, seating herself in a chair next to Clare. Georges stood with his back to the fireplace, which had a low arch and blackened iron crane. He remained in the half shadows sporting his usual blank expression, but his eyes took in every detail of the place.

"You've been so kind," Clare said. "Your son-in-law said you might find a place for us to stay tonight." She glanced up at Georges as if for confirmation. None was forthcoming.

"Ah, poor Paul," she sighed, "he has had a hard time. But he can be, how shall I put it, wild." Her soft eyes engaged with those of Clare's, and many unspoken words were exchanged in that moment.

"I understand, Madame," Clare replied. She reached out and held the good woman's hand in her own. "The Lord has never been easy on mothers, even though his own loved him more than most," she said.

"You speak well, my lady, but please call me Madeleine."

"And I am called Clare. This is Georges, my dear friend who tries to keep me out of trouble." A wry smile crossed both feminine faces, but Georges's face remained as unreadable as ever.

A silence came over the room; all that could be heard was the crackle of the low fire. Above their heads a bed creaked, then all was silent once more.

"I think there are many stories to be told, Clare, but first drink up your soup—I'm sorry, but it's all I have prepared at the moment. After that we must find you both somewhere to sleep." She automatically looked up at the ceiling, "It would be good if we didn't disturb my husband; the dear man needs his sleep." She stopped to fold the unruly tress of hair back into place, and a slight weariness crossed her face. "He worries too much." She stared into the fire, as if seeking some solace from those pale red coals.

Clare slept deeply that night, yet woke well before dawn. The house was silent and cold. She crept out of bed and went into the kitchen, where her cloak was hanging near the fireplace, dry and warm. She smiled as she enclosed herself in it and silently thanked Madeleine for her natural kindness. Looking around the room, she picked out things that she remembered well from growing up in Marco and Laura's kitchen: for instance, an old dresser with tokens and talismans of years past—sacred memories of a family grown and gone.

She put a small handful of dry kindling on the fire, which roused itself from its whitened slumber to let a few flames lick the brittle offering.

She walked to the window to see if there were any stars still in the sky, but it was jet black outside. Tiny dots of rain sometimes coalesced on the pane and raced a drunken course to oblivion at the bottom. Others seemed to just wait on the glass. She reached out a finger and traced Kristopher's face on the pane, then leaned forward and breathed on the window to see his face appear. She smiled as it stared back at her, then slowly faded away. "Be safe, my love," she prayed aloud to herself.

Resuming her tour of the kitchen, she saw that there were ample provisions for the couple who lived here. In fact it appeared to be a kitchen where people were imminently expected, with place settings for several people. The larder contained sweetmeats and a host of dainties that children would enjoy. The kitchen was scrupulously clean, too, which told Clare that Madeleine was a hard worker, as well as a generous spirit. But of a man, there was no sign to be found anywhere in that homey room. Perhaps he kept his tools in another spot, she thought to herself. She was reluctant to enter the rooms behind the other door that led from that snug space.

Clare sat down in the chair and stared at the hearth. She didn't hear anyone enter the kitchen. "Please," was the first word she heard. "Please don't let me disturb you, lady." The voice piped in the throat of a white-haired man. Clare made to arise from her chair. "No, no, no," he said, indicating animatedly that she must stay where she was. "That's my favorite place at this time of day, and I'm so glad that you're enjoying it. I call it my dreaming chair," he said, and he gave a small smile as he scratched at his white goatee. I'm Jean-Claude, by the way, and I think you've met my good wife Madeleine already." His smile moved his creased features, and for a moment he appeared almost youthful. "She works too hard," he went on, "I worry about her. I need to make better provisions for her in case . . . ," his voice faltered. "But no matter," he said, rousing himself from the precipice of chronic anxiety, "Can I get you something, my lady?"

"Please call me Clare," she said gently, "and no, I am happy to sit and enjoy your fire and your company, Monsieur." Jean-Claude stood behind her with one hand on the back of her chair. Silence embraced them both, and they abandoned themselves to the alchemy of the flames.

"I see you've met." Madeleine's voice eased their minds into the present moment. As if by some secret signal, Georges appeared from the outside door. He closed it quietly, shook his coat before taking it off and hung it on a hook on the back of the door. "The horses have been seen to, my lady. It's drizzling out, but I think that will clear with the light of dawn." Turning to Madeleine he asked, "May I be of assistance, Madame"?

"How did you get out there without me seeing you?" Clare interrupted.

"You were busy thinking, my lady, and it seemed inappropriate to disturb you. If my memory serves me well, I believe you have an appointment later on this morning?"

Clare smiled at the faithful Georges. "Which means I'd better get off my behind and get dressed to go out." She started to stand, but was stopped by Madeleine, who said cheerfully, "Not before I've fed you, my dear. This sort of weather is much easier to endure if you've got a stomach full of hot food." The good woman shooed the others out of her way, whilst she prepared and served food to break their fasts.

"Now," she said, with a satisfied look at the empty bowls in front of her, "time to greet the day. Georges," she said kindly to the sentry by the sink, who was wiping the last traces of food from his face, "perhaps you'd be so kind as to bring some more wood in for the fire. And husband dear, perhaps you'd be so very kind and sweep the hearth clean, so that I can begin to prepare soup for later in the day?" Both men obeyed her gentle requests, leaving Clare to wander back to her room and prepare to meet with Odysseo.

As she walked to the back of the house, she passed a small door. She was intrigued to find it secured by a very large lock. "It's Jean-Claude's private room, my dear," Madeleine said, as if answering Clare's unspoken question. She had appeared in the corridor behind Clare and was carrying a dry towel and a bowl of steaming water. Her face was disturbed by a rare, agitated expression. "Jean-Claude likes to hoard things. Sometimes I think he loves money more than he loves his family. He keeps his treasures in there. Not that I know what they are. He goes off to nearby towns to 'trade' as he calls it. When he's been successful, he brings his treasures home and locks them in there. He says it's for the family. But he keeps it locked away. Even from me." She looked at Clare, and the tiredness in her voice spoke volumes.

"Men are such strange creatures, aren't they?" Clare said. "You think you know them, and then you realize you never really quite know all of them, if you get what I mean."

Madeleine held out the bowl of water. "Here," she said, "there's nothing so nice as splashing your face with hot water in the morning. Here, take it before it goes cold." The light had returned to her eyes as she draped the clean towel over Clare's shoulder. "I suppose we're just called to love them, not to understand them, Clare. Do you have a man in your life?"

Clare's face flushed, surprising even her. "I didn't think I had, but now I'm beginning to think I do. Thank you for the hot water," she muttered, turning toward her room to hide her embarrassment.

Having finished her ablutions, Clare quietly returned to the kitchen. The two men stood like bookends at either end of the fireplace, contentedly sipping on some hot soup. Madeleine had tidied the breakfast things away. "I never asked what you thought of my son-in-law last night," she said haltingly.

The sound of Georges clearing his throat indicated to Clare that perhaps he'd better do the talking. "He was well, Madame. I would perhaps observe that he is not fully content with his present position. During our conversation, he gave the impression of holding you both very close to his heart." At this, a knowing look passed between Madeleine and her husband, leaving a smile to illuminate their features. Georges cleared his throat once more, "I had the impression that perhaps the young man might be about to do something impulsive." A small log tumbled from the fireplace and smoked benignly on the clay hearth. Jean-Claude pushed it back with an iron. "He mentioned the Americas," Georges announced. This time the look that flashed between husband and wife reflected fear. Madeleine was the first to recover. "He's a dreamer like so many young men. What hope do they have in this country, where what little they have is taken from them, and yet they have no recourse to justice? The king says much, but does so little."

"Be quiet, my dear," Jean-Claude hissed. "Walls have ears, and even though our new friends seem sincere, a word let slip carelessly, and we could all find ourselves without a place to rest our head. Even worse, we might have no heads at all." He glanced to where the corridor was and where his private room of treasures was. "We must be very careful."

"You need have no fear of us," Clare said, going over to embrace Madeleine. "We have our own concerns, but I promise that we will do whatever we can to be of service to you and your family."

"I believe you, my dear," Madeleine replied. "But these are uncertain times. You must be careful, too."

Clare looked across at Georges, who appeared to have been sculptured from marble, such was the apparent lack of interest on his face. "Time to go, Georges," she said, and the two took their leave. "We'll meet again, Madeleine. Thank you, Jean-Claude, you have a pearl of great price next to you. Your daughter is doubly blessed to have you both." Jean-Claude's haunted look, which had lingered in his eyes since glancing at the door guarding his treasure, dissipated. "Yes, yes," he muttered as he dragged his mind back to the present moment. "Yes. Of course. Pearl of great price. Thank you," and he forced a smile back onto his greyed features.

Clare and Georges rode off along the muddy track in the grey light of the morning. The rain had stopped, and the clouds were beginning to break up. I think it's going to be a nice day, Georges," she said. "Thank you for being so kind to those dear people. What strange times we live in."

"Strange indeed, my lady," was all the good man could muster.

"Did you get the impression that something heavy lay on that poor man's mind?" she asked, whilst gazing around her in the morning light.

"I believe that money can corrupt the minds of the poor, just as much as it does the wealthy, my lady."

They both rode on in silence. The horses' breaths were like dragons' breaths in the air. Holly bushes with ruby red berries colored the bare hedgerows. Their green, glossy leaves provided a stark contrast to their barren white-thorn friends. Startled rabbits stood and watched the riders approach, before scampering off into their warm, dark burrows.

"We should get to the forge in plenty of time," Clare said. She sighed deeply. "I never thought France would look so beautiful in winter. Just look at the light the sun makes in the hole in those clouds." They both stopped their mounts and stared spellbound at the beauty in the sky before them. The opening in the clouds grew wider as the cumulus curtains drew further apart. A pale-blue sky spread above the riders as they continued on toward the village.

They saw the signs of the smithy in the sky, too. A fine wisp of smoke like a silvered string rose from its fires to the heavens. Then they heard the song of the smithy—the ringing tocsin of metal upon metal.

"I'll beat this red until it's black," Clare softly sang to herself. She repeated the phrase several times, and an irrepressible smile emerged on her face. "Marco used to sing that when I was growing up," she said to Georges.

"Really," he replied stolidly.

"I'll beat this red until it's black. Hit it hard, hit it true," she sang. She was still singing as they approached the forge, where a mule was tethered to the rail outside the wooden building. Nearby, sitting on a stack of wood and chewing on the bone of some indistinct beast sat Odysseo.

"Well met, my lady," he heehawed. "Forgive me for not getting up, but when it doesn't pay, I prefer to stay seated."

The sound of Clare's pure laughter shook Georges and delighted Odysseo. "I'm glad you know your real station in life, little woman," the dwarf shouted at her, then he honked with great laughter.

"Oh Odysseo, if you weren't so old, I'd ask you to marry me."

"If you weren't so honest, I'd probably accept," he honked back at her as Clare slipped from her horse and ran over to give him a kiss and a hug.

Georges stayed where he was and watch the scene unfold. He felt uncomfortable in the presence of such ugliness and found himself not trusting the little man.

But for Clare, there was much joy at their reunion. For his part, Odysseo never dropped his guard as his eyes probed the surrounding area. "Your cousin, little Duchess, is slippery as an eel, and it wouldn't surprise me if he slipped out from under a rock at any moment," he said. "I've met some cruel people in my life, but that man is definitely in the top three of them." Clare's senses sobered immediately.

"Where's Kristopher?" she asked.

"To be quite honest, which isn't my natural state, I don't know—yet. But Philippe is worried. He's made a big mistake by seizing someone who is an emissary to the king. That's about the only advantage we have. I think Philippe is moving your friend from place to place just to keep you off the scent, but my guess is that he'll send him to Paris." He paused, "That's what I'd do if I were in his position. It's much easier to hide a man in a big city."

Both of them lapsed into silence. Clare thought, Georges watched, and Odysseo worried.

"This is all too much for me, Odysseo," Clare confessed. "What do you think I should do?"

"One thing's for certain, you can't do this by yourself, and I can't be seen to be helping you. But you're right, you need help." He scratched at his chin, his eyes constantly darting this way and that. "Get Rosso here. In fact, get as many of your friends as you can here. Make the excuse that they're artisans coming to help you decorate your château. After all, I hear that redheaded ex-monk is quite the painter these days. And didn't you say that Marco was a smithy? Make that a wrought-iron worker, and he'll have more work than a one-armed caulker in a shipyard." A conspiratorial grin spread across his handsome face. Then he battered his hat and stamped his feet in celebration of his genius.

"Oh yes," he whooped, " nowadays the French love their Italian maestros, especially the king. Once he hears about their creations, hey presto, all the people follow his lead, and they'll love you, too." He stopped. His face fell, "Rosso can paint, can't he? And Marco can twist iron, can't he?"

It was Clare's turn to howl with laughter. "Oh course they can, my little genius. Of course they can."

"I need something to write on," Clare declared.

"I think I can oblige you there, little lady," Odysseo said, twisting his large satchel around to the front of his giant torso. His stunted arms delved into the depths of the satchel and plucked out a quill and some parchment. "Always good to have this on hand if an unexpected promissory note is on offer," he grinned devilishly. Then he foraged once more until he found a blackened vial with a blackened cork stopping its broad neck. "Ink," he announced, "the very lifeblood of binding contracts." Clare took the quill and the paper and dipped the quill into the vial proffered by Odysseo. He ignored the splashes of lampblack and gum that dribbled down on his big fat fingers.

Clare gave orders to Georges as she wrote. "Go into the village and send a message back to Marionette to say that I've been urgently recalled to St. Germain. Tell her that all our things should be packed, and she should bring them to the château. Then find a reliable messenger and get him to deliver this urgently to Mario. He'll know what to do next." She finished her missive and shook the parchment to dry. When the letters were fixed, she rolled it up and gave it to Georges. For a brief moment, they both found themselves holding an end of the document. Georges gave a slight nod, went to his mount, and left.

"Talkative sort, isn't he?" snarled Odysseo, once Georges was out of earshot. "But still, that's far better than someone with a loose tongue. Can you trust him?" he asked, still watching the disappearing Georges.

"As much as I trust you," replied Clare.

Odysseo burst out laughing again and beat his chest with his fat hands crying, "Oh, I do like you, little lady. I do like you."

Fifteen

A CONSPIRACY IS PLANNED

CLARE AND GEORGES WALKED their mounts along the driveway toward the Château Villepreux. They were both keenly eyeing the fields around them for signs of trouble, but even to Georges's well-trained vision, everything seemed to be running smoothly. He cleared his throat.

"Yes, Georges?" Clare asked.

"May I be so bold as to say, my lady, that the last few days have been the best of my life." As he spoke, he continued to look straight ahead, and not a muscle in his face had altered in the slightest. Clare cast a swift sideways glance at him and smiled to herself.

"That makes me very happy, Georges," she replied.

"Thank you, my lady."

Nothing more was said on the matter as they moved closer to the château, where the fountain was bubbling clean water into the pool at its base. A gardener approached and uncovered his head, acknowledging his mistress.

"Welcome home, my lady, Monsieur Georges."

"Where is Signore Mario?" Clare asked. The gardener shot a knowing look up at Georges.

"I think he may be in his office, my lady. He had a late-night meeting with Monsieur Pinot, and by all accounts is still asleep in his office." Clare looked at Georges, who continued to stare straight ahead. The two of them walked their horses to the stables and gave them over to the stable lads to rub down and feed.

"Who is Monsieur Pinot, Georges?" Clare finally asked. The good man cleared his throat.

"I believe, my lady, that Monsieur Pinot is the name of a grape that is often distilled into intoxicating liquor. Some seem to find it quite palatable, but for myself, I prefer one of Marionette's tisanes."

"Oh, dear Lord," Clare expostulated, "does that mean Mario's drunk?"

"I believe it does, my lady. But before we leap to the wrong side of the fence, may I just observe that the household seems to be functioning perfectly, and all the orders you gave appear to have been carried out. Perhaps it was just an aberration?"

"We'll soon find out," Clare said, as she mounted the steps two at a time.

Mario was in his office, sprawled across his desk and snoring loudly. An upturned wine decanter lay near one outstretched hand. Papers were strewn all around him, and in the midst of these Clare found the message she had written to him at the forge.

"Mario!" she barked in a voice loud enough to disturb the dead. "Mario, explain this!" she added, waving the letter in front of the hungover young man's face. He blinked his bloodshot eyes as he tried to shield them from the light threatening to explode his desiccated brain. He was struggling to his feet when the benevolent Georges pushed him back down and offered him a large glass of water. Mario downed it in one long gulp, wiped his face, and then stared sheepishly at Clare.

"I'm in love," he said meekly. "She's so beautiful, she outshines Aphrodite herself. Look," he pointed to the papers on his desk, "I've been writing poetry to her all night long. She's the most . . ." Clare cut him short.

"And what about this, you drunken, lovelorn fool?!" She thrust her message under his nose, anger bubbling just beneath the surface of her face.

"Oh that," he meekly replied, "I didn't dare send the original in your handwriting. So I copied it and sent that instead. I didn't want the original to fall into the wrong hands. You never know who might see it." He looked up at her with innocent, if glazed, eyes. Silence filled the room.

"Mario," Clare shouted, "you're, you're . . . you're nothing short of a genius!" She went around the desk and hugged him hard. "You stink of stale wine. Go and wash," she ordered, "then we can talk some more." Mario rose unsteadily from his chair and walked to the door.

"And Mario," Clare called to him. He stopped and looked at her, "Thank you, Mario."

Georges cleared his throat as if on cue. "Go on, Georges," Clare pre-empted him.

"If I may be so bold as to observe, my lady, that Signore Mario continues to amaze me." Blinking twice as if to emphasize this wise insight, he bowed slightly and added, "But perhaps a brief reconnoiter belowstairs might be appropriate?" The words were left hovering in the air.

"Certainly, Georges. See if you can find out what's been happening in our absence." She turned and looked out Mario's office window onto the stable yards. The normal noise of the day eddied through the air. *Waiting will be the hardest part,* she thought to herself. *Kristopher.* She allowed the name only a brief presence in her consciousness before she slammed the door shut on it, to block out the anxiety that threatened to flood in. "Where are you, Rosso?" she said to the sky.

She rummaged amongst the papers on Mario's desk, and picking up a random sheet read,

> *Come, let me speak softly of the love we share.*
> *Not of the love I have for you or the love you have for me,*
> *But the love that lives in the spaces of our lives.*
> *The love that illuminates our moments*

Nourishes our hearts
And feeds our dreams.

It made her smile. Love. She picked up another,

Our love is so precious
So very much beyond the grasp of words
So, so exquisitely gentle and painfully shy,
Yet it will outlast the jeweled stars in their
     obsidian vault
And all the sophistry from men's mouths,
Which is carried off with the morning
     breeze.

She remembered Rosso telling her how he'd found Mario drunk in a church, and how he'd been madly in love with some passing vision of beauty. Dropping the parchment back on the desk, she picked up the empty decanter and stood it up straight.

She left Mario's lovelorn sanctuary and went to her own room. Her head was buzzing with things she needed to do, and she needed space to sort them all out. But what she needed most at this moment was time to think and time to plan.

Not much happened in the following weeks. The king returned to Paris, winter tightened its grip on the countryside, and Clare watched the long graveled driveway for any sign of her friends. Kristopher seemed to have vanished from the face of the earth. All seemed locked in by the grey skies and the cold damp air.

A royal messenger arrived. She thought the message might have news of Kristopher, but it announced that the king was to be married again to a lady of a very different ilk to Queen Claude. It was reported that His Majesty had shaken off his grief and was now planning to party. In her heart, Clare hoped that she would be quietly forgotten at her château at St. Germain-en-Laye. Each day she prayed that she would soon get news of Kristopher's whereabouts.

Marionette was a constant source of strength; she sensed when something was troubling her lovely lady and admonished her if she didn't eat: "You can't win wars on an empty stomach," she wagged her finger at Clare one day, and before Clare had a chance to respond, Marionette added "And when it comes to dealing with men, life's a constant battle, believe me."

"Do you think Kristopher . . . ," but before she could finish, her mentor held her finger to her lip, warning Clare that even in her own home, this was a name too dangerous to mention.

"I'm sure that when your friends finally arrive," she went on in a loud, businesslike fashion, "they'll have the appetites of giants, and your little Marionette will be hard-pressed to fill those bottomless pits. But I've never failed yet," she smiled confidently.

"It will do my heart good to watch them eat your food, Marionette," Clare said, smiling back at her. "Let's hope we don't have to wait too long."

And, fortunately, they didn't.

Georges appeared silently late one morning to announce, "My lady, there's a one-armed giant at the front door asking for you. I thought . . . ," but his words were cut short by a shriek of delight from Clare. She rushed past him, her skirts held high in a most unduchess-like fashion. She sped across the flagstones of the cavernous hallway and out the half-open door. She launched herself at the Dom and hugged him as if he were the Savior himself.

"Oh Dom, oh Dom," she kept repeating, between hugging him and kissing his massive grinning cheeks. The dear man laughed and hugged her in return until they were interrupted by a discreet cough from Georges.

"Perhaps my lady might like to invite the gentleman inside," he said, hovering by the open door until the two of them had disappeared back into the château like naughty schoolchildren.

"How did you know to come? Who sent you?" she asked as questions tumbled out of her mouth one after the other. The Dom stopped her flow with another hug that swept her off her feet, almost crushing her chest at the same time.

"Whoa there, little lady," the good man said, "there's enough time to answer some of those questions over a nice refreshing beverage, I think." He gently restored her feet to the flagstones, and they marched into the drawing room with gleaming smiles on their faces.

Clare had just asked Georges to bring refreshments when the distant sound of the doorbell interrupted them. Georges retired to answer the call, and Clare turned to pepper the

Dom with a thousand more questions. He sat next to her with a look of supreme pride on his face. Ignoring all the questions she fired at him, he quietly took her hand and said, "You look beautiful. I am so proud of you, my little lady; if only Rosso or Marco could see you now."

At that point Georges reappeared with his usual unreadable expression, slightly disturbed by something or someone. "There's a monk at the door, my lady, asking if you would like to have your confession heard."

"A monk," Clare replied, mystified, "asking if I want to give my confession?"

"Yes, my lady. A monk with red hair." Georges was again surprised by his mistress shrieking and running for the front door, only this time she was shouting "Uncle Rosso, Uncle Rosso." Once she had reached her quarry, she repeated the exercise of flinging herself at him and hugging him half to death, but this time there were more sobs than kisses. "I've missed you so much, Rosso. You won't believe what it's like to be rich and powerful. I hate it. It's so good to have you here."

Leading her back across the hallway by the hand, Rosso fairly gleamed with happiness. The reunion with his fellow conspirator was all the more sweet with Clare sitting between the two of them.

They were sitting quietly enjoying the refreshments that Marionette had brought them, and their stomachs were indeed feeling quite content at what they had received, when Georges appeared again. They heard his cough and all turned toward him. Something glinted in one of his eyes and unusually for him, he repeated his cough. This time it really did give the impression that he was clearing his throat. "There's a blacksmith at the door, my lady," he said, oh-so-very-quietly.

Clare turned ashen as she sat between her two mentors. She rose slowly, and as she walked past Georges, she softly touched his arm and looked up questioningly into his eyes. He nodded, and she proceeded across the hallway and stopped at the front door. Marco stood there. The silhouette of his broad back was outlined by the sunlight he was gazing at. He turned. His uncovered head had a shock of white hair, but his great and good face was full of love and happiness. He was holding his hat in his massive hands, and he looked a little sheepish. They looked at each other as only a parent can look at his long-missed child, and as only a child can look at her most loving father. Clare took the final two steps that separated them, and they embraced silently, together as one in that secret place where the heart's true home really exists.

"My blessed daughter," was all the good man said.

"Papa," came the reply.

When they returned to the drawing room, there was laughter, there were tears, and there was an endless stream of questions and barely believed answers.

Midway through their reunion, there was a knock at the door. At the words "Come in" from Clare, the door opened to reveal Mario carrying a bundle of parchments and seemingly on the cusp of asking her a question. When he became aware that she was with company, he immediately fell mute.

Rosso rose from his place next to Clare and walked across the room to him. The young secretary hesitated as his mind tried to place this ascetic-looking monk. Suddenly his eyes grew wide, and he whispered, "Is it really you, Rosso? What happened?" Rosso came up to him and relieved him of his paperwork, placing it on a small nearby table, and stood with his hands on his young protégé's shoulders.

"You've grown, Mario. My trust was not wasted on you. Clare has been telling me all about you." He pulled the youth close to his own chest and spoke softly in his ear, "Thank you." Then after a pause he repeated the words, "Thank you," and nothing more was said. He put his arm around Mario's shoulder and introduced him to the others. All the while, Mario was looking askance at Rosso. Finally he stammered, "You're not really . . . ," before his voice faltered.

Dom beamed and said, "The man's a holy father, you should see his two beautiful children. As for the cloth, there aren't too many monks who are as Christian as this farmer is! Come to think of it, there aren't too many artists who are . . . ," and a look of bewilderment knotted his brow. The others laughed as Dom tried to untangle himself from his fleetingly wise moment. "Good try, Dom," said Marco, "I was going to say the same thing myself, but you said it so much better!" Dom reddened to the roots of his hair.

"Clare," Rosso asked, "Would you care to show us around your home? I've a feeling that word of our arrival will soon reach your cousin's ears," and we really don't have much time to make any plans, so it'd be good to see what's at stake here."

"Of course," she said, smiling. "No time like the present." Linking Marco's arm through hers, she took Mario's hand and asked him to lead the tour, as he knew more about the house than she did.

"You want to see all of it?" he asked, looking a little uncertain. "You mean everything, warts and all?"

"Absolutely," Clare replied, still quite giddy at her newfound happiness.

"As you wish, my lady," the young man said, and he led them through the ground-floor rooms. The public rooms were grand indeed, full of gilt leaf with oak-paneled recesses. Two large glass chandeliers hung in the dining room, glinting in the sunlight released by the newly opened shuttered windows.

Floor-to-ceiling doors led from the main drawing room to the terraced gardens outside. Naturally, Rosso examined the paintings in the rooms closely. He lifted a couple of the frames away from the walls and looked behind them. His face wore a worried expression.

"Any problems, Uncle?" Clare asked him.

Mario interjected, "Perhaps we should wait until we've seen everything," he smiled back at her. Clare was too happy with all her men around her to be greatly concerned, and the party moved on.

"Belowstairs, too, if you please," Dom said to Mario. The young secretary darted another look at Rosso, as if seeking his permission. Rosso nodded.

"If you must, Signore," he replied, and they headed down to the kitchen and the store room. As they descended, the smell of damp ascended.

"Just as I thought," murmured Dom, so Clare couldn't hear him. As he walked into the kitchen, he picked a flake of plaster from the crumbling wall, revealing black mold behind it. The kitchen itself was large and well stocked. All the utensils hung in pristine condition from hooks in the ceiling. This was under Georges's sphere of influence, and naturally everything was perfectly organized.

Marco walked over to the kitchen fire, which had been damped down since breakfast. He leaned into the fireplace and looked up the vast chimney. "How many fireplaces are in the château?" he asked Mario.

"Counting this one, there are nine altogether, and that's not counting the two in the stables."

"Any idea when they were last swept?" Marco asked.

"Not for some time, Signore," Mario replied, and once more he shot a look at Rosso.

"What's troubling you, Mario?" Rosso asked. "What is it that you're not telling us?"

"I'm a young man, Signore Rosso, and I've never run an estate before. All I've ever known is singing, my poems, falling in love, and getting drunk. I'm a young man," he pleaded with them all. "Here, I'm the Italian upstart, but maybe I've come to enjoy the challenge." He shrugged his shoulders. "You ask me what the problem is? It's that sneaky serpent Philippe with his plots and threats . . ." The young man paused for dramatic effect. "He is going to steal this place from my lady." Mario assumed the air of someone who knew something the others didn't. "It appears that her cousin Philippe has big gambling debts, and he needs money, lots and lots of money if he's not going to lose everything. So he's plotting against my duchessa here. If I ask for a chimney sweep, suddenly the chimney sweep has too much work and cannot help me. If I need help to fix broken plows, suddenly the blacksmith gets sick and cannot leave home. With that weasel around whispering promises in one ear and threatening vile retribution in the other ear, it is very difficult to get anything fixed here." He threw his arms in the air with intense Italian drama.

"It's not only the chimneys and furniture that need attention, I'm afraid," Rosso said, ending the silence that had followed Mario's declaration. "From what I've seen of the artwork, it's in a pretty poor state, too. It's suffering from what I would call 'loving neglect.'" He looked around at the others, who now seemed more somber than before. "If you were to ask me, then I'd say that nothing much has been done to maintain this place for years. If I were a guessing man, then I'd hazard a guess that someone's been milking the estate behind your predecessor's back, and I think we all know who to point the finger at."

"That's exactly what I've been saying. Philippe has been taken off the tit that he's been sucking on for years, and he wants it back. Your cousin is a very dangerous man, my lady," Mario said. He folded his arms across his chest in an attitude of finality.

"I think your secretary speaks wisely," Marco commented. "I know little of the estates of powerful men, but greed and villainy are common to all men in all situations. We need to be very careful, especially as he appears to have the ear of the king, and he's holding your friend somewhere." He put his arm around Clare's shoulder. They were all deep in their own thoughts.

The sound of a throat being cleared brought them back to the present. "Refreshments are being served in the small drawing room, my lady," Georges intoned, and he opened the door leading to the vaulted hallway.

"That man's been reading my mind," Dom whispered to Clare.

"He reads all our minds, Dom, but I know his heart's as true as yours."

Marionette had laid out some dainties and her famous tisane on a card table by the bay windows. Dom was about to comment on how small the dainties looked when the door opened again, and the bewitching smell of a country soup preceded that good woman into the room. A huge smile stretched Dom's features, "How did she . . . ?" he said to no one in particular.

"What?" inquired Clare.

"If I'm not mistaken, then that's game soup, my absolute favorite. The dear lady must be a mind reader." Marionette blushed at the compliment.

"Traveling men need feeding up," she riposted, "much the same as children do!" She looked straight at Dom.

"Well said, good lady," said Rosso, entering the fray. "Thank you for caring for our beloved Clare and for Dom's stomach, too." He then formally introduced each of them to Marionette, who wiped her hands on her apron before shaking each of their hands in turn.

"It's about time someone gave the poor lass a hand." She looked at them one by one before predicting, "If I'm any judge of character, which my brother Georges seems to think that I am, then I'd say that your cousin Philippe is in for a merry ole time, my lady." With a twinkle in her eye, she dropped a swift curtsey and left.

Sixteen

THE ART OF DEFENSE

FOR THE REST OF THE DAY, they walked the land around the château, discovering the extent of Clare's inherited holdings. In addition to the two hundred acres around the main house, which was mainly forested and of little worth except for its hunting value, she held the leases to over seven hundred acres of good farmland. It was the income from these lands that should be making Clare a very wealthy lady. But through fear and force, Philippe had been bleeding the farmers dry.

"Just imagine if some of your income was used to restore your home," Rosso commented, "it would be a veritable palace. But is that what you really want?" he asked?

"No, Uncle. Farmers' lives are hard enough without having a parasite like Philippe sucking the life blood out of them. I've no need for a palace! Surely there must be some other way?" She stared at the countryside. "It's beautiful isn't it?" A thrush settled in a tree nearby and began to sing. "There *must* be something we can do!"

"Well, I suggest that we all try to get a good sleep tonight, and then tomorrow we'll have a council of war, and then I think we need to make some plans," Rosso said.

"Great idea," replied Dom. "What time's dinner? I'm starving!"

Marco nudged his friend, saying, "Your stomach is a bottomless pit. I don't think even Marionette will be able to fill it."

"I'm a growing lad," he replied in mock hurt, and then he engulfed Marco in a big one-armed bear hug. He lifted the well-muscled blacksmith clean off his feet before they both tumbled laughing onto the grass, causing the rest of them to join in the laughter.

When they returned to the château, Georges stood at attention by the front door. "I've taken the liberty of arranging accommodation for our guests close to Signore Mario and myself, my lady."

Clare's face colored. "But the upstairs guest rooms . . . ," she said, "surely they would be more suitable for my friends and family, Georges?"

"Monsieur Georges is correct, Duchesse," Mario interrupted. "The rooms he speaks of are dry, warm, and near the kitchen. I am afraid to say that the upstairs rooms are, how shall I say, less than welcoming. In fact, it is possible that the guests might freeze to death in this weather. We cannot light fires in the rooms because birds have nested in the chimneys." He spread his hands wide to explain the seriousness of the affair. "I think also that perhaps they would be happier nearer the kitchen, especially those who like Marionette's food," and he beamed at Dom, who immediately returned the compliment.

"A man after my own heart," he replied.

"So is my room the only one fit for nobility?" and she blushed deeply as soon as she'd mouthed the words. "No, please don't get me wrong, but what if we have guests?" she said, flustered. Marco embraced her saying, "We know what you're trying to say." Then holding her hand, he turned to his friends and in a serious tone continued, "From what I've seen, there is a great deal of work to be done before anyone visits this place. If, I'm not mistaken, I wouldn't be surprised if Cousin Philippe found some pretense to shame Clare as soon as he possibly could."

They didn't have to wait long before Marco's prediction became a reality.

Following their tour of the house, Rosso had taken on the job of renovating some of the paintings in the rooms and hallways. He also showed Clare how some of the damage could be used to their advantage. Pointing to where the paint had chipped from the doors to the library, he said, "Look here." Then lifting a piece of old gilt paint from the vast double doors, he continued, "See here underneath, the old paint is blue, and if I'm not mistaken, I would guess that the rest of the doors down here will be exactly the same."

"But it would take months to renovate all of them, and it'd probably take an army of painters to do it," Clare replied, a deep crease furrowing her forehead.

"Aha," Rosso interjected, "now there I think you're wrong. You see, I think we can turn that flaking into our advantage. If I'm correct, then I can make these doors look delightfully 'distressed' and give the impression of cultured wear and tear. It should be a fairly simple thing to match these colors, and by the sparing use of some gilt leaf, I can make these doors like individual works of art. There'll be nothing like them in all of France."

"Oh, Uncle," Clare said, throwing her arms around his neck, "can you really do that? Silly me," she said, "of course you can. You can do anything once you've turned your mind to it."

"If you think I'm clever, then go and talk to that father of yours. He's got a genius of an idea which makes my attempts seem quite humble." Clare looked at him quizzically. "He's in the forge, if that's what you were about to ask me." Leaning forward, he gave her a light kiss on the forehead. "Go on," he added, "he's waiting for you!" Clare turned and left. As she opened the towering front door, she turned back to look at Rosso, who had already begun chipping away pieces of the old paintwork. Standing in the doorway, Clare's hair was illuminated like a halo by the morning sun. The chill winter's breeze made her pull her wool shawl closer to her neck. Georges saw it all from the shadow of the staircase. Clare saw him, too, and blew a kiss in his direction before heading off to find Marco.

Marco's forge—as it had become known since he'd first fired it only a few days earlier—was glowing red, and the man himself stood before the furnace, just watching. The glow was reflected in his face, and his leather apron showed signs of previous encounters with flying embers and white-hot metals. He held a pair of pliers in one hand and a hammer in the other. He seemed lost in contemplation as he stared at the glowing embers. "I thought I'd see you this morning," he said, without stirring his gaze from the heart of the heat. "Been talking to Rosso?" A smile turned up one corner of his mouth, making him look more youthful.

"You should smile more often, Papa," Clare said, "It makes you look very handsome." She came and stood behind him where she could shelter from the heat, but slipped her arm through his. "What are you making?" she asked.

"It's a surprise," he said, poking the lump of red-hot metal that was being transformed deep within the coals.

"Not for me, I hope. I have the best present in the whole world with you, Rosso, and the Dom being here," she said.

Marco smiled more fully, but still his gaze refused to budge from the glowing piece of iron. "No, my dear, this little gift will be fit for a king. Just give me a few days, and I'll have something to show you." After a short pause, he asked, "Has Rosso told you about his new painting?"

"He's told me about what he proposes to do with the doors. I'm not really sure I understand what he's going to do, but neither of you have ever let me down, which allows me just to feel excited." She squeezed Marco's arm tighter.

"No, not the doors," said Marco, lifting the almost-translucent piece of iron from the fire, turning it in the pliers for a moment, then putting it back deep in the flames as if dissatisfied with its behavior. "The portrait of the cardinal," he went on. "The two of us were talking, and we think that Philippe is going to use his influence with the king to discredit you. At some point, you'll no doubt have to present yourself before His Majesty, and if you just happened to have some very special gifts for him, then Philippe might not get what he expects, eh?"

"Men!" said Clare, giggling and encircling her papa's waist with both arms. "Always plotting something!" She gave him an extra-hard squeeze.

"Careful, there," Marco laughed, "you can't go around crushing blacksmiths to death in their forges, you know." He leaned his head sideways and rested it on her head. Marco closed his eyes and soaked up every molecule of scent from her hair. "I love you, Clare," he whispered. In a more serious tone, he finished, "This is a very dangerous game we're playing here." He gave the bellows a couple of pumps, and the flames roared from the white-hot hell before him. "We're playing with a fire that I don't understand, and fires can do terrible damage."

Clare gave him one more squeeze. "But if the wind turns to our advantage, Papa . . ." She kissed him lightly on the cheek and left him to his work.

Seventeen

THE KING IS COMING

THE VERY NEXT DAY, a courier arrived from the king. He dismounted and said, "His Majesty is to hunt this weekend in the Forêt de Cruye and intends to visit your forests, too. He has been informed by Duke Philippe that the hunting is particularly good in this area. Naturally, His Majesty will be stopping for refreshments." Making a sweeping bow before Clare, the courier mounted his horse and cantered back up the long driveway, the quartz chips sparkling under the horse's iron shoes.

Clare stood on the top step of the entrance, and her heart fell. "How can we be ready in just a few days?" she muttered to herself. She looked around at the tall Doric pillars that held up the canopy. Once they would have been a marvelous white, but now they were dull and grey and crusted with scabs of lichen. Thankfully Georges took great pride in the large flagstones that formed the terrace, so they were scrubbed clean each day. Even the great iron urns at each corner looked dowdy and unkempt in the wintry light. *They'll need some greenery*, she thought to herself.

She turned and entered the hall, wrapping her woolen cloak tightly around her to keep out the cold, damp air. Inside it felt even colder, with the fire from the drawing room failing to extend its warm, welcoming fingers further than the open door. Rosso had been busy, and the results of his labors were beginning to take shape. The once shabby-looking woodwork was now looking clean and chic, in a style she had never seen before. "You're a genius, Uncle," she said, amused and amazed at the subtle transformation.

Rosso straightened up, holding a heavily laden paintbrush in his hand. He smiled at Clare and gave a mock bow, saying, "Praise indeed, my lady."

Clare smiled at his humor, but then her face fell. "It's not going to work, Uncle. The king is coming on Sunday, and it's impossible that everything will be prepared in time. Even Marionette won't have enough food to feed his whole retinue." There was a pause as the news sank in. "Apparently it was my dear cousin's suggestion that the king call here whilst hunting." She could barely conceal the sarcasm in her voice as she spoke of her cousin.

"There's no point stopping now," Rosso said, returning to daubing paint on doorways. "There are still four days to go, and anything can happen in that time. Have a little faith, my love." Even though the words sounded good, neither truly felt the strength of them. Clare left to inform the others and stir them all to greater activity, so for the next two days, there was a great hive of activity around the château. But it was also noticeable that there were far fewer workers to help than there had been just the week before. Philippe's threats and coercions were having their effect.

On the Friday before the royal visit, the same courier on the same horse rode up the driveway. This time he wore a heavy canvas cloak to protect him from the rain that fell in sheets. Thrashing his hat against his cloak to beat out the wetness, he attempted to resurrect its sodden plumage as he stood under the château's canopy. Georges invited the good man to step inside out of the elements, where he dripped on the hall floor instead. Georges also sent a message to Marionette to bring some hot refreshments for the bedraggled man.

Once the man was warm and refreshed, he was led into Clare's small reception room. She indicated to him to come and stand close to the small fire. "Thank you, my lady, you are most gracious." He glanced around the room and took in the heavy drapes that framed the bow window overlooking the forlorn rose beds outside. The oak-paneled room smelt of potpourri laced with lavender. Two high-backed chairs were drawn up close to the fire, which was covered by the fine filigree of an iron curtain hanging in front of it. "I've never seen that before," said the courier.

"My Italian smith made it for me. He's quite handy at such things," Clare offered, in a slightly offhand way. "Enjoy the fire for a moment whilst you tell me your news." At that, she parted the iron mesh, and the heat from the fire leaped into the room like a hungry beast. A broad smile covered the messenger's face as he lowered himself into the enfolding armchair.

Above the fire was a lively portrait of the previous duchess, her piercing eyes daring anyone to not like her.

"That's very good, too. Who painted that? The glaze looks very new," he said.

"Oh that," Clare replied in a steady voice. "I have an Italian artist staying with me. He's helping restore some of the paintings. He seems to have a good eye for detail." Turning to the messenger, she finally asked, "So what brings you to Château Villepreux twice in one week, sir?"

"Ah yes," he answered. "The king sends his sincere regrets, but due to an unfortunate riding mishap, he won't be able to hunt this weekend. In fact, he won't be able to ride for some weeks. He sends his royal affection and asks that you prepare to receive him four weekends from now."

"If my memory serves me correctly, that will be the first weekend after Ash Wednesday," Clare said, looking up at her grandmother in the painting. "Will His Majesty be keeping Lent this year?"

The courier looked a little flustered. "I would suggest that you prepare yourselves for any eventuality, my lady," he replied. "Kings often seem to do unexpected things," he finished. But whether he was talking to Clare or to the flames, she was not quite sure.

When the messenger had left, Clare almost skipped to where Rosso had set up his easel by the tall, west-facing windows. He was working on the cardinal's portrait. She was about to speak when she stopped and gasped. "Uncle.

That's incredible. You have captured the essence of the man perfectly. He looks so wise, and yet there's something about the eyes that . . . ," her voice trailed off as her mind scrambled for words.

"Uncertainty is what I was aiming for," Rosso said, taking a step back from the small canvas. "With power and old age, uncertainty must play on your mind a great deal." The two of them stood staring at the picture. "Did you have any news from the king? he asked, taking a deep breath and approaching the canvas once more.

"Yes," Clare said excitedly, "Excellent news. The poor man fell off his horse." She tried to suppress a smile, but failed. "I don't think he can be hurt too much, but he can't hunt this weekend, which means he can't visit Villepreux." She clapped her hands and twirled around once before continuing in a more serious tone, "But he will be coming in a month, which gives us more time to get things done."

Rosso squinted at the tip of his paint-laden brush, which he was placing ever so carefully at the corner of the cardinal's mouth, "That is indeed a great relief," he said, "but we still have a vast number of things to do." Straightening himself slowly, he turned to Clare, palette in one hand and brush in the other, and beamed. "I'm really very happy for all of us. I wish I could give you a hug, but I don't think the paint spatters would add to the beauty of your dress." They laughed, and Clare kissed him lightly on the cheek.

"Have you seen Mario anywhere? I need to tell him the news and see if he's heard any tidings of my friend." Rosso watched her face cloud as she thought of Kristopher.

"He must be someone very special, little one," he said quietly.

"He is," was all Clare could allow herself to say.

"Well, the last time I spoke to Mario, he was telling me about a beauty he'd met at the market yesterday. Apparently, she has the most perfect ears in all the world! I suspect that our young poet is composing sonnets in his office as we speak." Leaving Rosso to return to his work, she left the drawing room and went in search of her secretary.

She knocked lightly on Mario's door and was greeted by a voice shouting "Enter!" Obeying the young man's command, she went in, causing Mario to rapidly rise from his chair and push something under the papers strewn over the surface of his desk. "I hope I'm not interrupting you, Mario," she said.

"No, my lady," he replied, looking a little abashed, "I was just jotting down a few notes." Mario was dressed in a black soutane, which looked fresh and clean. He now sported a well-trimmed black beard in the fashion of the French beaus of the time. His eyes were clear and his hand steady, suggesting that his impulsive affair with Monsieur Pinot was currently in abeyance. Clare cast her eye around the room. The walls were spartan and freshly limed to keep the air clean. A low shelf held a small pile of papers that were neatly piled and tied with a blue ribbon. Beside the window stood a tall cupboard which was closed, the key remaining in the lock. At the back of the door leading to the yard hung a wet-weather cloak that had recently been cleaned and a broad-brimmed hat devoid of any plumage.

"I see you've been tidying the place up a little," Clare observed.

"I believe that it merited a certain reorganizing, my lady," and he smiled meekly. "You wish to inform me of something?" he asked.

"I thought you should know that the king won't be able to visit this weekend," she paused dramatically, "and it's such a shame." She glanced at the yard door as she indicated that someone might be on the other side. Mario smiled and mutely acknowledged her. Clare went on, "I have just been informed that instead, His Majesty will be gracing us with his presence on the Sunday after Ash Wednesday. Perhaps we could take a walk through the gardens and discuss the arrangements?" Mario nodded. He arranged his papers into a small pile, placed them into desk drawer and locked it. He then pocketed the key, and went to open the door, saying, "After you, my lady. He waited to follow her out as Clare dipped her head under the low lintel and exited into the sunlight.

"How is it going?" Clare asked, once they had reached the safety of the far end of the rose garden. A statue of Apollo stood guard nearby.

"Another gardener failed to turn up for work today. That makes four we have lost this week, my lady. Inside the house, it has been not so bad. Georges treats them well and had already dispensed with the less reliable ones shortly after we arrived, but he still works every hour of the day. The man never rests."

"And Marionette?" Clare inquired.

They headed over the lawn toward the reflecting pool. They took seats on a bench facing down the pool, whose dark waters mirrored the tall cypress hedges surrounding it. They sat staring into the still surface, and Mario lowered his voice as if out of respect for the quietness of the place.

"The whole world loves that woman, and who wouldn't? She may not cook Italian food, but my God, she is an alchemist with herbs and spices. I have no doubt that His Majesty will leave with a heavy heart and a heavier stomach." The still surface of the pool was laced by the arrival of a tired bee that landed on its surface. Mario picked up a small twig and patiently waited for the frantic insect to attach itself. He then placed the bee on the bench beside them to dry its wings in the lukewarm sunshine. "Marionette is the queen of bees when it comes to preparing a feast."

"Any news of Kristopher?" Clare asked tentatively.

"I think you saw that letter I put out of sight?" Mario said, without withdrawing his gaze from the surface of the pool. "It was from an Italian priest who is visiting Paris. I had been told to expect him by a friend back home." He looked sideways at Clare. "This priest tells me that he thinks your friend has been moved again. A military friend of Philippe's has Kristopher locked up in his cellar. This military man is not a popular person." He said no more, but at that moment the sun disappeared and the surface of the water turned inky black. A chill breeze sent its icy fingers through the hedge, and Clare was forced to draw her shawl closer over her shoulders. "That is all I have to report," he said.

"If he is still alive," Clare said, her face fixed like a mask, "then I shall talk to the king about him," she said. Mario remained silent.

Rousing herself from her torpor, Clare suggested they pay Marco a visit in his forge and see what news he had. Mario stood and offered her his arm as they slowly strolled back across the lawn The rhythmic sound of bellows being pumped, and the low sound of voices greeted them as they walked through the open doors. Marco was holding something with his pincers deep in the fire, whilst behind him a young man, his back turned, stood slowly raising and releasing the forge bellows. "We thought you might like some company," Clare said cheerfully to her papa. She stopped in her tracks as the young man turned around. "Paul," she cried. She turned to Mario as if looking for an explanation.

"It was Monsieur Georges's idea, my lady," Mario said, raising his palms toward heaven and shrugging his narrow shoulders. "What could I do?"

Clare turned back to Paul saying, "Forgive me, dear Monsieur Paul. You are very welcome in our little family here in Villepreux. I hope Papa is not working you too hard." Marco appeared to be deaf, watching whatever was deep in those flames.

Paul shifted his weight in embarrassment. "It is you who do me a great honor, my lady. Me and my family," he added. "Monsieur Marco is the best teacher I ever had."

"A bit slower please, Paul. Almost there," Marco said, raising his left hand, but not taking his eye off the fire. Straightening up and pulling the object from the flames, he said, "There. All finished." Before their eyes was a perfect golden bird, still glowing orange from the heat of the fire.

"That's beautiful," said Clare in utter astonishment. "Papa, I have never seen anything . . . ," and words failed her.

"Signore Marco, you are a genius," whispered Mario as the white-haired smith slowly turned the little creature at the end of his long pliers.

"A little patience, eh, Clare?" He smiled at his daughter as the golden glow of the bird deepened. "The next job is to create a fine iron cage for this little bird to sit in, and then it'll be a gift fit for a king!"

"Oh, Papa," Clare said, putting her arms around his waist just as she'd done as a little child. "I'm so very proud of you."

"Careful, my dear," Marco said smilingly. "This bird still has a ferocious bite to it whilst it's hot. It needs to cool down slowly, if it's not to lose its luster. Now that I have Paul here to help me with the bellows, I should have the cage put together before the end of next week." Without looking at his new apprentice, he said in a stage whisper, "He's a smart young man, that Paul." The straightening of Paul's spine suggested that the comment had been clearly heard.

"I've received some news from the king," Clare continued, her arms still around her papa's waist and her eyes fixed on the mesmerizing flames. "The poor man has had a fall and won't be able to visit until after Ash Wednesday." Only the slight movement of Marco's body told Clare he knew what that meant.

"Bless him," Marco said, "I trust it's nothing serious."

"At least now we'll have time to prepare for him properly," Clare went on in all seriousness. "I never would have thought that running an estate would be such hard work." Mario cleared his throat. "You've been around Georges for too long, my friend," said Clare, releasing her papa and looking at Mario.

"Speaking of work, my lady, if you no longer require my presence, I have plenty of things to do."

"I'll come with you back to the house, there are one or two details I need to talk to you about," Clare replied. And saying their farewells, they left.

"She's a very special lady, Monsieur Marco," Paul commented. For the first time since before she had stopped by, the old smith took his eyes off his forge and gazed at the empty doorway through which Clare had just exited.

"She's not just a special lady, my friend. She's *my* special lady."

Eighteen
AN UNEXPECTED
ARRIVAL

ROSSO WORKED ON his painting of Cardinal Villepreux, and Marco completed his glorious golden bird
in its fine filigree cage. Mario marshaled the few remaining gardeners to create an entrance fit for a king. Inside
the house, Georges reigned supreme, and soon the old
château appeared to flex lithe limbs from its long-forgot-
ten youth. Stores began to appear in the kitchen, and the
gamekeeper was hard-pressed to keep up with Marionette's demands. "The damned woman must think I'm a
magician or summit," he muttered. But at heart, he loved
Marionette dearly—a fact clearly demonstrated by his
enlarging waistline, which threatened the few remaining notches in his worn leather belt.

Clare was in the small reception room looking over some papers when Georges appeared and made his presence felt in his usual manner. Looking up, Clare acknowledged him with a smile. "Yes, Georges?"

"There's been a minor commotion at the gates, my lady. A poor wretch has turned up in a dreadful state and claims that he is acquainted with you." As an afterthought, he pronounced, "He's French."

Mario and Clare looked at each other askance.

"I've taken the liberty of taking him to the kitchen, where he's currently being attended to. I thought you should be informed, my lady." He made as if to leave.

"Did he give any name?" Clare asked.

"Jean-Claude, I believe," said the stately Georges.

It was Mario who first remembered the frightened youth on their coach journey to Paris, but it was Clare who made the connection with the military man and the last sighting of Kristopher. "Take me to him," she said, lifting the sides of her skirts and striding swiftly to the door. Mario made to follow her, but she commanded him to remain and finish the urgent paperwork. He shrugged and stayed at his desk.

Georges led her across the hallway and through the narrow door at the side of the grand stairway, then down some steep stone steps lit by a guttering candle. Belowstairs, they entered the world where hard work made upstairs life flow with seemingly effortless ease. They entered the kitchen, where a litter had been placed by the fire. Marionette was stooping low from her stool and feeding spoons of broth to the bundle of rags lying at her feet. Rosso had appeared out of nowhere and was holding the boy's head. He looked up, and deep concern was writ large on his face.

"Someone's given this boy a terrible beating," he said, "but thank God, he'll live."

"There, there," Marionette cooed at the boy, "just another spoonful and you can rest easy, my lad." The boy slurped the spoon clean, and Rosso gently lowered his head to rest on a rolled-up cloak. "Once his stomach's happy, we'll clean him up and give him a fresh set of clothes. The poor little beggar's been through hell and back, if you ask me," the good woman said.

The young boy seemed to swoon, but woke suddenly with crazed eyes "Where's the lady? I need to see the lady," he yelled.

"Shh, little friend," Rosso said, hugging him close once more and rocking him ever so gently. He looked to where Clare was standing. Her face was frozen with fear. Seeing the broken look in the boy's eyes had ripped apart the shrouds covering her own childhood suffering. She remembered the beatings, the cruelty, the utter feeling of despair and betrayal that had destroyed her early years. Rosso saw the look in her eyes and held out his hand to her. "It's OK, little woman," he whispered. "You know you're safe now. Come closer. He needs you."

Clare took a step toward that tragic sight. Her knees bent and she clasped Rosso's hand. Squatting next to her uncle, she felt the serene power of his unconditional love spreading up from her hand and into her own heart. She looked at him. "Thank you, Uncle," she said, returning the gentle pressure of his grip. As if shaking off the specter of a nightmare, she picked up the boy's hand with her free hand. The three of them were linked in a scene that would be long held as a treasured memory by those who witnessed it. "I'm here, Jean-Claude," Clare said, "You're safe with me." A tranquility came over the boy's face, and he slept.

After a few moments, Clare looked up and quietly asked for some blankets, sheets, and pillows from her room so that they could make him comfortable there by the fire. "Bring in a settle for me, too. I'll be sleeping close by until he gets his strength back. Marionette and I will take care of him now." Clare looked across at Rosso, who'd leaned back against the chimney breast and repeated, "Thank you, Uncle." His eyes filmed with tears.

"I remember," he said softly. "I remember it all as if it had only just happened." He looked down at the boy saying, "He needs a lot of love, Clare, and I cannot think of a more pure heart to provide it than yours." He squeezed her hand one final time and released her. Straightening up, he said in a louder voice, "I must be getting old. All this kneeling and squatting is hard on an old man like me." The tension in the air was released immediately, followed by the clearing of a certain throat and the statement, "If you don't require me for the moment . . . ," as the shadow dissolved into the darkness of the servants' staircase.

Mario, who'd left the study to see if he could help in any way, was the next to leave. "I will go to Signore Marco and inform him about the boy, and then I will return to my work, my lady."

"Thank you, Mario," Clare replied without turning. "Thank you, all."

After a few days of care in the kitchen, Jean-Claude was able to move to a room upstairs next to Clare's room. Marionette went with him as the child was still having nightmares. With her motherly care, his strength soon returned, and his wounds healed. His face continued to bear the traces of deep shadows in its pallid, pensive features. His naturally black hair had been cropped short in the manner of a convict, revealing the scars on his scalp, still livid against the white skin. His thin arms and feeble legs soon gathered strength from his walks with Clare around the gardens. It was on these walks that she learned he had a keen and quick mind: questions sprouted like seeds in the fertile soil of his mind.

On one of the turns around the garden, he spoke of his parents for the first time. Clare felt a steel grip tighten around her heart. The memories of childhood are never forgotten, just buried deeper than most. "Daddy was a soldier," he said, out of the blue. Clare kept her mind clear, and her pace steady. She said nothing. "At least I think he was." Pause. "At least that's what Maman told me." Another pause. Another silence from Clare. "Stepfather told her never to talk about him, so I don't know much about him really." Another pause. "Maman was very pretty," the young boy said, wringing his hands. "He blamed me when she died. He said she worried so much about me that she just wore away to a shadow. He said he'd make sure that I didn't cause him to wear away, but that he'd teach me how real boys behave, even if he had to beat it into me." He went silent for a few moments. "I think I'd like to be a soldier like my real papa," he said. "Was your papa a soldier, Mademoiselle?" he asked, looking up at her with sad yet hopeful eyes.

Clare held his little hand in hers and stopped walking. She looked up at the house and then down at this poor lost child. "Yes, my father was a soldier," she said, after some thought. "But I never knew him. My real papa is over there in the forge. He and Maman took me in when I'd been abandoned. They loved me back to life, just like I'm going to love you back into life, my serious little man." Grabbing his other hand, she began to swing him slowly around in the air, making circles on the grass, until they both fell down giggling. Sitting up in the meadow area, they looked back at the imposing château and saw the white apron of Marionette standing by the kitchen looking for them. "I think someone wants to feed you again. Come on, we'd better hurry or the Dom will get there before us." Gathering her skirts about her, she chased the little boy back toward the house.

By the time they reached the kitchen, Marionette had Jean-Claude's food ready for him. The Dom was already seated and playfully made to take the young boy's plate. "Hey!" the boy cried, distraught.

"I was just checking to see whether Marionette had given you enough," the gentle giant said, sliding the plate back toward its rightful owner. Soon the two of them were eating happily and smiling at each other. Mario entered during their fun and games and went over to where Clare was watching over them. Mario waited for a few seconds and then said softly to her, "Still no news of Kristopher, my lady," he said. The sound of a fork hitting a pewter plate made them look suddenly toward the table. Jean-Claude had gone pale and was swallowing the remnants of the food in his mouth.

"I'm so sorry, Mademoiselle," he said pleadingly. "I'm so sorry," and he burst into tears. Clare went over to him and placed her arm around his shoulder. The Dom stopped eating and stared at the little lad.

When he had finished crying, he looked up at Clare and said, "You won't send me back now, will you?"

"Of course not," replied Clare in a firm tone. "Your home is here. Just let anyone come and try to take you away from us!"

"It's just that the man asked me to give you a message, but I forgot it until now." Suddenly time hung suspended. "He beat me because I talked to him." Quick glances shot between all the assembled adults.

"Who beat you?" Clare asked softly, "and who were you talking to?"

Jean-Claude looked down at his half-empty plate as if staring into a forgotten abyss. "My stepfather beat me for talking to him. He said I shouldn't lower myself by talking to such scum. He said that's why they'd locked him in the cellar, because that's where scum and vermin live. Then he said that I needed to be taught a lesson, a lesson I'd never forget." Clare held him closer and whispered, "He'll never lay one finger on you ever again, Jean-Claude." From across the table, the Dom added, "He'll have to get past me first, little man." His face was set like granite as he spoke.

"Who was the man in the cellar, Jean-Claude?" Clare went on in her calming way.

"He was Italian like you. He was nice. He always spoke kindly to me and said that the first thing he'd do when he escaped was to take me away from my stepfather." In a quieter tone, he added, "I think he'd overheard some of the beatings I'd been given." The only sound in the room was the sound of Marionette sniffing into her apron and wiping her eyes.

Looking up at Clare again, he said, "The man said that if I did get away before he did, then I should take a message to you." The lad grinned for the first time. "When I told him I was going to run away from home, and about you and what you'd said to me on the coach, Kristopher told me he knew you as well." At the mention of his name, Clare sat weakly down on the bench next to the boy. Marionette came over and put her arms around them.

"So the boy knows the house where Kristopher is," said an astonished Mario. Marionette's face informed him that perhaps he should remain silent, at which he shrugged and folded his arms.

"Tell me more about Kristopher," she went on.

"They thought I hadn't heard him being brought to our house," he said seriously. "It's funny how adults think because they don't see children in a room, they can't hear what's going on. But I heard them bring him in late one night and take him to the cellars. Normally I'm never allowed to leave my room, but a few days later when the house was empty, I went down to see who they'd put in the cellars."

Jean-Claude knuckled his eye for a moment and then added, "They don't usually keep them there for very long before they disappear again." Looking across at the Dom, he confided, "Kristopher's stayed there the longest that I know of."

"Is he still there?" Mario couldn't stop himself, but Marionette's look did. Again he shrugged and returned her admonition with an air of innocence.

"I think so," said Jean-Claude, looking up at him.

"How is he?" interjected Clare. "Have they hurt him much?"

"I think he's alright. He told me that he'd been gagged and bound before he arrived, but now he just had some chains on his feet, and anyway, they daren't touch him because he had powerful friends who were close to the king himself." Jean-Claude's eyes opened wide and he puffed out his chest as if he was a close confidant of His Majesty. Returning his gaze to his plate, he sighed. "I'm hungry," he said. Picking up his fork, he filled his mouth and looked around at the others in the room. Having cleaned his plate, he looked at the Dom, who was still deep in thought, saying, "If you don't want the rest of yours, Dom . . ."

A smile cracked the good man's features. He replied, "Over my dead body." A lightness returned to the kitchen.

"Mario," Clare said in an even conversational way. "Could you ask Marco to meet with us in your office once he's finished what he's doing? Come and get me when you're both ready. Dom, can you be there, too? And ask Georges to come with you. I'll go and find Rosso." She looked half-expectantly at Marionette.

"My place is here feeding this bottomless pit, my lady," she said, folding her arms across her ample chest. "That should keep me busy for the rest of the day." Jean-Claude grinned up at her.

"What about tomorrow, Marionette?" the boy cheekily replied.

Clare was pacing up and down the narrow piece of carpet that went from Mario's desk to the bookshelf on the opposite wall. She was oblivious to the once-grand design beneath her feet. The emblazoned white stag had long been trampled by muddied boots and scraping furniture, and the proud beast had receded into the carpet pile as if concealing itself from the humans who blindly trampled over it. Georges was standing at attention by the door. Whatever thoughts filled his mind, no one could decipher, yet his bright eyes took in every detail around him. He made a mental note to straighten the small likeness of the Parisian scene that hung crookedly on the wall opposite him, and to suggest that it might be brighter in the room if the windows were cleaned.

In reality, most of the light from the window was obstructed by the large frame of the Dom, who was studying the activities of the gardener currently working toward that part of the house where they were. He was pushing a barrow with a rake and shovel. A small pile of moldy leaves sitting in the bottom of the barrow seemed to give credence to his activities. A throat was cleared. "I agree with you,

Monsieur Dom," Georges intoned. "That man is, I believe, in the pay of our lady's cousin Duke Philippe. It might be wise to suggest that we need more wood for the kitchen fire, and perhaps he should be directed to take it from the wood pile behind the stables."

A smile danced around the Dom's lips. He rubbed his stump against his stubbled chin and moved toward the door. "Back in a minute," was all he said.

"I didn't know there was a wood pile there," said Clare, rousing herself.

"It's an aphorism, my lady," Georges replied, looking straight ahead. "I suspect that the Dom will explain to the gardener with great clarity that his horticultural duties would best be carried out a long distance from the house. After he's been fully acquainted with the situation, I doubt that we will be bothered by any more eavesdroppers." Clare thought of saying something, but decided to hold her tongue.

A few minutes later, the Dom returned and entered together with the other two men. Marco came in with his finished golden bird in a cage. The Dom was telling him how he'd suggested that the gardener might find alternative work for the morning, and Mario closed the door behind them all.

"Thank you all for coming," Clare began, "Rosso will be here in a minute. He had to finish the glaze on his portrait, which shouldn't take him long." She hesitated, then went over to Marco, embraced him like the little child she once was, and buried her head in his shoulder. Marco stroked the back of her head, and the two of them gently rocked from side to side. He whispered something in her ear. Clare looked up into his eyes, and they began to sparkle.

The door opened, and Rosso appeared, cleaning his hands with a paint-stained rag. "Having a family meeting?" he said, with a wide grin.

"We know where Kristopher is and who's holding him," the Dom began. "That little lad's stepfather has him. Though how anyone could call that man a father is beyond my comprehension."

Rosso looked at Clare. "What would you like us to do?" he asked simply. "I doubt that this person will hand Kristopher over if we knock on his door and ask for him. And if this man is in league with Philippe . . ." He looked at the others for ideas. Clare gave Marco's hand a squeeze and moved to stand behind the desk.

"I'm the reason you're all here. You are the dearest people in the whole world, and yet I find I have placed you all in great danger. If Philippe had his way, he'd take the château from me and lock me away in some dungeon until I rotted in hell." She looked at each of them with steel in her eyes. "That I could take, but the thought of him hurting one hair on any of your heads would rip my heart to pieces." Rosso blinked, the Dom rubbed his invisible hand on his chin, and Marco seemed to be smiling. Georges and Mario stood like sphinxes on either side of the door, listening intently.

"So here's my plan. Dom, as soon as the king's party has left, I want you to take Jean-Claude and Marionette and leave immediately for Rosso and Agnes's cottage. Mario, I want you to leave immediately for Marseille and get word to Admiral Doria. Tell him what's happened to Kristopher, where he's being held and by whom, if the admiral hasn't heard already. Rosso, Georges, and Papa, we need to prepare the château for when the king arrives. I want to make him feel like he's at the château of one of his most loyal subjects." The only sound in the room was the trembling of the window shutters in the stiff breeze that had sprung up suddenly. "We need to keep this to ourselves, so make your plans well. When things start to happen, we'll need to move quickly."

"Rosso, I need to talk to you about something, can you wait after the others have left?" Marco gave her a hug and left, leaving the king's gift on the desk. Mario inclined his head, stole a swift look at Georges, and followed Marco out. The Dom went up to Clare, put his hand on her shoulder, and said quietly, "My little lass, you've become a mighty lady. Bless you." And he blessed her with a kiss on the top of her head. Clare reached up and touched the cheeks of the gentle giant and in a whisper said, "Thank you."

Georges stood by the door like an immutable spirit. "If I may be so bold, my lady," he proffered, staring straight ahead at the uneven picture on the wall. "These are unusual times that may call for unusual actions. It may come to pass that those who choose to follow your orders suffer as a consequence of your actions. There are some in your employ who might not be able to comprehend the significance of your orders, and yet suffer as a result of your decisions. May I inform those parties as to their possible choices under such circumstances?"

Rosso stepped forward. "I don't think even the good Lord can predict what may happen tomorrow. Even His Majesty was knocked from his horse just when he thought he'd be coming here. What will happen as a result of Clare's choices, I'm not sure even God fully understands yet."

Clare moved forward and nestled in close to Rosso. "Trust me, Georges. If my plan works, then no one will get hurt, unless they bring it upon themselves."

"My lady," Georges replied, inclining his head. The loyal man moved across the room to straighten the painting and then left.

Nineteen

A ROYAL OCCASION

THE AIR OF ORGANIZED chaos which reigned in Marionette's kitchen appeared to have infected the whole household. Yet by the time that the royal herald arrived, the final finishing touches were complete. In the calm before the storm that was about to crash into their little world, everyone looked around and smiled with satisfaction.

The gardens in front of the house had been manicured to perfection by Mario's young hands. The kitchen was a veritable movable mountain of food awaiting the royal entourage, and surveying it all was Marionette, with the help of her chief taster, the Dom, and his able assistant Jean-Claude. "Hands off!" the rubicund lady said, slapping the Dom's hand away from a pile of pastries. "That's for His

Majesty, she said, "not for one-armed, one-eyed bottom-less pits like you."

"Marionette," said the Dom, "You are a genius." And whilst he gave her a hug, Jean-Claude reduced the pile of pastries by two!

Upstairs, Georges had brilliantly marshaled his re-maining loyal servants, and the rooms literally shone in the morning light. Clare slid up quietly behind him and put her arm through his. "None of this could have hap-pened without you, Georges. I owe you so much. What-ever happens, I want you to know that I will always want you near me." She squeezed his arm as she spoke.

"As you wish, my lady," Georges replied without moving a muscle—apart from those in his throat which reflected the deep feelings he held for his young mistress.

Marco and Rosso appeared from belowstairs. Each gave Clare a hug and acknowledged Georges with an incline of their heads. "Great job!" said Rosso. "I suspect that even the king himself will be impressed."

"I believe that the artisan painter lately arrived from Italy has made a considerable impact for the good on the presentation of the premises," Georges responded, as close to a compliment as he could provide.

"Where have you put the king's gifts?" Clare interrupted the men's banter.

"In the minor drawing room, my lady." It was Georges who proffered the answer. "I thought it might prove more intimate for the king to receive the gifts from my lady in private."

"A wise suggestion, Georges. Thank you. Now all we have to do is wait."

Waiting seemed to stretch the time, and the low grey sky offered no respite from the gloomy pace. Then the yelp of a hound was heard in the distance, and the wheels of motion really began to spin. Water was boiled, linen smoothed for the final time, goblet-laden trays brought out onto the portico, and carafes of wine and water set up like soldiers along the low palisade wall that enclosed the two sides of the entrance.

Clare and Georges stood waiting, she by the steps and he by the door, as the sound of barking increased and the dull drum of hoofbeats echoed from the forest. Rosso and Marco installed themselves in the minor drawing room and watched through the diamond windows.

A hunting horn sounded, and just as the sun broke through the clouds, a kaleidoscope of color erupted from the green landscape as the king and all his mounted hunters burst into the adjacent field. The sun's rays flickered on the battle points of the spears and were reflected in the golds of the riders' tunics. Soon the jostling throng was crunching the quartz stones that covered the driveway and surrounded the fountain. At a signal from Georges, liveried men appeared from nowhere and carried trays of refreshments and drinks to the still-mounted men, and to the few women riding with them.

Soon, stable lads appeared with stools to aid the safe dismount of His Majesty and his female companions, whilst the more athletic riders slid from their mounts and stretched their aching limbs.

Clare went down the steps and curtsied low to the king. His Majesty offered her his hand and helped her to rise. "She gets prettier and prettier, eh, Philippe?" he said, in a leering aside to the man in black standing next to him.

Her cousin grinned at her, then looking around added, "You seem to be taking good care of my inheritance, dear Cousin. Thank you."

Clare never took her eyes off the king, saying, "I am the king's good servant, and thank God that I can offer him hospitality. There is still much to be done here if it is to be restored to its former grandeur. I hear that gambling debts nearly reduced it to ruins."

She turned to her cousin and said, "If you were ever to inherit the château, my lord, then I hope you will be satisfied by what you find. But believe me, I intend to live to a ripe old age." Offering her arm to the king, she led him up the steps and into the house, leaving Philippe all alone in his own world.

The main reception room had been prepared by Rosso and was fresh and bright. Long gone were the lecterns holding the illuminated manuscripts that Cardinal Villepreux had shown him all those years ago. A full fire filled the massive grate and the room felt comfortable, despite the cold air coming in through the open doors leading to the rose garden. The walls of the room were paneled with oak and inlaid with veneers of rosewood depicting scenes from Homer's *Iliad*. Fresh boughs of pussy willow filled tall vases, whilst specially pressed spring flowers smiled from small frames discreetly placed around the room.

The king stood by the fire and indicated that Clare should occupy the seat nearby. "You've done a remarkable job, my lady," Francis said. "I hear that you have some Italian artisans helping you restore Château Villepreux."

"Yes, Your Majesty," she replied. "In fact, they've created some humble gifts for you to take back to the Louvre with you." She nodded in the direction of the silent Georges, who had appeared on cue at the doorway. He inclined his head and went off to bring Rosso and Marco into the royal presence.

"Your cousin seems very keen on you being married, my lady," Francis went on, "and I think it's an excellent idea. He has a son of marrying age. I think it would be a very good match, don't you?" he said, but Clare's response was delayed by Marco and Rosso arriving with their gifts. Each of them gave a suitable bow to Francis and approached the king.

When he unwrapped the small portrait of the cardinal, the king's eyes opened wide with delight. "What an excellent representation. You have caught his expression perfectly, Monsieur, he said. Looking up, he asked, "What do they call you, maître?"

"Rosso, Your Majesty."

"Well, you have great skill, Monsieur Rosso. I shall treasure this. I knew the cardinal well, and he was a loyal advisor to me in difficult times." A small fissure creased his forehead. "And what have we here?" he asked, untying the ribbon around the box that Marco had placed on a nearby table.

"A small gift for your wife, Your Majesty," the black-smith said.

As the king pulled the cage from the box he let out a peel of laughter, "She will surely enjoy the thought put into this, Monsieur. And your name . . . ?"

"They call me Marco, Your Majesty." Not being sure what to do next, he bowed again and backed away to where Rosso was standing.

"Well, Monsieur Marco, you have great skill and not a little wit as well." He looked at the golden bird and spoke to it directly, "Well, little bird, now that we have you in a cage, I think we should take you back to Paris with us, don't you?" As the last word left his lips, he turned to Clare and said, "So you'd better pack a case to bring with you, my lady."

It was Clare's turn to look confused. Then she under-stood. She looked to the door where the inscrutable Georges stood and summoned him to attend her. She indicated to him that she wanted to whisper in his ear so he bent down to attend to her orders. It was all done in a few seconds. Georges straightened himself, inclined his head toward the regal presence and left the room.

"I like silent people," the king said to the little bird. "Silent people don't tell other people's secrets, do they, little bird?" He handed the cage to the royal attendant and briskly said to Clare, "My coach should be here by now, Mademoiselle. You will accompany us to Paris." With that, he left.

Clare rose and followed him. She waited a few moments in the hall, looking at Marco and Rosso whilst waiting for Marionette to appear with her case. All the time Philippe stood grinning at them and admiring all the work that Rosso had done. "Yes, Cousin, you've certainly made a big impression on the old place. I shall quite enjoy it all again once I've moved back in."

Twenty

JUSTICE IS DONE

WHEN THE ROYAL coach arrived back at the Louvre in Paris, the postillion dismounted and, bringing the royal stool, placed it by the carriage door. But the door remained shut. The servants who had lined up in their fine liveries stood on the steps, whilst a cold breeze tugged at their clothes and mottled their skin. But still the door remained shut. Eyes began to glance sideways at other eyes, and lewd suggestions were whispered between lesser servants, causing a few to suppress giggles.

Then the carriage door flew open, and His Majesty descended with a stony expression on his face. He reached up for the hand of the Countess of Villepreux to help her down. In a loud, icy voice he informed her, "When the royal entourage returns to Paris, I shall expect your final decision, my lady. Until that time, I suggest you remain in your apartment." Turning on his heel, he left a curtseying countess in his wake.

Clare followed the king into the palace, trying to avoid the accusing eyes that monitored her every step. An official had been summoned by the king and given instructions as to where Clare should be housed. He approached her, acknowledged her presence, and said, "Follow me, please, Countess." Waving toward the rear of the carriage, he indicated to a baggage boy that he should bring Clare's case. She was trembling so much inside that the grandeur of the palace was lost on her. She missed the sculptured golden eagle perched on the bottom banister on the sweeping staircase, which led to the first level. Portraits of former monarchs gazed down on her ascent with imperious disdain, but she glided past them, impervious to their frosty looks, her eyes focused on the heels of the servant who walked before her.

They passed down a long corridor to a white door at the far end. The servant opened the door and indicated that she should enter. Clare walked slowly into the room and was surprised at how light it was. Three tall windows occupied one wall and gave a clear view over the park in front of the palace. She saw troops performing their drills in a square to one side, like silent mannequins in some other world. The room was well-appointed with a couch, two high-backed chairs separated by a finely crafted occasional table, and a highly polished circular table with four dining chairs where she supposed she would be taking her meals.

Through the only connecting door, she could see her bedroom. There was a single bed that had been freshly prepared and fresh flowers on the bedside table, confirming that the king knew that she would be a guest of his before he'd left to hunt.

"Just ring the bell if you require anything, Countess," the servant said, as he closed the door behind him. No lock was turned, so Clare quietly opened the door to see if a guard had been left. There was none to be seen. *A golden bird in a gilded cage doesn't need locks or guards to keep it secure,* she thought and busied herself as she settled down to wait.

Back at Château Villepreux, Marco and Rosso had been shaken by the events of the morning. "We can't just leave her," said Marco to Rosso as he paced up and down the small drawing room. He was about to reply when a throat was cleared in the doorway.

"I believe that we should continue as planned," the inscrutable Georges began. "As requested, I have informed Marionette that she should leave this very evening with the boy." He paused for a moment. For one of the very few moments in his long life, Georges began to struggle with his emotions. "It was my lady's express wish that we trust her, gentlemen." It was hard for Marco and Rosso, who'd spent many years protecting their little girl, to now abandon her to her own judgment. "There was one final matter," Georges said, regaining his normal emotionless expression, "Monsieur Mario is to follow her to Paris and seek to gain admittance. I shall inform my young colleague of his instructions." Rosso was the first to speak.

"Not only do I trust that young lady, but I trust you, too, Georges," he said. Marco's nod indicated that he, too, trusted the austere Georges, though the events of the morning had rattled his intent.

"If that is all, gentlemen?" was the good man's reply. Receiving no response, he inclined his head and left.

Rosso and Marco stared at each other in silence, and then left the room for the final time to carry out Clare's fragile plan—a plan that depended so much on good luck and blind faith. And like all men of faith, they had their doubts!

Later that evening there was a knock at Clare's door. "Come in," she called. She was sitting at the polished round table reading a pamphlet lately distributed and written by the German priest Martin Luther. Although she'd been shocked by its less-than-subtle attack on Mother Church, she was inclined to agree with the monk that there was some truth to what he was saying. The door opened, and Mario walked in, looking very pale. He bowed to his countess, who rose and walked over to greet him.

"How is everyone? Papa? Rosso? Georges? Are they all safe? What's happening at Villepreux?" Clare stopped herself. "Forgive me, Mario, you must be exhausted. Come, sit here, and I'll order some refreshments." Before he could refuse, Clare had rung the bell pull and ushered him to the small table.

Mario placed his hat on the table and threw his cloak back over his chair, revealing his lean frame. "So far everything has gone according to your wishes. Marionette and Jean-Claude left at the same time as I did. They took the small cart and plenty of provisions." A smile crept over his lips.

"What sort of things, Mario?" Clare asked archly, knowing the tastes of her secretary.

He shrugged his shoulders and leaned back in the chair. "Oh, just a few things to keep them comfortable on their long journey. Perhaps some wine that they do not have in Italy. Things like that," and he took an unusual interest in his fingernails whilst Clare tried to look at him severely.

"And the others?"

"They are doing as you wished, my lady. Though now you are a guest of the king, they worry that you might be in danger." He looked at the door as if he expected some guards to appear at any second. "For a poor Italian boy, coming into such a place as this almost drove me to drink," he said, as a grin spread wanly across his face.

"Will you be sad to leave France, Mario?" she asked.

"It has beautiful women and beautiful wine," he said simply, his brown eyes glinting in the candlelight. "Perhaps in time I might become bored . . . ," he said. "It seems to me that France is such an easy place to fall in love." He placed both hands flat on the table and looked at Clare. They remained looking at each other for some moments.

"Mario," Clare began, "If you got a chance to stay, do you think you might learn to like it?" Mario held her gaze for a few seconds more and then seemed to deflate as his bravado evaporated.

"Who would take me in?" he asked. "I have no friends here, no patrons."

"But if you *did*, would you like to stay?" Clare persisted. A smile rose up over Mario's face like the warmest sunrise on a summer's day.

"The women, the wine," he said, spreading his arms again, "Such temptations are difficult to resist!"

A knock at the door was followed by the head and liveried body of a servant. "You called, Countess?"

Clare arranged for food to be brought for Mario, and while they waited, Clare recounted what had transpired on her trip to Paris with the king. Mario's eyes widened as she told her story.

"But how can that be?" Mario gasped. However, he was interrupted by another knock which heralded the arrival of his meal. The two of them were silent as the food was arranged on the table before them.

After the servant departed, he said, "This Duke Philippe is no better than a rat. No, he is worse, he is a slimy snake in the grass . . ." Clare raised her hand to stop him speaking so loud.

"We must be very careful, Mario." She leaned in close to him, whispering, "We must not give them any evidence to use against us." Righting herself, she added, "and perhaps marriage to the duke's son may be the only solution to our problems." She stared at Mario who looked down at his plate. Sullenly he pushed it away from him.

"I seem to have lost my appetite, my lady." Clare reached across the small space and held his hand.

"You'll need all your strength, Mario, so please eat. After you've finished, I want you to take this back to Villepreux." She pushed an envelope across the table to him with her free hand. "Open it once you've left Paris. Your instructions are inside. Then return here as fast as you can and tell me," Clare paused, seeking the correct phrase to use, "how things are progressing there."

Her eyes pleaded with him as she squeezed his hand one more time before releasing it. "This isn't just for me, Mario. It's for all of us." Lowering her voice for one last time, she said, "Many lives depend on what happens in the next forty-eight hours."

It was just after midnight when Mario set out from the Louvre. At that late hour, the streets seemed empty. Yet even as he rode through the outer parts of Paris, he felt hidden eyes watching him. But before long, he was out in the dark of the countryside. No moon illuminated his path. Low clouds had resumed their natural position, and a sensation of claustrophobic blackness enveloped him. Mario rode slowly along the rutted road, knowing that one slip could lead to a fall or lame his horse.

When he rode up the path to the château, everything was deathly quiet. He shivered. His nerves felt as tight as the string on a long bow, so he urged his mount to walk on the manicured lawn to silence its steps. Not one light showed in any of the black windows before him. It was as if all life had been sucked out of the place.

He dismounted on the lawn and tied his horse to a sapling. Slowly he made his way to the rear, where light glowed through the shuttered window of the kitchen. He let his muscles relax and made for the haven of Marionette's empire, where a soft light glowed from a solitary candle. It occurred to him that she had left already, so who was in the kitchen? He put his ear to the door and listened. A smile appeared on his face. Someone was singing! And much to Mario's great amusement, the ditty being sung was in Georges's voice.

Mario knocked and called out at the same time, "Mio amico, Georges. It is your drinking companion, Mario, with news from our lady." Silence greeted him.

"Georges, it is I, Mario. Let me in, old friend. It is very dark out here in this damned country of yours." The sound of a chair falling over was followed by the sound of scrabbling at the door.

"Who is it?" came a querulous, yet slurred, demand.

"It's me, Mario. I have news from the countess."

The door was unbolted and flung open. Silhouetted in the doorframe was a very disheveled Georges beginning to fall backward. Mario leaped at him before he hit the flagged floor. "It is not right that a man should drink alone, Signore Georges." He helped his companion over to the table, lifted the fallen chair and let his friend down into it. "You sit here, and I'll pour myself a drink, and then we can tell each other our stories".

Georges slumped down and let his head fall on his chest. "It is so hard saying goodbye to one's life," he said, letting out a soul-draining sigh as he spoke. "I needed some liquid courage, but then my courage turned to liquid," and he began to giggle like a child. Then the giggles turned to sobs, and in a moment he was transformed before Mario's eyes into a tired, lost man whose sole purpose in life had vanished. In that moment, Mario saw himself twenty years hence, and he was devastated.

He stood for a few moments, whilst Georges's shoulders heaved, and tears coursed down his long face. Mario took the two paces needed to reach the desolation and squatted down before him. Mario gently took his own kerchief and wiped away the tears from poor Georges's face. "It is a brave thing for a brave man to cry," he whispered. "And you, my dearest of friends, are a very, very brave man. I salute you, and you have my eternal respect." He remained there whilst the heaving subsided. Eventually Georges's heavy head slowly lifted, and his bleary, bloodshot eyes fixed themselves on the younger man.

He cleared his throat, and Mario smiled a little smile of hope. "I think perhaps that I should retire to my chamber," said Georges, still slurring his words. Struggling to his feet, he staggered once before correcting himself and making for the door. Opening it, he stopped in the darkened portal, turned and said, "Sir, I may be drunk, but you are a true gentleman. I am honored by your words, sir, and I shall take your friendship to the grave with me." Then turning, he proudly made his way into the blackness with only his feet making any noise.

Mario turned to survey the kitchen. He picked up the decanter and poured himself a glass of wine. "Magnifico," he muttered to himself. "Trust Signore Georges to save the best wine for himself," and he downed the goblet in one. "Perhaps just one more," he smiled, "it would be such a shame to waste any of it," so he poured himself another. "Ah," he exclaimed as he stretched his arms, "such nights as these are made for poets!" Then picking up the single candle, he made for his office. Stopping at the doorway that had so recently consumed Georges, he turned, went back to the table and picked up the decanter before resuming his voyage into the miasma of the night.

The sun had been a long time in its ascent before any soul roused itself in Château Villepreux, and that soul belonged to Georges. No gardener had appeared, no tradesman had crunched up the driveway, no dairyman had stripped the cows of their milk, even the cows themselves seemed to have disappeared. Only Georges's bleary eyes gazed out of the empty windows across the lands of the Villepreux estates. He knew what he had to do, and it broke his heart to do it.

In Paris, Clare stood in front of the royal court awaiting the arrival of the king. All eyes seemed to be probing her, some with naked lascivious intent, others with obvious disdain, yet all the eyes belonged to men. Somehow, the antagonistic attention strengthened Clare's resolve.

There was a sudden stir at the rear of the throne room as the doors opened, and in walked His Highness. He was accompanied by his entourage, including Duke Philippe himself, now positively glowing with insidious delight. The group walked past Clare as if she didn't exist. The king sat upon his throne, still listening to the whispered words of his advisors. Finally, there was silence in the great room, and only then did Clare feel totally alone and very exposed.

"Advance, Countess de Villepreux," the king called to her. Clare obeyed. She approached the throne, resting in the curtsied position for what seemed an inordinate length of time before commanded to rise.

"Your choices are limited, I believe, Countess," His Majesty began. "You either marry the son of Duke Philippe, who I am sure will prove to be a most suitable man once he is fully grown." Smug giggles could be heard all around her at the king's words. "Or . . . ," as the word clattered around, Clare's pulse pounded in the paneled throne room walls as if the first rush of an avalanche was about to descend on her. "Or," he repeated, "you can renounce your claim! But be aware, my lady, that should you renounce your claim, then not only will Château Villepreux, and the ground on which it stands, revert to Duke Philippe here," His Majesty paused again and looked knowingly in Philippe's direction, "but you will be exiled from France for ten years." A tremor of murmurs suggested that this announcement had not been expected by the court, and for the first time, some of those in attendance darted sympathetic looks in Clare's direction. Philippe himself couldn't believe his luck and leered trium-phantly in Clare's direction.

"Well, what is your choice to be, Countess?" His Majesty asked, after the court had been silenced once more.

In the quiet of that moment, Clare felt a strange peace come over her. She looked at the men around her wearing ermine cloaks over their withered frames. She saw the symbols of power luridly displayed on their fingers, around their scrawny necks, and in the gaudy clothes they wore like dissipated peacocks. And she compared them with Marco, with Rosso, with Laura, and with Sara, and knew which life she would rather choose. Facing her king, she steadied herself before speaking.

"It has been my honor, Your Majesty, to spend a short time in your great country, tasked with restoring the house of my father to its former glory. In those works, I have taken great pride, and I humbly believe that I have enhanced their treasured memories. My father was a soldier and his father, too, but I would rather follow the path of my other grandfather, Cardinal Villepreux." She was halted in her speech by the sudden chattering of the courtiers, who were amazed by her announcement. The king himself seemed surprised.

"Carry on," he said, indicating to those gathered that they should be silent.

"My grandfather Cardinal Villepreux was a man of great wisdom and great integrity; my only sadness is that I never really knew him. But others that I trust have told me of his great inner strength and his belief in the power of higher purposes rather than that of earthly pleasures. It is these that I choose now." Clare stopped for one final look around that gilded cage with all the king's brightly colored songbirds perched around the periphery.

"I choose exile," she said.

The room erupted into uproar, and she had to shout above the din, "Yet I will always remain loyal to my king, to my family, and to my heart." Turning to Philippe, she said in a powerful voice, "May you reap what you sow, Cousin." Then she stood and waited for the king to speak.

"So be it, noble Countess," he said, rising from the throne. "Noble words demand noble actions. If anyone here disturbs the countess during her journey into exile, or at any time until she returns again, my wrath will be severe." Many were amazed at what the king was saying, but they dared not antagonize him, deciding instead to nod sagely in agreement. "Now get out," he said, waving Clare from his presence.

The former Countess of Villepreux left the royal presence and went straight to her room. She packed her few things and waited serenely for Mario's return. By afternoon when he had not appeared, she began to pace up and down the room, making frequent detours to gaze in every direction from her windows. "Where are you, Mario?" she muttered to herself. "Where on earth are you?"

Later, as the leaden grey sky darkened, and an evening chill oozed its way into her room, Clare rang the bell and asked for a fire and for light. "Does my lady need any food?" the servant asked, but was greeted with a silent shake of the head. As the laid fire was being lit, a demon draft blew down the chimney and filled the room with smoke. As if on cue, there was a knock on the door, and Mario appeared, even before she had a chance to answer. The servant looked up from sweeping the hearth and sucked in her breath suddenly at the sight before her. The shock on Clare's face was quickly suppressed as she ordered the maid to leave. Once the door had clicked shut behind the girl, she rushed over to him, saying, "What in God's name has happened?"

Mario stood there with tears coursing down his blackened face. His hair was singed, his clothes smelled of smoke, and he had filthy bandages wrapped around his blistered and burnt hands. She put her arms around his shoulders and led him to the chair, went and poured him a goblet of wine, then squatted down at his feet, looking up into his face.

"It's gone," he said, with a dark expression on his sooty face. "Only the walls and the chimneys are left. Once the roof caught fire, I knew it was the end. The sound of it crashing down was awful." He stared straight ahead, but what he saw seemed to terrify him. "The heat was like the fires of hell, but he wouldn't come out." Clare's heart froze.

"Who wouldn't come out?" she shouted. Nothing came from Mario's mouth. Clare moved to her knees and began to shake him. "Who wouldn't come out?!" she yelled again.

As if disturbed from a dream, Mario said, "Georges," and fell silent again.

"What happened, Mario?" Clare shouted. "Mario, tell me what happened. Did anyone try and get him out? Mario, talk to me. Mario . . ."

Mario began to speak slowly.

"When I got back last night, no, early this morning, Georges was very drunk." He smiled weakly and looked at Clare. "Can you believe that? Georges intoxicated and singing like a crow! I made sure that he went safely to bed and then I retired to my study." The look that he gave Clare suggested that he was being economical with the truth.

"There's something else that you're not telling me, Mario," she said. "I need to know everything."

Mario licked his lips as if trying to remove the taste of the previous night. "Maybe I did finish off the wine that Georges had left in the decanter, and maybe I did fall asleep, too." His eyes pleaded with Clare for forgiveness.

"What happened next?" she asked with a steely expression on her face. "I need to know everything," she demanded.

"You know where my office is, my lady. The smoke took a long time to get there. The smell of it coming under my door made me choke and woke me up. At first, I thought that perhaps there was a fire in the kitchen, but when I opened the door I saw nothing but a wall of smoke. But the noise . . ." Again a haunted look came over his face. "I will never forget that noise. It was like an animal roaring. I slammed the door shut. There was no way out that way, so I climbed out through the window and ran around the front. It was horrible. Flames were coming from every window of the upper floors, and the chimneys, they were spitting fire like mad volcanoes. It was hell on earth." He ran his fingers through his hair and looked at where his boots had once been and saw only burned flesh.

"I saw Georges through the open front door. A burning beam had fallen and was blocking his way. He just stood there like a statue. It was like he was waiting for you to come home, my lady. So stiff and formal. So Georges. And then he just turned and disappeared." On Mario's face was a mixture of wonder and shock. He returned his gaze to stare at his bandaged hands as if surprised as seeing them so.

"What happened next?" asked Clare, collapsing back on her heels in resignation and despair. Mario raised his head slowly and stared at her. His soft brown eyes had tears in them.

"What could I do?" Mario sighed and shrugged his narrow shoulders. "I had to try and save Signore Georges." Clare's hand flew to her mouth as she suppressed a shriek of hope and tears flooded her eyes. She forgot to breathe, but automatically reached out and gripped Mario's knee. He dropped his head again and spoke to his reddened feet, caked in wet clay. He began to shiver, a shiver so violent that it shook his whole, frail frame. Clare recovered herself and ran to the bedroom, dragging the cover off her bed and wrapping it around her secretary's shoulders.

"I'm so sorry, Mario," she said, "Shall I call for the physician?" He shook his head.

"Not yet, my lady. Perhaps when I've finished my story, it will be time enough." A wan smile crossed his face. Then he grimaced as he tried to pull the blanket closer around him. His shivering lessened, allowing Mario to continue his tale. "I threw my cloak into the fountain and put it over my head. I ran around the house looking for somewhere to get in. All the windows were shuttered: most had smoke coming out or around them."

"Then I came to the window of your small drawing room. There was no smoke from there. It was my only chance. The shutters were still closed, but that big statue outside? It made a great battering ram." He smiled at his bandaged hands. "I never thought I was a strong man, but I knocked

Apollo off his plinth, and he smashed through the doors for me!" Clare resumed her place at his feet.

"So I climbed through the broken wood and glass, inside all was as it should be. Even the fire in the hearth was as it should have been. Your chair was in the usual spot, and there was even a vase of fresh flowers on the small table next to your chair. It was as if he was expecting you back at any moment." Mario looked at Clare before saying softly, "I think Signore Georges loves you as only Signore Georges can." It was Clare's turn to feel warm tears again in her own eyes as she returned his smile. "Then, suddenly, there was a terrible crash from the hall. I went to the door and opened it. And I looked straight into hell. There were flames everywhere. Flaming wood was dropping from the roof. Even the walls were on fire."

"The heat beat me back. Then I discovered the cause of the crash. It was the chandelier that had fallen from the ceiling and trapped Signore Georges underneath. Then a flaming plank fell, and I couldn't stop myself." A terror mixed with stunned disbelief shadowed his eyes.

"Go on," Clare said softly after a pause.

Mario looked around as if he'd lost something. "It . . . when I had dragged him to your little room, I thought he must be dead, but then he said to me, 'Leave me, Mario, save yourself. Be good to her.' Then he passed out. I dragged him out through the doors and into the garden. I ran to the stables to find something to cover him with. When I was certain he was still alive, I thought to myself there is only one thing to do."

"What did you do with him, Mario? Where is he?" A curious look came over his face. For a moment, Clare thought it might even be a blush.

"There is a young lady I know, she was very kind to me once when I became a little emotional, and she brought me home recently. You might remember her, my lady?"

"Go on," said Clare, a grin tickling the edges of her lips.

"I put Signore Georges in a cart full of hay, and I brought him to Paris. At first, I was going to bring him here, but then I said to myself, 'Mario, the king may not like burnt servants in his palace,' so I then I thought that perhaps my lady friend might help." A roguish grin gleamed in his face. "I think she must love me, because she was very firm with her papa and mama. They are looking after Signore Georges and told me to come to you immediately."

Clare threw her arms around the young man's neck, causing him to wince in pain. She desisted immediately. "I'm so sorry, Mario, I forgot. Do you hurt very much? Here, have another drink of wine."

Mario looked askance at her. "Are you sure, my lady?"

"Consider it an order, Mario," she replied, happily filling the goblet to the top.

Clare's mind began to hum with all the information she'd heard in the last few minutes, but she made her mind up quickly. "It won't be long before the king and my cousin hear of this, and the sooner we leave, the better. I have His Majesty's protection until I leave France, but that might not prevent some less principled person from trying to organize an unfortunate accident to happen to me." She rose to her feet. "Can you walk, Mario?"

"I am Italian, my lady. Where love is concerned, all else is secondary," and he struggled to his feet. Finding her cloak and carrying her own bag, Clare led Mario from the apartment. She ordered the footman in the hallway to have a coach brought to the front of the palace. He stared in amazement at Mario, but bowed his wigged head at her and obeyed immediately. On his return, he kindly helped Mario down the steps and up into the vehicle.

"Thank you, sir," Clare said. "Please inform His Majesty that the Countess Villepreux has kept her part of the bargain and is leaving France."

"Yes, my lady," came the reply, and he quietly closed the door on the two travelers.

In a room in another wing of the palace, a group of men were playing cards. A footman entered and stood by the door waiting for permission to advance into the presence of His Majesty.

"Come," the royal voice called out. The man approached and whispered in the royal ear. The faintest hint of a smile quivered at the corner of the king's lips, but he kept his focus on the cards before him. He leaned forward and picked up a card in his turn, then he laid down his cards on the table saying, "I believe this is the winning hand, gentlemen!" He beamed at his fellow players who, having checked their own hands, conceded defeat. Duke Philippe pushed his chair away from the table with a black look on his face and stood up.

"Count me out, sire, that last hand cleaned me out," he scowled.

"Not your lucky day, is it, Philippe?" The king gathered in the glittering pile of coins with a wide sweep of his arms, adding, "It seems I have the Midas touch today. By the by, my lord Philippe, I had a very interesting conversation in the carriage yesterday with your pretty cousin." Philippe stood stock still, uncertain as to what was to come next. He'd played recklessly at cards, thinking he was about to come into a great fortune.

"You've piqued my interest, Your Highness," he said.

"A bright young lady with a quick mind, that! The vixen will make a fine wife for some lucky gentleman." He was concentrating on making a tower out of the gold coins he'd just won. "But not to anyone that you know. Or at least, I don't think you know him, do you?"

"You have me at a disadvantage, Sire," Philippe said, becoming uncomfortable at the way the conversation was heading.

"No matter," Francis said, appearing to lose interest in the conversation.

Then addressing them all, he said, "You know, it's funny how one little letter can make all the difference to what we think we know, eh?" The puzzled expressions on their faces, particularly Philippe's, showed that they had no idea where the king was leading them in this strange conversation.

"Take the letter *s*." He picked up a coin and said, "I have the 'coin,'" and then he showed the coin to all those present.

He then picked up a handful of coins. "Now I have the 'coins.'" Again he showed the treasure to all assembled.

"You speak in riddles, My Liege," said Philippe, becoming irritated by the king's seemingly childish behavior.

"But what if I said you owned the ground on which Château Villepreux stands. Without that little *s* there's really not much to inherit, is there?" A terrible insight flashed into Philippe's mind, freezing his ability to think. His Majesty continued with just a faint flicker of exultation on his face, "Your wise little cousin took it into her mind to gift her king with all her lands in France: lock, stock, and every last barrel of it. I'm afraid you won't be able to repay all your debts with what's under your house."

"How dare that bitch . . . ," exploded Philippe.

"There, there, my lord, when you gamble in games with high stakes you have to be prepared to lose, and I believe that you've just lost to a very intelligent player."

A weasel look fixed itself on Philippe's face. "There are still plenty of treasures in that old house. More than enough to . . ." He was cut off by the royal hand being raised, as the king wished to say something else.

"Regarding Château Villepreux, my lord. I've just received some dreadful news." He paused theatrically to gain maximum attention. "I understand there's been a terrible disaster. The chimneys caught fire, apparently due to some past neglect, and the place has burnt to the ground. With God's good grace, no one died, but everything else is lost. I am sorry to report that when you visit your ground, all you will find is a charred wreck!"

Twenty-One
THE CHASE

THINGS MOVED RAPIDLY after that. At the house of Mario's friend, Clare and Mario found poor Georges looking as if he were close to death in one of the guest rooms. The father of Lucette, for that was the infatuated maid's name, was a kind and enlightened man.

Monsieur De Montreal forwent the usual pleasantries and led Clare to Georges's bedside. "Is he going to die?" she pleaded, dropping to her knees by her faithful servant's bedside. "Dear God, please don't let him die because of me," she implored. Laying her hand on his, she was reassured to feel some warmth in him yet. Looking over her shoulder, she said to her host, "Please forgive me, Sir, I am distressed and forgot my manners. I am eternally in your debt for what you have done for Mario and dear Georges. Thank you, Monsieur," she said.

The good man raised his hand to stop the flow of her words. "I am happy to assist where I can, Mademoiselle. And no, I do not think that your Georges will die. In the past, I was lucky enough to travel extensively in Persia and the East, where I saw much and learned even more. I spent some time with the Muslim physicians there, which leads me to believe that much of the quackery performed by the so-called physicians of Paris is far more likely to kill than cure."

Monsieur De Montreal went on to tell Clare that he was also a keen correspondent and counted amongst his friends Paracelsus, a native of the alpine region of Unterwalden on the shores of Lake Lucerne in Switzerland. From Paracelsus, he'd learned the secrets of tincture of opium, commonly known as laudanum. Correctly used, laudanum was a great reliever of pain.

"My daughter would never forgive me if I failed to help one of her young man's friends. In fact, it is I who should be thankful to you for allowing me to help someone as attentive as your clerk here." His eyes twinkled as he looked over at where his daughter was gently caring for Mario, who'd been led to a seat and was now having his bandages changed. "Here," Monsieur said to him, "take a sip of this. It will ease your pain." Mario did as he was told and soon began to experience the benefits of the drug.

Georges moved his head and spoke. "Am I dead, my lady?" he asked of the room. Then, moving his head from side to side, he added, "Are we all dead? It's very dark in here." Around his head, a bloodied bandage was covering his eyes.

Mario looked up. "That burning plank? It was lying on his face."

Georges would never see his lady again.

Monsieur came to where Clare was kneeling and whispered, "It is not unusual for some to experience a dreamy state when taking laudanum. Some even tell me of visions they've had, but in most cases, the dreams are harmless. Let him have his dreams for the moment. He will have to live with the truth for a long time, so let him enjoy the dream."

A slight color had returned to Georges's cheeks. "No, dear Georges, you are definitely not dead, and neither is Mario, and neither are any of your friends. It's finished, Georges. Everything. We are free to go. The king has his lands in France, and I have a few remaining possessions of the cardinal's in Rome, and that's where we're going once you are fit to travel." Georges made to rise from his bed, but Clare firmly held him down. "Rest my beloved friend, rest. When you are stronger, then we will go. You are safe here with me." She felt Georges squeeze her hand before his whole frame relaxed, and he slipped back into a deep sleep.

"Apart from the burns to his face and hands, I could find no other serious injuries. If he rests well overnight, he should be able to travel in your coach on the morrow or the next day, my lady," Monsieur said.

"May I stay here with him, Monsieur?" she asked.

"I will see to it that a settle is brought in for your comfort."

"Thank you."

"I think Mario is recovering at a remarkably rapid rate, my lady," the good man said happily, "it's not often we have someone so gifted and so, well, delightful, in our humble home. If I'm any judge of a man, I believe that young man should go far."

Clare smiled. "Monsieur, you have fine judgment. I have the king's word that he will go far. Mario will prove to be a force for great good in this country."

The following morning, Clare was awakened by the sound of falling furniture. Believing that she was still in a dream, she was slow to realize that Georges had just knocked a chair over. He'd removed his bandage, revealing the awful damage done to his face. The skin had been scorched white around his eyes, with his eyebrows and eyelashes having burned away. Watery blisters hung like bags from his cheeks, and the hair on his forehead was singed black. His eyes were open and vacantly staring, urging his brain to see something.

"Am I blind, my lady?" he asked.

Although there was an instant desire to deny his terrible injury, Clare could not lie to him. "Yes, Georges, you are." It immediately struck her that Georges knew that she was there, even though he couldn't see her. "How did you know I was here, Georges?" she asked.

"I heard you breathing first, my lady. Then I smelt you." It was a beautiful moment for both of them. "Is there anything you want, my lady?" he asked, staring a few feet to the right of her.

Clare suppressed a smile. "Yes, Georges, there is. Could you come with me to Rome and help me set up home there?"

"Certainly, my lady" came his formal reply. "Would you like me to arrange the coach for you?"

"I believe that Mario might be able to manage that, Georges," she said, her face almost cracking open with her smile. "Perhaps I might get someone to help you with a fresh set of clothes, Georges?" she proffered.

"Certainly, Mademoiselle. I surmise that my current ones may be in need of some cleansing." Clare could no longer contain herself and rose to gently hug her indestructible friend.

They parted from Mario with much emotion. Clare had told him of the arrangements she had come to with the king. Mario was to enter into royal service with special instructions to deal with Roman affairs. "Affairs are my lifeblood," Mario smiled at Clare. "Soon I shall be Ambassador to Il Papa, eh?"

"Well if you do, then be very careful, my friend," she replied.

They left him with orders to call in to see them whenever he came to Rome, and then they were gone.

"My heart is breaking," he said to young Lucette. She slipped her arm around his waist and guided him back into the house. "But I think it will soon get better."

On the road south, Georges asked for news of Marionette, Rosso, and the others. Clare reassured him that she had sent ahead with news of their journey home. "I didn't mention you were hurt, though. I thought that worrying about you wouldn't help anyone. Anyway, by the time you get home you face should almost be healed." His blindness was not mentioned. Both of them knew that it would be a hurdle to him, but not a complete obstruction.

"And your friend Kristopher, my lady," Georges asked in a quiet tone. "Will we be seeing him soon?" The irony was lost on him.

"I hope so, Georges. I sincerely hope so!"

Twenty-Two

ROME

TWO MONTHS LATER, a man in a light cloak walked down a busy street toward the piazza. He heard the market before he saw it. Then he smelt it, and finally, the square opened out before him to reveal it. There were sellers shouting, animals sending up their several sounds, and buyers ambling from stall to stall looking for bargains. But the man's intent gaze was not searching out any of the colorful produce or the colorful people going about their business. His eyes searched the surrounding buildings, and his ears listened for another sound altogether. When he heard the sound he sought, his face brightened, and he headed for Marco's forge.

Marco looked up, his face ruddy from the fire and his arms gleaming with sweat. "Signore Marco?" the stranger asked. The blacksmith put down his hammer and approached him.

"Is it you?" he asked. The answer was a simple nod. "She's been waiting for you. She's not here, though. Just behind Santa Maria Maggiore, there is a road heading north. Go along there for half a league and you'll find a small house there. You can't miss it." Marco grasped the man in a powerful embrace and tears filled his eyes. "Go now. Don't waste another second." The stranger bowed and headed off toward the ancient church whose tower stood like a beacon of hope above the miasma of Rome. As he reached the corner of the piazza, he turned and shouted back to Marco, "Will you send a message to Rosso please, and tell him I'm here?" The smithy signaled back in the affirmative.

Passing the great Church of Santa Maria Maggiore, the man slowed and listened intently. It was quiet, so he carried on.

After half a league, he found her house. It stood by itself and, although small, it exuded a sense of peace and tranquility with its green gardens and bright windows that seemed to smile at passersby. He took the path to the door, mounted the three stone steps, and stood there with his knuckles poised to strike. He could hear his heart pounding in his ears.

The sound of his knuckles on the oaken door calmed him, and the pounding abated. He waited. He turned to take in the view of the pretty garden where sparrows had grown fat and cheeky with the attention given to them by their new mistress. As he watched them, he failed to hear the door open.

It was the sound of someone clearing his throat which caused him to turn suddenly.

"May I help you?" asked the man standing before him. The man stood ramrod straight, although in one hand he carried a light cane. He stared straight past the stranger and into the distance, which unsettled the visitor until he noticed that both of the man's eyes were white. He was blind.

The man cleared his throat again. "If my senses don't deceive me, sir, I believe you've traveled a great distance, and if that's the case, then I think you should come in immediately, as my lady has been expecting you." He stood to one side and let the stranger in. "Follow me, Sir," Georges said, and tapping his cane before him, led the way across a cheery hallway to a half-opened door on one side. Light danced into the house, and flowers shared their scents from vases on side tables.

Georges knocked and entered. "There is a gentleman here to see you," he said, allowing a big smile onto his face. Clare rose and stood by the fire trembling.

"Is it . . . ?" she asked.

"Yes, my lady. It is." Standing to one side, he allowed Kristopher to enter. Then he quietly closed the door behind him and left.

"You expected me?" Kristopher asked.

"Mario sent word," she replied, not daring to move a muscle lest she begin to shake with joy. "Francis kept his word?" It was her turn to ask a question.

"Indeed, His Majesty was very kind to me." Kristopher replied, "Your friend Mario helped fill in all the gaps of your story. I didn't realize he was so close to the king?"

"Mario makes friends with both princes and paupers," Clare replied with a smile. Kristopher moved toward her. He offered both hands to her, and she gratefully took them into hers. Their happiness couldn't have been more complete, and they smiled until their cheeks ached.

"I love you, my little ragamuffin. I love you more than any words could say," Kristopher said, raising one hand to lightly cup her pink cheek.

"And I love you beyond all my dreams, my pirate captain," she said, smiling back at him. A thought flashed through her mind. Kristopher was still a captain in Admiral Doria's fleet.

"When do you have to return?" Clare asked, her expression falling a little.

Kristopher moved his lips closer to hers and said, "Never my love, I've come home for good . . ."

About the Author

"I spent all my life learning the rules. Now that I know which ones are irrelevant, life is simpler!"

AFTER MORE THAN thirty years as a busy family practice physician in Perth, Duncan Jefferson retired from his practice and started traveling. He still practices medicine part time, as a relief doctor traveling to the most remote corners of Australia, and in between assignments he and his wife travel the world.

Duncan has walked the famous Camino de Santiago, and now volunteers his time as the chairman of The Pilgrim

Trail Foundation, which is organizing a similar, contemplative-style walk in Australia called the Camino Salvado.

VISIT HIM ONLINE AT

WWW.DUNCANJEFFERSON.COM